No Regrets

Book One of the Wedding Dress Promise Series

RONNIE ROBERTS

Copyright © 2014 by Ronnie Roberts
All Rights Reserved.
This is a work of fiction. Any references to real people or places are used fictitiously; other names and places are products of the author's imagination. Any resemblance to actual people or places is entirely coincidental. No part of this book may be copied or reproduced without the author's express permission.

Edited by Jason Whited
Cover Art by Prospero
Published by Pajama Therapy Books – 2014
ISBN-13: 978-150-2990051
ISBN-10:1502990059

Books by Ronnie Roberts:

No Regrets
After the Party
The Wish List
The Contract
The Fixer Upper
Saving Piper
The Sweet Spot
Nailed It!

Special thanks to my husband, Rob for his steadfast support, to my BFF, Sharon for her Ninja Beta Reader skills and to Cairo for providing the words that made writing Shannon so much fun.

TABLE OF CONTENTS

A Game of Chicken 1
A New Path? 9
Soap Opera 18
Who Are You? 28
Snip! 33
Through the Lens Sparkly 41
Disclosure 49
Pupcakes and Mini-Meats 60
The Bingo Dauber Solution 68
Metamorphosis – Part A 75
Warm Milk 86
Big Developments 96
Escape 102
Walker House 111
In the Attic 120
Sexual Healing 133
School's Out for Summer! 140
Birthday Party 149
Aunty Darby 161
Metamorphosis – Part B 168
Tide Pool Reflections 174
To Market, To Market 183
Inside Darby's Trunk 190
Into the Abyss 196
After the Party Excerpt 215
About Ronnie Roberts 221

A GAME OF CHICKEN

WHAT WAS he up to? Darby eased off the gas, her eyes flickering away from the road back to the kid on the dirt bike. For a moment, his bike wobbled, threatened to toss him to the ground, but then it straightened and surged forward, peeling across the open field, leaving a huge plume of dust in his wake as he raced toward the highway. Was this some crazy game of chicken?

She gripped the steering wheel convulsively and watched his approach with her heart rising in her chest. If she sped up, she might miss him. Or should she slow down and let him cross, and hope for the best? A quick check of her side mirror showed a red truck gaining on her fast. Didn't he see the bike streaking toward the highway? She glanced at the boy again. From this angle, she couldn't tell which of them would arrive at some incalculable point of intersection on the blacktop ahead—his bike or her van.

"Don't do it, kid," she begged out loud. Did he seriously think he could cross the highway in front of her and make it safely to the other side? Hitting the ditch alone would send him sky high.

Registering the long stream of traffic coming her way, she moaned, "Oh, God." Did they even see the kid? Then from behind her, the red truck's horn blasted. Instantly she knew if she didn't stop—right now—she was going to hit that stupid kid. Her choice taken from her, she stood on her brakes, her tires howling in protest as she fought to keep her shuddering van out of the path of oncoming traffic. Come on, come on ….

The truck behind slammed into her van, snapping her head back against the headrest and blasting her body forward like a bullet. The seatbelt slapped her back against the seat, emptying her lungs with a painful whoosh. She was traveling down the highway broadside now, tires squealing as she fought to drag air back into her body. With a never-ending metallic scream, her van achieved an impossible-to-maintain angle, throwing her against the door, the driver's side window scary close to the ground, riding precariously on the driver's side wheels. It was going to roll!

She brought her knees up, covered her head with her arms, bracing herself for disaster, then inexplicably ... miraculously ... the van slowed, defied gravity, and with a lumbering thump landed back onto all four tires, stopping dead in the middle of the highway. A lifetime of terror in mere seconds.

Loose camera equipment rained down from everywhere, but Darby felt nothing. Opening her arms, her eyes found and locked onto the boy on the bike. In slow motion she saw the bike leave the field, fly across the ditch, slam into and up the bank, tossing the kid backward onto the ground. In a vacuum of paralyzing silence, save for the tick, tick, tick of the cooling engine, she stared at the boy, praying for signs of life.

Her windshield exploded. She screamed, her heart exploding inside her chest. Glass rained all around her, stinging her arms, her face, clattering across the dash, thudding on the upholstery, pinging on her strapped-in laptop. When it was over she tentatively opened her eyes, then jerked back in horror at finding the hot, twisted metal of the bike lodged scant inches from her face—somehow suspended above her. "Get out!" her inner voice commanded.

She released her seatbelt. The boy needed her. She yanked a first aid kit from under the passenger's seat, saw she was bleeding but not enough to get her attention.

Naturally, her door was grossly distorted and cemented closed. She pivoted, aimed her boots at the door and kicked it out, the last of the windshield shattering harmlessly onto the dash in the process. Slipping to the ground, her long skirt caught on a jagged piece of metal and tore from hip to hem. Cool air rushed against her bare skin. She barely noticed, taking in the lines of traffic that were now stopped on both sides of the highway, with people emerging.

She darted around her van and dropped down into the ditch. A broad-shouldered man with his hair tied back in a sun-streaked ponytail was already leaning over the boy, talking to him urgently.

"Andrew. Can you hear me, son?"

This was the boy's father? How had he gotten here so quickly? She fell onto her knees beside him. "I'm trained in first aid and can help."

She saw the boy's eyes were open, and he looked frightened, his skin so pale it blended into the shock of blond hair plastered against his head. He looked to be in his early teens. "Don't try to move. My name is Darby. Can I check you out? Don't nod your head, use your voice." He was slow to answer yes—a totally normal response to having been slapped to the earth like a bag of marbles. She ran her hands up and down his gangly limbs, searching for and finding no bleeding or obvious broken bones.

"You have any allergies? React to any medications?" She included the father in this, and he shook his head no. "Cool.

"He does have a rare blood type." The father indicated a silver medic alert bracelet on his son's arm.

"Good to know," she replied, and scrambled around to above his head, glad of her ankle-length cotton skirt to save the skin on her knees. She leaned down until her elbows were on the ground and her hands were positioned on either side of his head. She gripped his head and held it firmly. "Okay, Andrew. Did I hear right, your name is Andrew?"

The boy answered yes again, this time more quickly.

"I'm going to immobilize your head until the ambulance gets here. It won't hurt even a little bit. It's only a precaution, just in case you've hurt your neck or back." She glanced up at the father, grimacing at the action. "You called 911?"

"Yes. They're on their way."

"See, Andrew, things are looking up. You're okay, and I have yet another opportunity to look really awkward in front of total strangers. This is such a flattering position, with my butt stuck out in the wind at such a rakish angle."

"W-what?" Andrew murmured faintly.

People were beginning to arrive, saying they had called 911 and offering water, blankets, pillows, even a ham sandwich on rye, with the promise of low-fat mayo—this offer from a distressed little woman with mussed silvery hair, the proffered sandwich in her hand already half eaten.

Darby laughed and said, "Awesome. Now my butt looks like I need low-fat mayo."

Andrew laughed too.

"There you go. You're going to be all right," Darby said with a smile, exchanging an encouraging glance with the boy's father as he wrapped an offered blanket around his son. A distant siren sounded, approaching fast.

He said, "You were driving the camperized van?"

"A used-to-be camperized van, thanks to the idiot who just rear-ended me. I'm homeless now."

He looked startled. "Homeless? You live out of your van?"

"Yup. I'm a photographer. I'm here for the summer, getting shots for a government contract I'm hoping to get. This is not the stellar beginning I'd imagined."

"Huh. Well, the idiot behind you—that would be me."

"Oh." Darby craned her neck to look at the worried expression in his blue eyes then away. Once again, she'd put her foot in her mouth. "I shouldn't have said that."

"I was trying to get Andrew's attention, get him to slow down, stop, anything but cross that damned highway. He—he's going through …" he faded off, his expression bewildered.

"He's a teenager."

"Yeah, something like that."

"Sorry about the comment. Of course you were trying to stop him."

"I'm sorry too—about your van. I'm glad you're here, though."

"Just doing what anyone would," she answered, then tried to soften her earlier complaint. "I'll figure something out about the van. Got a used car lot here in Brennan's Point that sells cheap vehicles?"

Two paramedics appeared with a stretcher loaded with gear and climbed down the crumbling bank of the dry ditch. Placing the stretcher beside Andrew they pulled apart the strapped-in bundle of supplies and began asking questions. Both Darby and the boy's father pointed out the medic alert bracelet. Very quickly Andrew was fitted with a neck brace and loaded securely into the stretcher. Then to Darby's surprise, the paramedics turned their attention toward her.

"Hey, I'm a just bystander. I'm okay," she protested, shrugging them away. "Take care of Andrew here."

"That's maybe the adrenaline talking? You've got several cuts," one medic warned. "You should have your family doctor look at you at least."

"I'm not from around here. But ..." She held up her hand in anticipation of further argument. "I will go to a walk-in clinic. I promise."

Andrew's father pulled out his wallet and extracted a business card. "Do me one more favor? Call this number, and my man Clint can arrange for both our vehicles to be towed. I'll cover the cost."

She glanced over her shoulder at the wrecked red truck, her tan-colored sadly misshapen camperized van, which now sported an orange crown of twisted dirt bike, and the cops directing traffic around the two battered vehicles, then down at the card. It read Joe MacKinnon of MacKinnon Marina in Brennan's Point. She looked back at him. He didn't look old enough to have a teenage son, let alone run a marina, what with the long hair and permanent vacation tan. But then, what did she know? Life was funny that way.

She held up the card. "Sounds fair. I'll talk to the cops too." She nodded after the departing paramedics. "Now go with Andrew. I'll make sure the vehicles are taken care of."

■ ■ ■

JOE SPRINTED down the street toward the walk-in clinic, hoping he wasn't too late. Once he'd gotten home from the hospital with Andrew this afternoon, Clint had told him towing the two vehicles had taken forever, what with the Annual Memoir Writers' Conference in town. Apparently, these visiting writers were terrible drivers who liked to bump into one another on a regular basis. The two local tow companies had spent an extremely lucrative day extracting these same writers out of their troubles, at rates jacked up just for such occasions. And these very same writers were now currently ensconced in every available hotel and motel room for miles around, which he was guessing Darby would be discovering once she left the clinic. She probably didn't know just how homeless she actually was.

Swinging open the door, he scanned the crowded waiting room, his eyes skidding to a stop. Seated alone in a corner, surrounded by two bulging duffel bags was the small woman who'd come to Andrew's rescue this morning. She wore a pale blue T-shirt that read, *Cloud 8 is Cheaper, Less Crowded, and Has a Better View*. A long tear in her stained cotton skirt revealed a slender, tanned leg.

Her head was resting on the wall behind her chair, and she appeared to have fallen asleep, the cuts on her forehead and left cheek having already formed scabs. A scattering of more scabs and bruises trailed the length of both of her arms. Regret washed through him. She had been driving innocently down the road, minding her own business one minute, then was up to her neck in his family drama the next. She had all the cuts and bruises while Andrew was walking around as if nothing had happened to him.

He could see more than one patient was taking the opportunity of her closed eyes to openly drink in her appearance. She was certainly different, not someone you'd normally bump into a small town such as Brennan's Point. The blue outfit she was wearing was nice. He'd lay money down it had started out the day–before he'd rear-ended her–clean. But paired with hiking boots …. Her poker-straight, jaw-length hair was tricolored, dyed first black on the bottom, with a band of electric red in the middle and honey blonde at the crown.

She wasn't shy with the eyeliner, either, evidently believing the blacker the better. Her fingers ended in black polished nails, her hands now sporting several colorful drugstore Band Aids, obviously an attempt to cover the worst of the cuts she'd gotten from this morning's accident. He knew her eyes, when open, were an intense green and able to take in and understand everything around her. She was quite unlike anyone he'd ever met.

"Darby Walker?" The receptionist called out.

Darby started in her chair, winced, and brought a bandaged hand up to her neck. She had been hurt!

Joe strode across the room. "Darby, you okay?"

She looked up at him, seeming slow to recognize who he was. "Um. Joe, is it?"

"Joe MacKinnon." He couldn't help his disappointment when she didn't know him. He, for one, wasn't about to forget their meeting.

"Darby Walker," the receptionist repeated, her tone edged with impatience this time.

"I'm here," Darby called out, struggling from her seat. Joe extended his hand, and she took it, rising to her feet with a low moan. "God, I'm so stiff. I feel ancient." She stretched tentatively, and he saw instantly when the action incited more pain. "Sorry–is Andrew okay?"

Andrew she remembered. "He's good–better than you, apparently. How about I stay with your stuff while you go see the doctor, then we can talk."

Darby looked puzzled. "About what?"

"Later." He nudged her toward the exam rooms. "Go see the doctor. I'll wait here."

It was a long wait, with Joe becoming more concerned as the minutes ticked away. He knew Stuart well–you were in and out with Doc Turner. He was a no-nonsense doctor, getting to the point immediately and then on to his next patient. It was why his clinic was so popular; he knew his stuff and didn't waste time holding your hand.

Making a liar out of him, Doc Turner appeared in the waiting room with one arm around Darby, who was now wearing a thick neck brace, and holding her hand. When his gaze landed on Joe, he jerked his head for Joe to join them. Darby's expression was mortified. Joe hurried forward.

"Hey, Joe, you looking after this young lady?"

"No!" Darby protested.

"Yes," Joe answered, ignoring her.

"Good, because if someone doesn't take responsibility for her, I'm admitting her into the hospital right now. She has a pretty good case of whiplash and needs a place to stay to rest. She lost her camper this morning, I understand?"

"She did. I rear-ended her when Andrew took off on that stupid bike this morning and got himself into trouble."

"You know about the conference, then?"

Darby's expression went from embarrassed to mystified. "Conference?"

"Yeah," Joe answered her. "There are no rooms available anywhere. I was going to talk to you about it. I have lots of room for you out on my ranch."

"But I hardly know you!" Darby protested.

"We have a live-in nanny—Melody—so you'll be okay. No ulterior motives."

Now Darby snorted. "Do I look worried? That's not my point."

Doc Turner faced her. "You weren't listening, young lady. It's the hospital or the MacKinnon ranch, your choice."

"Ranch," she blurted out at once.

A NEW PATH?

DARBY BEGAN to have second thoughts once she was seated snugly between Joe MacKinnon and his neighbor, Leo Crabtree, in a rumbling old truck that had to be completely devoid of shocks. Thumping over a particularly wicked pothole, she gasped in pain and grabbed Joe's denim-covered thigh. Their gazes collided. "Sorry." She grimaced, slow to take her hand away, afraid of the next thump. The ride out to the ranch was proving worse than the accident.

"Here." Joe MacKinnon tucked his jacket behind her head as a pillow then put his arm around her shoulders and held her gently but firmly against him. "Maybe this will help. Over her shoulder, he said, "Leo, could you slow up a bit? Darby's feeling every bump, I'm afraid."

Leo nodded and eased off the gas pedal.

"Thanks," Darby murmured, shifting restlessly on the slippery bench seat. Doc Turner had said Joe MacKinnon was a good man; she'd never have considered this new arrangement, bizarre as it was, without the doctor's recommendation. And, the universe had placed this path before her, and it was up to her to follow it to its natural conclusion. She wondered what the next few days would reveal.

As Leo's truck eased along the narrow dirt road, she tried distracting herself by ticking off what she knew about the man who was cradling her in his embrace so earnestly, his expression a study in concerned regret. He was a dad. He owned a marina, and apparently a ranch. She slid her gaze toward him. He was pretty tall, about six two or so, and he was physically fit—his thigh muscle had felt thick and hard when she'd grabbed it—oops! She couldn't help a secret smile of appreciation. And he had another one to match it.

Here in the cab, she knew that he smelled good too—and that counted for a lot. Darby hated men who perfumed themselves six ways to Sunday with men's cologne. A man should smell like a man—a clean man, mind you.

"Leo, would you mind opening your window a crack?" she asked, shifting in her seat slightly, silently astonished at her intensely inappropriate tallying of Joe's masculine attributes. Still… her assessment marched on. Brushing at the dirt and grass stains on her skirt and pulling the torn edges together over her thigh, she slid another sideways glance at him.

She normally didn't appreciate blond men. Was it the surfer dude vibe she didn't like, maybe? Joe's intelligent expression saved him from that unfortunate category. Joe looked to be more of a seasoned sailor with his sun-streaked hair swept back from his tanned face, his blue eyes framed by crinkly laugh lines. She could imagine him guiding a sailing boat through swift water, could see waves wash across the deck and his gaze focused out to sea. Okay, was it time to add novel writing to her résumé?

She asked, "You grow up here, Joe?"

"Nope. Been here just about six years now. We came just before Shannon was born." He adjusted his arm behind her shoulders, his thigh still pressed against hers. Held virtually motionless against his side, she felt the soft movement of his breath on her hair and imagined her crumpled clothes growing moist from her body heat penetrating his.

"Shannon?"

"My daughter. She's five."

"That's a fun age."

Joe smiled and nodded, and silence descended into the still-too-warm cab.

Darby tried again. "Brennan's Point's a nice little town. Everyone seems to know everyone else."

He nodded, and the quiet yawned over them once more.

Their visit to the wrecking yard to get her remaining possessions had been enlightening, as had the clinic. Same thing at the marina and at the drugstore, when they'd filled her prescriptions. Joe was obviously well liked and respected, but she couldn't help noticing quickly hidden glances of surprise behind many of the greetings she received after he introduced her. Did everyone know about the accident already? Were her scabbing-over cuts more gruesome than she thought?

"Here at Brennan's Point life is slower, and people rely on one another." Joe's husky voice brought her back to inside the truck cab.

"I've been here before. I spent some time out on Idle Island, just off shore from here. My friend, Laura Winthrop, owns it."

Joe's face opened up. "Hey, I know Laura; she keeps her boats at the marina. I like her."

"I kinda like her myself," Darby echoed. Mindful of her stiff neck, she turned slightly toward the older gentleman at the wheel. "Sure good of you to rescue us, Leo."

"No trouble a' tall," Leo answered, staring straight ahead and concentrating on his driving. She couldn't fault him there—he was now steering carefully around every pothole he encountered. Good thing, as all her precious photography equipment, which had recently been tossed around like popcorn inside her currently-deceased van was thumping in place in the back of his truck. She prayed her gear would survive the experience; especially the printer, which had cost the world.

Shifting gingerly in her seat again, Darby managed only to become wedged more firmly against Joe's hard torso, and it occurred to her that he was maybe enjoying himself a little too much. Giving his knee an ungracious shove, she said sweetly, "I wonder, Mr. MacKinnon, if you might move your legs over a bit. We hardly know each other after all."

"Why, Miss Walker, I'd certainly like to accommodate you, but as you can see, this cab is small and I am large. Beggars can't be choosers, now can they?"

She was very aware of his size, thank you very much!

Since she could do nothing about the seating arrangement, and certainly didn't want him to let go of her and allow her to feel every damned bump Leo wasn't successful in avoiding, she took interest in her surroundings instead.

The road they were traveling ran parallel to the shoreline. On their left was a mix of majestic, dark cedar trees, paler, almost sage-colored scrubby pines, and beautiful arbutus trees, their twisted and peeling trunks burnished a beautiful red in the sunlight. In the shaded base of the trees the ground was covered with gigantic, waist-high ferns while the open, sunny areas were populated with stands of giant purple lupin. Pretty.

On the right side of the road was a bank of opportunistic rough broom that separated the road and the shoreline. Standing as high as the ferns, the broom was ablaze with glorious yellow flowers, which looked beautiful along the sea edge, but Darby knew it for the invasive plant it was, brought over in container ships as packing material between furniture by early Scottish settlers. The locals hated it, waging a never-ending (and losing) war against its prolific spread across southern British Columbia

Beyond the brilliant yellow hedge, she could see it was low tide. Closest to the road, and sloping gently seaward, ran a band of pea gravel, then a pale band of larger, rounded stones that faded into the wide expanse of an exposed, hard-packed sandbar. Huge beds of glistening bronze seaweed were draped across the ripple-patterned sand. Shallow pools of sparkling water collected sporadically along the bar. She knew from experience the pools would be warm from the sun and teeming with life. It reminded her of her Art in the Park days, teaching kids down at Stanley Park, because the YWCA was under the misbegotten impression she was eighteen at the time—oops, did I say that?

"Pardon?" Joe asked.

She looked at him blankly. "What?"

"You said 'Oops.'"

"Oh. A memory popped into my head. This place reminds me of teaching kids photography down at Stanley Park along the seawall when I was fifteen. I loved it. It didn't pay much, but it put a roof over my head."

Just then they plunged back into forest, and the interior of the cab darkened. Her eyes were slow to make the adjustment; for a moment she couldn't see Joe's face. She could, however, feel him—very, very well.

"You've been on your own—in Vancouver—since you were fifteen?"

"Yes. I graduated with my class, same as everyone else; I just did it a bit differently."

"The hard way."

"You could say that. The good news is, my experience with the Art in the Park program and the recommendations I received from those four years earned me a full scholarship at the Vancouver Institute of Art. And that's where I met your friend, Laura. See? Full circle. Small world." Her eyes had adjusted to the low light. Joe's expression was astonished.

He whistled softly. "Vancouver's a tough town."

"Life presents pathways we can either follow or not. I believe every path was meant to be explored. It's all good."

"Huh," Joe grunted.

She could see he wasn't comfortable with "New Age" speak. She had him stumped all right. It was fun, she had to admit. She loved fighting her way out of the box people liked to place her in. She was different; she knew it, and she liked it.

Leo's truck broke from the trees, back into sunshine. Darby blinked against the brightness as they came to a halt before a rambling, white bungalow-style house with a wraparound porch that faced the ocean. Gentle slopes of what had to be acres and acres of cleared and fenced land stretched from the low hills behind the house and reached down to the sea. A big, red setter bound up the beach and greeted the truck with a great show of welcome.

"Oh, Joe!" Darby practically fell out of the truck after him in her eagerness to drink in the view, regretting her haste immediately. "Ouch!" Doctor Turner had told her to keep moving, but the leap from the truck had been a mistake. Chastened, she slipped a hand under the hot collar and massaged her neck gingerly while Joe and Leo unloaded her gear. When they began grunting and rolling their eyes over the avalanche of cases and boxes that were the sum total of her life, she turned away and absorbed the panoramic sight of gently sloping land, the constantly moving Pacific Ocean and the islands beyond with her photographer's eye. This was stunningly beautiful. She could take pictures all day long and never tire of it.

Moving carefully, she crossed the lawn to where it met the sandy beach. The warm wind rippled across the sand, wrapping her thin skirt snugly around her. She raised her hands to hold back her hair, breathed in the fresh, tangy sea air, and let her body soften and sway with the breeze. It felt so right to be here. She turned to find Leo's truck gone and Joe's deep blue eyes assessing her. She stared back, evaluating him just as intently. She knew that together they were about to embark on a strange voyage. Where would it take them? She smiled and said, "It's a breathtaking sight, Joe."

"It is."

She saw that he was very human, and maybe just as baffled by their situation as she was. He'd gone after his escaping teenage son and returned with an injured house guest. Now that's what you'd call a bizarre day. Obviously, she was meant to be here, was meant to meet Joe and his family–there was some purpose here she did not yet see.

As she walked toward him, she saw him read the message on her T-shirt and smile. Mindful of her bandaged cuts she tucked her hand into his arm, turned him around, and steered him toward the house. "I'd love to take some shots here. Would you mind?"

"Not at all. There are riding and hiking paths through the woods beyond that ridge," he indicated past the cultivated portion of the property to the rising bluff. "Though there are some old lime caves up there I don't suggest exploring. Stick with the horse trails."

She leveled a stare at him. "Do I look like I'm going horseback riding any time soon?"

"True." He smiled and shrugged.

She waved toward the sloping hills. "This is all MacKinnon land?"

"All MacKinnon land," he confirmed, unable to suppress the pride in his tone. He bent and ran his hand along the flank of the setter. "And this is Buddy. What he lacks in good judgment, he more than makes up for with enthusiasm and loyalty."

Darby held her hand out to the dog. "Hi, Buddy."

"Daddy, Daddy!" A child's voice preceded a blur of blue that shot out from the house, across the porch and launched itself from the top of the stairs with complete trust, through the air and into Joe's arms. "Melody's gone, and Andrew's being mean to me," the tiny girl reported. "He says I have to clean up my own ..." She caught sight of Darby. "Who's that?" Her arms tightened possessively around her father's neck.

"This is Darby Walker, Honey. She's going to stay with us for a while and get better. She hurt her neck and back today, helping me with your brother."

The screen door slammed again, this time behind a rangy teenage boy who stood on the deck, looking them over. It was Andrew, upright, and much taller than Darby realized, though, she was short, making almost everyone else taller in comparison. He seemed none the worse for wear. Gone was the frightened boy of this morning, replaced by a sullen teen.

"Not another one," he muttered under his breath. Darby caught the words and resentment in his expression and posture and recognized at once teenage angst at its finest distillation. Poor Joe.

With Shannon in his arms, Joe swung around to face his son. "What's Shannon talking about? Where's Melody?" He sounded both defeated and alarmed.

Andrew's eyes flicked from Darby to his father. "She's gone. Took all her stuff and left about an hour ago."

"Another one?" Darby prompted. It seemed Melody had left an unfortunate lasting impression on Andrew.

Joe eyed his son balefully, but directed his words to Darby. "We've had a problem keeping the nanny position filled for any significant length of time around here. Good thing Mrs. Russell is willing to pinch-hit for us." The boy shook back his overgrown mop of blond hair and squinted into the air with a show of disinterest. To his son, Joe said, "Darby's going to be staying with us for a while. She was hurt helping us this morning. We owe her this much."

Andrew shrugged. "That's cool."

"If Andrew gives you any trouble, just let me handle it." There was a message to Andrew in Joe's voice.

"Hi, Andy. Nice to see you upright." She placed her hand into his and received a limp-wristed return to her handshake. "I'm sure you and I will get along just fine." Swiftly he pulled his hand away and shoved it into the pocket of his worn jeans. He may have said 'cool', but she knew it wasn't. Anyone with eyes could see he didn't want her here.

"And this is Shannon." Joe's face fairly shone with love for his daughter. The exchange of looks between father and daughter tugged on Darby's heartstrings. Shannon was a lucky little girl. Giggling, Shannon buried her face in her father's collar and peeped out at Darby. Joe set her on the ground.

Darby held out her hand. Shannon slipped hers into it, her open expression full of curiosity for their new house guest. Darby registered surprise as she gazed into Shannon's upturned face, a child-like mirror of her own! Framed in honey-colored hair, she had the same green eyes, small freckled nose, bow lips over small even teeth, and stubborn pointed chin. Her face would one day lose its chubbiness and become heart shaped as was Darby's. She wondered if Joe saw the uncanny resemblance. What did the children's mother look like?

Joe held the door open for Darby. "Coming, Andrew?"

"No, I have to feed the horses."

Still clasping Shannon's little hand, Darby climbed the two steps up onto the porch and followed Joe into the house.

It was cool and dark inside, with a beautiful open concept design and decorated in soothing earth tones. The floors were a mix of ceramic tile and polished hardwood, with well-placed, hand woven rugs. The walls were clad with paintings, weavings, and row upon row of well-used books. The tables were made of oak and pine and were littered with hand-thrown clay pots and plants, toys, books, and electronics. The furnishings were massive and, under different circumstances, might have looked inviting to curl up on.

But everywhere she looked it was a disaster! The place looked like a toy bomb had gone off, followed by a clothes bomb, then a pizza box bomb. She could see the kitchen—even from this distance—was in great need of TLC. Suddenly she was homesick for the cute little two-burner stove in her van. She could have a decent meal whipped up on it in half an hour; cleanup was a breeze. Then she'd lie down in her fresh, comfy bed, which suddenly she longed to do. She was exhausted.

Pivoting on her heel, Darby took in the magnitude of the domestic disaster before her. "You are kidding me," she said.

Joe had the grace to look sheepish. "We've had a little trouble keeping up. I'll be giving Mrs. Russell a call first thing in the morning."

"I've seen crack houses that are neater than this," Darby blurted before she could stop herself, letting go of Shannon.

"You've seen crack houses?"

She glanced at him swiftly, and hissed in a sharp breath of pain. Sudden head movement—not okay. "I watch 'Cops' on TV like everyone else. Do I look like I've been inside a crack house, for heaven's sake?" It was a lie, of course, but just a little one.

His eyes flickered up to her hair and back to her face.

"Don't even go there," she warned, and turned her entire body this time, to survey the room. "So this is what it means to be a single parent in Brennan's Point."

"I've been busy at the marina throughout the spring, and now the summer; the season's booming this year," Joe defended. "The last nanny wasn't working out, but I simply could not cover all the bases. So," his gaze followed hers with regret, "I settled for a nanny with no housekeeping or cooking duties required, so the kids would at least be watched until things slowed down and I could take time for the home front. Unfortunately, it seems Melody decided today is that day."

Darby was beginning to get the picture. "I'm guessing Andrew's bid for freedom and both our vehicles being totaled was a real day topper. And now you're stuck with me. I am so sorry, Joe."

He shook his head regretfully. "It can't go anywhere but up from here, right?"

Darby wondered if this was the real game of chicken fate had sent her way.

SOAP OPERA

AFTER DROPPING Darby's stuff in a pretty little guest room, which was under the stairs that led to the second floor, Joe attempted to order dinner from one of the local restaurants. Because of the conference in town, the restaurants were all slammed. He finally located one still willing to deliver out to the MacKinnon ranch, however, their order was going to be at least an hour, probably closer to two. Joe glanced at Darby, who'd been listening to his half of the conversation.

She murmured, "Okay by me." What was she going to do, haughtily point out that she was a guest here and demand better service? Turning away, her gaze swept the living room. She could see already the MacKinnon family was in a world of trouble. She wasn't a neat freak by any stretch of the imagination, but this …? She shuddered, registering too late that Joe had witnessed her reaction. She felt instantly contrite. "I-I'm sorry. I know this isn't easy for you."

He wagged his head resignedly. "What can I say? I live for the marina. The home front is in ruins."

Darby hesitated for a moment, then ventured. "And the kids? Do you … have time for the kids?"

He grimaced, looking around as if seeing his home, finally, as it actually appeared. "Not here. I take them out on the boat, to the marina. We fish; we horseback ride."

Darby waved toward the closed drapes. "It's a gorgeous day outside. Can I…?"

"Yeah, go ahead."

She picked her way across the carpet of toys and pulled back one side of the drapes. A billow of dust rose up from the cloth and lingered in the beam of light that slanted into the room. "Wow," she said, then checked that she hadn't offended Joe once again. When she saw no resentment, she said, "How about we open up a window or two and let in some fresh air?"

He strode across the room and flung the windows open. "Better yet," he pronounced with a grimace, "how about we take these damned things down and pass them through some soap and water?" He reached up and made quick work of unhooking the drapes. "Now that would be a novel idea, wouldn't it?"

"I could take the hooks off, if you like. They can be a little tricky," Darby volunteered. "We have a couple of hours to kill."

He looked over his shoulder at her. "What about your neck?"

"Doctor Turner said I should keep moving rather than sit still, actually. Nothing strenuous, but something gentle and steady would be good."

"Well, I'm not going to discourage you. I can use all the help I can get. Melody isn't coming back."

Darby arched an eyebrow at him and said dryly, "And that's a bad thing because …?"

Joe's shoulders relaxed and he began to laugh. "You know what? You're absolutely right. What the hell have I been thinking?"

"Like a man?"

"I'm a man … and I can change …" Joe's exaggerated beaten tone mimicked a favorite comedian. "If I have to …"

"You do that perfectly! Gotta love Red Green."

Joe pulled down the last of the drapes from the windows. Light poured into the house, revealing air heavy with lazy dust motes and a discouraging layer of dust on everything.

Darby swallowed thickly. They were breathing this air into their lungs. She longed to be back outside. Maybe she should have stuck with her first idea of hanging out in the bus depot for the night, then calling Laura about maybe staying out on Idle Island until she had her van problem sorted out. Yes, Joe was a nice guy, and yes, she could probably help out in the interim, but this … this problem ran deep–deeper than she was prepared to go. She traveled light.

After stuffing the drapes into the washing machine, they labored together through the next hour in the living room, Joe doing the heavy lifting and Darby moving carefully, sometimes only pointing and suggesting. Joe pulled out a huge garbage bag, the kind used for yard work, and started filling it as he made his way around the room, determining what went and what stayed. Darby followed with a wheeled laundry hamper, gathering dusty table runners and grimy throws and pillows. Some they threw away, some they decided could make it through the washer and dryer and come out okay. Shannon was given the task of gathering up all her Lego's into a bin and returning it to her playroom where it belonged. The dolls and stuffed animals followed. All the rest Joe boxed up and carried down to the basement storage for sorting another day.

Stuffed into various couch crooks and crannies they unearthed a seemingly endless supply of odd socks, children's clothes, doll clothes, towels, and bathing suits. The strange list of buried treasure went on: a snorkeling mask, a broken telescope, a dog collar, a glass paperweight, a hair brush, an interim summer school report card with Andrew's name on the top. Judging by Joe's expression, this last discovery had failed to be brought to his attention. So Andrew attended summer school? This spelled trouble.

Darby stopped short when she located and extracted an empty plastic ant farm from beneath the seat cushions of a leather chair. Mutely she held it up for Joe to see, her skin suddenly prickly. "Should we be worried?"

"There it is!" he declared. "I've been looking all over for that. We've been keeping the ants in the bathroom for a while now …" he stopped, laughing at her expression. "Relax! I'm messing with you!"

She tossed it at him.

"Nice!" He leapt away nimbly.

"If I had the strength I normally do, I'd 'a clocked you for sure," she declared weakly, her energy level abruptly at half-mast. She longed to lie down and close her eyes. She leaned against a door jamb and watched Joe strip the denim slipcovers from all the furniture, revealing beautiful neutral-grey upholstery beneath. Why cover it up, she wondered.

"I'm getting a bucket of soap and water for me, and some furniture polish for you," Joe said. "I'll scrub, you can do the lady-like polishing.

"First time I've been accused of being lady-like." She pushed away from the door jamb and wheeled the laundry bin toward the laundry room and switched over the loads. The wet fabric from the washer was heavy. With her neck so stiff, she was forced to drag the fabric from one machine to the other in small batches.

Back in the living room, Joe wiped down the walls, bookshelves and mill work while she moved slowly, spraying and polishing the furniture. She was growing to like the place. The furnishings were of good quality, and once cleared and polished, were lovely and welcoming. When Andrew and another boy around his age walked in from the yard, the surprise on their faces was almost laughable

Joe dropped his sponge into the bucket of now-black water. "Andrew, get out the Dyson and run it around the main floor." His tone had an edge it hadn't had moments before. "You're staying for supper, Dougie?"

"I guess …," the boy answered hesitantly, taking in the industry before him. Darby noticed his clothes looked a little worse for wear, his hair style the remnants of a haircut from too long ago.

Andrew scoffed, "Like you've got so many other options!"

Dougie elbowed him, and they wrestled their way back out of the living room.

"Dyson," Joe called after them. "Floors—all of them."

By the time the delivery man rang the doorbell with their dinner, the living room looked and smelled good. The drapes were still in the dryer, so the windows were bare, but they were clean. The room was actually very welcoming—a room Darby would want to spend some time in with a good book, or maybe a cup of coffee and an old friend.

Everyone, Dougie included, huddled around the large, square coffee table, loaded up plates from the cartons of food, and found seats where they could to settle back and eat. By now, Darby felt like she'd been beaten up and spit out, but kept it to herself. Joe looked so damned happy with the room and the people in it, she couldn't bring herself to say anything negative. Instead, she slipped first two pain pills, then the muscle relaxant into her mouth between bites of her dinner and waited for the effects to kick in. She'd sleep like the dead tonight.

It was inevitable she'd have to enter the kitchen sooner or later, so she took her own and Shannon's empty plates to rinse in the empty, and seemed seldom used, kitchen sink. There was plenty of counter space, though currently it was covered in crumbs and smudges with plenty of greasy dust toward the backs and corners. Forlorn, top-of-the-line counter top appliances were evident: waffle maker, blender, juicer, a one-cup coffee maker, a cappuccino machine? Darby frowned in puzzlement. And a Panini press, of all things.

It wasn't a horrible kitchen—the sticky hand-print-covered stainless steel fridge and dishwasher were commercial grade and expensive looking. It simply looked sad and abandoned, similar to how the living room had looked. She viewed the kitchen speculatively. With a good cleaning ….

Oh, but she'd be long gone soon. This was not her problem to solve. She had to find a new home on wheels and get herself out there with her camera. She had four short weeks to get her bid together for that contract. That was where her energy should be directed. Again she wondered if she would be able to find a replacement camper of some kind here in Brennan's Point or would she be forced to use precious time traveling back to Vancouver to search there.

She could save herself legwork maybe and go on line ….

Andrew appeared in the doorway with his plate of food half-finished. He hissed, "Don't get any bright ideas about staying around here permanently!"

Taken aback, Darby grasped the edge of the counter with one hand—too late she remembered its sticky edge.

"I know what your game is, and you can forget it!"

"My game?"

"He's not here, so you can drop the innocent act—and the stupid neck thing. I know you're after my dad." Andrew's voice fairly dripped with disgust. "The old 'love your kids, love you too' routine. I've seen it all before; there isn't anything you can do that'll surprise me."

"After your dad?" she echoed faintly.

Andrew rolled his eyes to the ceiling. "Give me a break. I see how you look at him. He's single, rich. Next you'll be all over him like a cheap suit." Pushing away from the door, he minced across the floor, voicing in a squeaking falsetto that only a fourteen-year-old whose voice was changing could produce. "Oh, Joe, I know how hard it is for you all alone with two children to raise. Let me take some of the burden from you, you poor man."

Darby burst out in laughter, stopping him dead in his tracks. She saw the hurt behind the anger in his young face and tried to muffle her laughter behind her other, still-clean hand. "I'm sorry, I don't mean to laugh at you. I'm just very tired. Believe me, I won't be 'all over your dad like a cheap suit.'" Hardly the expression she'd have expected from a fourteen-year-old – a seventy-five-year-old maybe …. A fresh burst of laughter bubbled up in spite of her efforts to be conciliatory. The very idea of her strapped down here in Brennan's Point was too damned funny.

"You will be sorry," he said. "Sorry you ever met my dad. I'll get rid of you just like I got rid of all the others. Just wait and see."

Darby sobered. "Look, Andy, your dad's safe from me, okay? I have plans of my own, and they don't include a husband, or a family. I have no designs on yours."

"You won't be around long enough to try." Then as suddenly as his expression had changed from neutral to hostile, his face was wiped of any sign of emotion. He picked up a slice of garlic bread and took a bite.

Joe walked into the kitchen with little Shannon draped over his shoulder, asleep, and understanding dawned on Darby. She watched Andrew's bland countenance in grudging admiration. Oh, he was good–smooth. Joe probably had no idea how strong his son's insecurities were and how he was dealing with them.

"I'm going over to Dougie's." Andrew shoved the last of the garlic bread into his mouth, and bolted for the door.

"Be in by ten, son." Joe turned back to Darby. "This is the last we'll be hearing from this one," he murmured, shifting Shannon gently. "You good for the night? I'm going to put her to bed, then call it a day myself."

"Absolutely," she agreed, turning on the taps and washing her hands. Her muscle relaxing pills had kicked in–thus the fit of giggles–and she was feeling absolutely no pain. In fact, she felt a bit spacey. A hot bath and a bed sounded perfect.

Back in the tidy guest room Darby reached into one of her duffel bags, hauled out her preferred sleepwear: comfy grey leggings and an oversized grey T-shirt that declared *Another Day Passed, and I Didn't Use Calculus Once!* on its well-worn front. Before she went into the adjoining guest bathroom, she glanced at the bedroom door, noting the lock was flimsy at best. Should she be worried? Put a chair under the handle? Ridiculous–as if Joe MacKinnon needed to break down bedroom doors to get a woman.

In the bathroom, she turned on the taps full force, adjusted the temperature, and added bath salts. She saw someone had thoughtfully hung a thick white terry robe on the back of the door. Nice. Spying a fat candle by the tub, she lit it with the lighter provided, then flipped off the overhead light. In the flickering candlelight the steaming tub looked heavenly. Removing the stifling collar with a satisfying rip of Velcro, she stripped off her grimy T-shirt, skirt, and undergarments and stepped into the tub. Her weary body sagged in the water. "Oh. My. God." Lying back against a folded hand towel, she closed her weary eyes and reviewed her strange day.

She'd come to take pictures and camp in the beautiful surrounding woodlands and instead was now living—if temporarily—with a strange family.

But there was something here, something she felt she should be recognizing, like something you see out of your peripheral vision, but when you turned your head to see it's gone. Not that she'd be turning her head much over the next several days.

She unwrapped the guest soap and began lathering her arms and legs leisurely, gently stretching her neck and back in the warm water. This was so much better than her customary bird baths in the van, which were necessarily brief, shivery, get-the-job-done affairs. With her toes she turned up the lever, adding more hot water into the tub, her weary bones soaking in the heat.

So what about that contract? Using the brand new post office box she'd opened this morning at the Brennan's Point post office as her contact point, she'd sent in her application along with the requested ten sample photos. If her ten photos were judged to be of the caliber Tourism B.C. wanted, she would receive an invitation to bid. That could happen within the next month, maybe within weeks. Then, she could pull out all the stops, send in her serious work—the pictures she'd been working on for the last three summers as she traveled around the countryside in her trusty camperized van. She sighed, taking a moment to mourn the old dear. It had seen her through many adventures, and now it was a heap in the local junk yard. Poor old thing.

Living in her mother's house wasn't an option, obviously. She'd made her choice about the estate months ago, and there was no going back now, no matter how much her circumstances had changed.

Lathering up the bar of soap, she stiffened. Holding her arms out before her in the flickering candlelight, she let out a stifled scream. Her arms were green!

Her legs—were green. Wherever she had soaped had turned a horrible, zombie, I-should-be-dead-by-now green!

She screamed out again in horror, scrambling to her feet with noisy splashes and reached for a towel, her neck sudden agony at her jerking movements. The door burst open. The overhead lights glared harshly. She snapped toward it and gasped in pain, clutching the towel against her wet body, momentarily blinded by the sudden bright light. Then she saw Joe and Buddy in the doorway, gaping at her in bewilderment. Joe's focus dropped to her legs and slowly worked its way up her body to her face.

"What in God's name have you done?"

"What have I done?" Her voice was edged in hysteria. Adjusting the towel frantically, she stepped out of the tub. "Look at me!"

"I am." The look on Joe's face made her throat close around her words. His eyes held hers for a heartbeat before he turned his attention to the tub. To put an extra edge on her discomfort, Buddy was now in the bathroom, his feathered tail whacking against the tub as he licked one of her wet green legs. She nudged him away, hugging the towel more closely and shivering. Joe had barely picked up the offending bar of soap when he looked up again.

"Andy's idea of a joke," he said with a frown. "I'm sorry, Darby, I should have warned you; he does make life hard on whomever I hire."

"You didn't *hire* me," she reminded him through clenched teeth. "You *hit* me with your stupid truck!" Buddy continued licking the water off her leg, and she gave him another ungracious shove, feeling the motion instantly in her neck.

"He thinks I'm trying to replace his mother and resents the hell out of it."

"Oh! My! God! Do you really think I want to discuss Andrew's troubles right here, right now, right this very second?"

Just then the towel that held together whatever scrap of modesty she could muster was yanked hard and pulled nearly out of her grasp. Buddy had a good hold on the other end of it and was shaking his head, tussling with his new toy. Darby screamed and pulled what remained of her cover to her breasts. Buddy dropped his end of the towel as if burned, and fled from the bathroom.

Furious with embarrassment, Darby gathered the towel tightly around her and turned accusing eyes to Joe. "You trained him to do that!"

At least Joe had the grace to look sheepish. "I did, as a matter of fact." His eyes widened in alarm at seeing the expression of her face. "But not off of naked women!" A beat of loaded silence lay between them. "That part was his idea," he added with a barely suppressed laugh.

"You think this is funny? Are you out of your mind?" When Joe opened his mouth to speak, she silenced him with a glare. "No, don't answer that. I'm out of my mind to even be in this hell hole!" She dropped her head back–which hurt like freaking hell–and wailed to the universe, "Seriously–why am I even here? And you'd better make it good!"

Joe raised his eyebrows. "Someone else in here I should know about?" When she didn't answer, he hastened to add, "You do have the right to be a little upset." At the daggered look she shot him, he amended, "Okay, a lot upset. But, Buddy does have a good excuse. We trained him to pick up forgotten towels from the beach and bring them home. He was doing what he thought was another towel rescue."

Darby narrowed her eyes and stared him down, watching for any sign he was lying. Nothing. It did seem as if he was innocent of setting this up. Oh, hell. She slumped against the edge of the tub.

All at once, she was monstrously fatigued. All she wanted was for Joe to be gone and this terrible day to end. "Okay, okay, I buy it. Pass me that robe." Her gaze danced away from his, coming to rest on the reflection of her face in the bathroom mirror. "Oh, my God," she moaned again, softly this time, flushing a bright pink under her new green mask. Not only that, she was sure Joe had seen the whole length of her body in its reflection. Could she be more embarrassed? The impulse to cover her face with her hands stopped when the towel began to slip to the floor. She felt tears pricking behind her eyes and blinked quickly to avoid that final exposure. *Come on, Girl. You're way tougher than this.*

Joe reached around her shoulders with the robe, bringing it snugly around her and bunching the cloth together at her chin. She shoved her arms hastily into the sleeves then let the towel drop to the floor. Cinching the robe tightly around her waist she waited for him to step back. He didn't.

"I'm sorry, Darby," he said softly, shaking his head. "You've had a terrible day."

"Yes," she answered, her voice faint and decidedly wobbly. She hated herself for it, and hated that he was hearing it. Struggling to inject some strength back into her tone, she said, "I guess I don't have my sense of humor quite in gear yet."

He bent to pick up the soap wrapper and read the printing. "Vinegar," he pronounced, frowning. "I think we have some."

"Great," she said, dropping Buddy's "rescued" towel into the hamper. "Could you get me some, please—sooner rather than later?"

With a nod, he turned and left, and it was all she could do to stop herself from slamming the door behind him. Where was her cell phone? She'd call Laura right this instant, beg her to come up from Vancouver at once and take her away from all this misery.

WHO ARE YOU?

JOE WAS back with a jug of white vinegar. She looked warily around for Buddy.

"Oh, don't worry about Buddy," Joe assured her. "With all your screaming, he'll be hiding for days."

"All my ..." Darby started to protest, but gave it up immediately. She was too damned tired and knew she'd never win. "Just give me the vinegar," she said weakly, recognizing with a sinking heart that Joe had full intentions of staying for this particular experiment. Ooh-kay. Let's get this over with. Soaking a facecloth with vinegar, she wiped at her arm, avoiding her newly formed scabs. It did lighten the green. She scrubbed at it some more, desperate for success. With relief, she saw her natural color return. "Thank goodness. I'm okay now, you can go."

"You're sure?"

"What—you're going to scrub the green off me?" she blurted. "I don't think so."

"I was thinking about around your eyes, actually. It's going to sting like hell."

"Oh." She looked into the mirror again. He was right, her eyes were surrounded in her normal heavy liner and the horrible zombie green. Charming. "All right." She dug into her makeup bag and produced a handful of cotton balls and her makeup remover. "Use these."

She sat on the edge of the tub and closed her eyes. She heard the sound of the toilet seat cover going down and Joe settling in for the task at hand. After a moment, she felt a cold wet cotton ball touch her cheek, then quickly move away.

"What about your cuts?" Joe's voice was worried.

Keeping her eyes closed, she answered, "They'll be fine. Even if they weren't fine, the green has got to go."

"True." The cool cotton was on her face again, this time brushing across her forehead, working from center to temple rhythmically, then her cheeks, jaw, then finally from over her nose and across her eyelids, then repeating the action, with pauses for what she guessed was changing out the cotton balls, sometimes soaked in vinegar, its scent sharp, other times with makeup remover, its scent sweet. Each stroke across her face and eyes was gentle and without impatience.

Now the cotton was gone, the room silent. She frowned, resisting the temptation to peek. "Is it working?"

"Hang on." She heard water run in the sink, and the sound of a cloth being rung out, then felt him return to her. Now a warm cloth was pressed against her skin, then gently drawn across each eye. The heat felt wonderful. "You look very different without your eye makeup," Joe murmured as he worked, his voice taking on an edge of wonder.

Darby smiled. "Without my war paint, you mean?"

A long silence followed as Joe worked. Finally he said, "Is that what it's called these days?" There was no answering smile in his voice. In fact, he sounded strange.

"I do. I draw on those lines and wear them like armor. It's my 'don't mess with me' look."

Quiet filled the room. "But not at night," he murmured, his warm breath fanning her face.

"There's no one to ward off at night," she explained. "At night, I'm safe." Though the irony of this statement was instantly apparent to her–she was naked under this robe, it was night and she was alone with a man she barely knew. How had she even gotten into this situation?

"You can open your eyes now." His voice told her he was still very close.

Slowly, testing for stinging, she opened first one eye, then the other and found Joe's unnaturally pale face mere inches away from her own. The shock she saw in his eyes alarmed her.

"What? It didn't come off?"

His eyes were dark pools of anguished confusion.

"Oh, no!" She pushed away from the edge of the tub to the vanity, afraid of what she would see. And saw–nothing unusual. Joe stood up behind her. Mystified, her gaze met his in the mirror, where he continued to gaze at her strangely, as if riveted. Her face looked like it always did, plus a few newly formed scabs across her forehead and left cheek from the windshield this morning, but nothing Earth-shattering, nothing that warranted his shocked expression of incredulous amazement. If that's what it was. Apprehension trickled up her spine. Something else was going on here, something she didn't know about, and maybe didn't want to know about. Why, oh why wasn't she safely down at the bus depot?

She moved to stand by the door and gripped the handle, a silent invitation to leave. "Thanks, Joe. I'll take it from here." She made her smile dazzling to encourage his exit, only it seemed to have the opposite effect. Instead of nodding and turning away, his eyes grew brighter, his expression a mixture of shock, and recognition and … yes, even what she'd call … horror?

Finally, he whispered, "Who are you?"

She stared back at him, not comprehending.

"I mean it, Darby, who the hell are you?"

"Are you freaking kidding me? I'm Darby Walker, the woman you slammed your truck into this morning. End of story."

"No! That can't be the end of the story. It absolutely cannot be the end of the story." He reached for her hand and pulled her from the bathroom, through her bedroom and out past the living room and down a hallway. "Come with me."

When she saw he was bringing her into his bedroom, she balked. "Hey, buddy, hold your horses …"

He shook his head, looking distracted as he scanned the room as if reacquainting himself with a place he hadn't seen in a very long time. "No, it's not what you think. I have absolutely no interest in you in that way."

She pulled back on his hand and raised her eyebrows at him. "And this is supposed to make me feel better?"

"What, you want me to jump you on your first night here?"

"No. But a gentleman would at least pretend that he wanted to."

He stopped short and swung his gaze toward her in surprise. "What?"

Darby could see he didn't have a clue what she was talking about. Men! She crossed her arms. "Okay, Mister. What are you freaking out about, and make it quick, otherwise I'm out of here in the next five minutes."

Now he looked at her, really looked at her. "This is what living on the streets in Vancouver does to a girl?"

Darby rolled her eyes around his austere bedroom, completely devoid of any personality. "And this is what being a widow with two kids does to a guy?" When he simply stared back at her, she softened. Obviously, Joe MacKinnon's head just wasn't in the game. "Look, what's your problem? I know something is bothering you. Just tell me what it is, then we can all go safely to our own separate beds."

"Right." He turned toward a set of double doors, seemed to reset himself, then opened them with a flourish, flipped on a light, and disappeared inside a huge walk-in closet. Since he didn't immediately come back out, she followed him in.

Evidently, Joe wasn't big on clothes. The rungs on all three interior walls were mostly empty, with a small section holding a lonely group of two, maybe three suits and six or eight shirts in various muted colors. These meager offerings were reflected around the room by the mirror-clad walls and splashed her apprehensive expression back at her from varying angles, again and again. She had to pull her eyes away, and concentrate instead on her host's frantic behavior.

Joe was pulling banker boxes feverishly down from overhead shelves, flipping off their tops, rummaging inside each before discarding it and moving on to another. Finally, he stopped, and with a satisfied grunt, came up with a shoe box. "Here." He dropped to the floor.

Darby found herself on her knees in a sea of open boxes beside him, peering into a shoe box filled with photos.

"These." He spilled them across what little floor space remained open and shuffled through them, looking for something. They were all pictures of the same woman—a blonde, pretty woman with a heart-shaped face, just like hers, and bow-shaped lips, just like hers, and intense green eyes, just like hers ….

Darby sank back on her heels and whispered, "Who is this?"

"Ah!" he said, satisfied. "This one; when she was twenty-five." He held up the photo for Darby to see, his eyes boring into hers, waiting for her reaction.

She gasped in recognition. It was Darby, only it wasn't Darby. This was Darby if she'd grown up in Middle America, all soft and blonde, a gentle smile on her face, wearing pale pink and cream-colored clothes; expensive, what Darby would term "white bread" clothes—lacy silk collar, tiny pearl buttons, and a slender, body-clinging linen skirt—in Darby's eyes, a fashion nightmare. But—this fashion nightmare could be Darby's twin.

"I'm twenty-five," she whispered, reaching out and taking the picture from his hands.

"So she was ten years older than you."

"Who is she?" she asked again, guessing the answer already.

"This was my wife, Nadine."

"Your wife ... Nadine?" she repeated stupidly, she knew, but couldn't help herself. Her brain was floating out there somewhere, unable to put the facts together. Why was Nadine MacKinnon almost her exact replica?

"You and I have some digging to do."

She raised her eyes to his. "We do?"

He stared back at her, assessing her it seemed, then said, "Nadine was adopted."

Darby dropped the picture as if it were aflame and scrambled to her feet, her neck protesting almost as loudly as her brain. This was not happening. "That's not possible. What you're suggesting—it's simply not possible," she whispered and launched herself out of Joe MacKinnon's Fun House of Mirrors.

SNIP!

JOE FOUND her in the dark, outside on the front porch, wrapped in the guest room quilt, and swinging on the porch swing urgently. Her collar was back around her neck, and one bare tanned foot, no longer green, propelled the swing. The rest of her was tucked inside the quilt, deceptively still, though he imagined her brain had to be racing a mile a minute. How could it not, with what he's just sprung on her?

"Darby?" he said, testing the waters. When she didn't balk, he emerged from the house, past the swing to the deck railing, and turned to face her. In the moonlight, her resemblance to Nadine hit him in the gut, though this time he was better able to cover it up. He simply couldn't afford to frighten her away. He needed to know all about Darby Walker, needed to know why she was here in his house. It was as if Nadine's ghost had shown up with urgent information and it was his task to decipher her message.

After a moment of silence, he asked, "Can't sleep?"

She burst out, "No shit, Sherlock! What was your first clue?"

He bobbed his head with an outward show of understanding, while frantically searching for a way to reach out to her, to calm her, keep her here. One little push, and she'd be gone, and with her would go Nadine's message. Nadine's message? He slumped against the railing, recognizing how crazy his thinking was. What weird trip am I on? He glanced up at Darby and was unable to tear his eyes away.

"Is this why everyone in town was looking at me so strangely this afternoon?" Darby burst out again.

Surprised, he answered, "Everyone?"

She nodded at him, her eyes wide and staring. "Yeah. How could you not see?"

"I was … distracted. Feeling bad about the accident and your neck, and …. Well, it doesn't matter now, does it? Obviously, they saw something I didn't."

She sighed noisily. "What a mess."

"No kidding."

Suddenly she smiled, then burst out in a laugh. "No kidding? That's all you've got?"

He found himself returning her smile. Who could resist? She filled up the space with joy when she smiled, the same as Nadine had done. His leavened mood faltered. He dropped his chin to his chest. "Yeah–that's all I've got."

"So what are we going to do?"

He shrugged his shoulders. "Where do we even start?"

"I can tell you that the idea of my mother adopting me–on purpose–given how much she did not enjoy being a mother, is beyond my comprehension."

"Could she have had a child before?"

"Never. I'd know it for sure. My mother never let an opportunity pass to grind me down with every piece of guilt at her disposal. I can't imagine her leaving something as juicy as her sacrificing a child on the table untouched."

He grimaced. "Sounds …"

"Crappy?" she provided. "In case you're wondering, my mother died last year, so there'll be no going and asking 'Mommy Dearest.'" She leaned back into the swing. "I'm sorry. That was rude, and uncalled for. My mother and I had a complicated relationship. But this much I know for sure–my mother did not have a daughter and give her away. If that were an option, I'd have been out the door the day I was born–good riddance."

"Bleak."

"Yeah."

"Maybe you were adopted?" He knew this was going around in a circle, but he couldn't help himself. There had to be some explanation as to why he was staring at Nadine's twin.

"You didn't know my mother. Trust me—not remotely possible." She eased her neck from side to side in a gentle stretch then frowned. "Maybe this is a massive, fantastical coincidence? They say we all have a twin somewhere in the world. Maybe Nadine was mine?"

He pushed away from the railing and paced the length of the deck. "I don't believe that for a minute."

"Yeah, me either," she admitted. "I'm all about what's meant to be, but when it slaps me in the face, maybe not so much."

"More like a punch in the stomach."

"So where do we go from here?"

He stopped pacing and searched her face in the darkness. "You're willing to stay, to help me out?"

"I'm willing to hear you out. I can see it's very important to you."

"It could be." He considered her for a moment, hesitant to dive into the heart of the matter so quickly, but hey, maybe this was his only chance. "Andrew isn't my natural son."

She was silent, obviously digesting this new information, then said, "Okay."

"He has a rare blood type, same as Nadine. I live in fear for that boy—he's always taking insane chances. Today was the perfect example. What if the accident had turned out differently? All I've thought about since the ambulance ride this morning is finding some way to stockpile his goddamned blood type for his next crazy stunt." He waved away her imagined protest. "I know I sound crazy—ghoulish even. Stockpiling blood? Who does that? But these are the mental pathways a teenage boy with an apparent death wish forces your mind to travel down. I know this is presumptuous, I know this will probably send you screaming out of my house, but I have to ask—do you know your blood type?" He winced at hearing the words come out of his mouth. No preamble, no smoothing the waters, just the direct hit—I want your blood.

Darby's leg was motionless now, the swing still. She was sitting upright, her gaze riveted to his, with emotions he could not name crossing her face. He waited for her to leap up in outrage at his suggestion that she become the blood cow for his reckless son. He wouldn't blame her, but he could not allow this opportunity to slip away.

Finally she said, "No, I don't know my blood type." Her tone was even, cautious, maybe talk-the-crazy-man-down cautious as you back slowly away from the high ledge he's standing on. Could he blame her?

He made himself laugh, the sound hollow in the darkness, and he wondered if he'd have had the courage to ask her in the light of day. But the subject was now on the table. He pressed on, "Since you haven't run screaming from the building, I'm guessing you're at least considering my proposal."

"Which is?"

"We find out what blood type you are, and if you're a match you donate blood, over time, which I stockpile locally for Andrew's next big adventure? Andrew's considered too young to donate. And Brennan's Point is a small town. Airlifting blood from Vancouver might take too much time." God, it sounded so frigging bad. Why wasn't she screaming and running from the building?

She surprised him instead with her next question. "Shannon's yours?"

"Yes."

"Nadine had Andrew with another man? You're Andrew's stepfather?"

"Yes."

She studied him in the darkness, then finally said, "You love Andrew."

"More than my life."

"I'll help you."

He couldn't believe his incredible good luck. "You're willing to help a stranger?"

"Yes."

"Just like that?"

"Yes."

"That's a lot of yeses." He couldn't help the grin that spread across his face. He wanted to grab her and swing her around the deck with pure joy. Either that or put his head between his knees until the sudden head rush that hit him now was gone. He stammered, "And … how we all might be related … that means nothing?"

"No. Well, yes, why Nadine and I look so alike is kind of weird, and seems to need exploring, even if only for curiosity, but that has no impact on my helping Andrew."

Should he press his luck and tell her the next idea that had been popping around inside his head like a Mexican jumping bean since finding Nadine's photograph in the closet? "We could do DNA testing between you and Nadine."

"How? I'm here, she isn't."

"I do have a lock of her hair, in Shannon's baby book. We could have that tested against yours, at a lab somewhere–wherever these things are done …" he faded off. The enormity of what he was asking of this strangely put-together mini-Nadine seemed suddenly too large to support. No one in their right mind would agree to this bizarre scheme. Yet he waited, his breath abated, for her answer.

Okay," she replied. "We can do that too. If I'm a blood match, I'll stay the rest of the summer. I'll donate blood, you can arrange for it to be stored, I'm guessing at the hospital? I'll do my photo tour of the area like I'd planned, and we'll wait to see what this all means."

"You serious?"

"Yup. Go get some scissors before I chicken out." She raised her hands to her head, dragging his gaze along with her black-polished fingernails as they combed though each colored section of hair in turn, first the honey blonde at the crown, just like Nadine's, so he'd guess that part was natural, then through the almost electric red and ending with ebony at the tips. She complained cheerfully, "I was just getting used to this new look."

He laughed in spite of himself. Darby may look like Nadine, but her mercurial personality and painted on "armor" were the complete opposite. Nadine would have sat here, heard him out, then stewed about his proposal for days, carefully considering all her options before choosing what to do. This was how she approached life: with consideration and caution. It had both assured him and frustrated the hell out of him during their time together. Nothing was easy with Nadine, always a production. Nadine's thoughtful and measured approach to life had also ensured that Shannon was delivered safely into this world, and for that he'd always be grateful.

He said, "All right. Let's do this." He reached out for her hand and pulled her up from the swing. She stood up easily, and he was shocked to find himself wanting to bring her all the way into his embrace, to feel her against him, even for a short while. He still missed Nadine, of course. Or maybe it was the feeling of another human being against his body, warm and welcoming, that he missed. It had been so long—too damned long.

He shuddered, appalled by his sudden, naked need to envelope this slender little woman with the big heart inside his arms. Geez, MacKinnon! Get your shit together! If she had any idea of this new path your brain is suddenly tumbling down, she'd be gone before you could say "blood bank."

She was gazing up at him, her eyes wide with questions. He saw her swallow before speaking and instantly realized that he made Darby Walker nervous, and for some unfathomable reason he was very happy about that fact.

It was as if he'd torn a veil from his vision and was seeing his world clearly for the first time in a very long time. Everything around him was brighter, richer, and pulsated with an underlying energy. He felt alive and charged up, and it seemed as if he suddenly possessed the power to move mountains or hold back the tides, or fly up into the sky if he wished it.

She whispered, "You're not about to sink your teeth into my neck to get your first donation, are you?"

Laughter erupted from deep inside his body, the sound warming, softening the cold places in his heart and rolling out across the night air, releasing him from the prison he hadn't even known he'd made for himself. He laughed with relief and gratitude. "Not with the damned collar on, I'm not. Mighty inconvenient, that collar."

Darby's eyebrows rose, and her chin tilted as she stroked the collar almost lovingly, falling in with his mood. "I'll be keeping it on for sure, then, Mr. MacKinnon—just to be on the safe side."

"Mac, my friends call me Mac."

She looked back at him speculatively then sighed with feigned resignation. "Alas, you will always be a Joe to me. I will call you Joe."

"You can call me Josephine Zahoolafat if your blood's a match." He led the way back inside the house to the kitchen. "We have scissors in one of the drawers in here. And Ziploc sandwich bags. And we'll need some way to label it."

He flipped on the kitchen light, and they rummaged around for the scissors and sandwich bag, finding both at once. Darby came up with a fine-tipped marker. Then, facing one another, Joe held the scissors poised in the air. He hesitated, considering her tricolored hair. Would hair dye affect the test results?

And how exactly did one chop into a woman's hair anyway? He glanced down and met her steady gaze. "Where should I cut?"

She shrugged. "Wherever."

Surprised, he looked over her small, shiny head doubtfully then back to her steady green eyes. She really did seem to understand and accept what they were about to do, as if she were merely meeting her fate. Was that what was happening here—was this fate in action? He lowered the scissors indecisively. "You're sure?"

"Is there another way?"

He pressed his mouth together before admitting, "Not really."

"Then cut a chunk from the root, so you get some blonde hair, the part I haven't dyed yet."

"That'll look ... not so good."

She raised her eyebrows at him with exasperation. "You think this is the worst thing to happen to me? It's hair—it'll grow back."

Before he could change his mind, he lifted a section of hair and snipped it away, the portion left behind springing into the air at the sudden loss of the weight of the rest. He grimaced and glanced down at Darby's face. She was not going to like this new look. Her placid expression did surprise him, however. Wasn't a woman's hair supposed to be her "crowning glory"? He really didn't understand women.

"Hey, maybe they need a hair root for the test?"

"You want me to yard some hair by the root?"

"Well, not a handful! Here, let me." She grasped a couple of strands of hair at her temple and with a grimace gave them a quick tug and dropped them into the plastic sandwich bags. "All done?" she asked, running her finger across her head to where he'd snipped, finding the nub of hair sticking into the air. Her expression transformed into horror. She wailed, "Oh, my God, not from there!"

He jumped back, dropping the lock of hair. "You said ..."

"Kidding!" she laughed, stroking the little nub back as if she could glue it down with the rest. "Just kidding. You've unloaded a truckload of family stuff on me tonight. Don't I get even a little chance to add in some drama of my own?"

He expelled the breath he had been holding. "Sure." Then he realized the hair was gone. No, not gone, the long, tricolored lock was resting on the swell of one of her rounded breasts, curled around the faded letter 'O' in the word

Another on the soft fabric of her nightshirt. The soft fabric that so clearly outlined nipples, hardened by …. His heartbeat kicked up a notch.

Cold. It was cold in here. This wasn't sexual, he assured himself, damping down the inevitable reaction the sight brought to his body. This was not the time or the place or the person he wanted to desire. The stakes were too damned high to risk following where his traitorous physiological reaction was leading. Darby's green eyes traced his gaze to her chest. Hesitant to touch her, to retrieve the lock of hair, he paced off time by reading her T-shirt aloud in what he hoped sounded as a half-amused tone, "Another Day Passed, and I Didn't Use Calculus Once. Nice."

She plucked the lock of hair from its resting place and slipped it inside the Ziploc bag, sealing it. "I thought so." Smiling, she handed him the bag. "There you go, Sherlock. Sleuth to your heart's content."

Did she really have no clue that he was one breath away from tearing that well-worn T-shirt away from her body? They could do a little of the new math– one plus one could add up to a multitude of interesting ways to spend quality time together.

He backed off, made a business of labeling the Ziploc with the marker, shaken by the strength of his reaction to Darby Walker. This had to be memories of Nadine, he told himself, knowing it had absolutely nothing to do with Nadine and everything to do with the little woman standing in the middle of his kitchen and filling the entirety of his home with her huge, all-encompassing sexuality, her sheer don't-mess-with-me, I-add-my-own-drama personality.

Or not.

He snorted and relaxed abruptly. He was full of shit. He was just plain horny! Time to return to your respective corners, people, and regroup.

Recovered, he turned back to her with a smile on his face. "You know you're in for a hell of a summer?"

"I know a lot more than you think I do." Her green eyes sparkled. "'Night, Joe."

And then she was gone, and he was standing alone in the bright kitchen with a Ziploc bag full of their future gripped in his hand.

THROUGH THE LENS SPARKLY

STILL IN last night's pajamas, Darby walked slowly. Shannon was tiring of their morning walk along the beach and was stopping more and more often to examine a myriad of finds along the way, staying with each for longer periods of time. Darby paused without protest, allowing Shannon to rest and play, while she drank in their surroundings. She loved the way the wet sand felt solid with each footfall, yet gave a little as well, and the gritty sound it made under her shoes. She loved how the sky was endlessly robin's egg blue, with small, highly placed puffs of cloud drifting dreamily by, when only an hour ago it had looked as if a storm was brewing.

Now, with the sun back out, the water sparkled, winking a bright Morse code to the sea birds gliding in the air currents overhead. Their answering cries, sometimes plaintive, other times shrill, served as contrasting punctuation to the low whistling rustle of the breeze through trees and grass. Where the sky and water met, distant rich, green islands dotted the horizon, the closest and prettiest of which was Laura's Idle Island, but then Darby was prejudiced.

Close to shore, the colors of the sea changed from greys and steel blues to a beautiful foamy green that seemed to reach for her with each sweep to shore.

Pulling her camera out from her fanny pack, she set up for another shot.

"Darby," Shannon asked, "can I take this one home? It has a pretty feather stuck to it."

Mindful of her collar, Darby squatted beside the little girl and regarded Shannon's latest find very seriously. It was a slender twist of driftwood that had been left by the tide the night before. Its grain was worn to high definition by the sea and finished to a gentle, grey patina. A white gull's feather, tipped with black, clung tenaciously to it in the breeze, defying gravity. "Shannon, why don't you sit real close, and I'll take another picture of you."

Darby had come up with what she hoped was a sure-fire method to keep the junk they'd cleared from the MacKinnon home out of the house permanently. Slow to pick up on her suggestion, Shannon had hauled an ever-growing load for the first hour of their walk, but had recently been talked into leaving her treasures for others to enjoy, as long as Darby took the agreed-upon picture of her with them.

While Darby focused the lens of her camera, a giant dragonfly flew into the shot, its wings beating a low whirling sound that seemed to vibrate the air. She clicked off a number of shots as the iridescent insect hovered over the driftwood before landing. It was an incredibly beautiful creature, with the sunlight glinting off its silvery translucent wings and subtly colored, segmented body. To Darby, it looked as ancient as the world and almost as wise.

"Oh, Darby," Shannon cooed softly. "Can I touch it? Can I keep it?"

"No, Honey. It's giving us a gift just by letting us see it. We never reach out to such a fragile creature. Mother Nature doesn't want us to touch; she wants us to know how wonderful our world is, and to love it like she does."

"I do love it," Shannon breathed reverently.

"I know you do," Darby answered softly. "You are a part of nature too, beautiful and free, just like this dragonfly. You remember that, okay? Mother Nature loves you the same as she loves this little guy."

Shannon giggled, and in the blink of an eye changed from wondrous human being to pure little girl, rolling onto her back in the sand and flinging her chubby little arms over her head, declaring, "Daddy loves me best."

Darby angled the camera to include Shannon and took more shots with the driftwood and dragonfly still in the frame, the sound of the camera whirring like the dragonfly's wings had only moments before. She'd thought her neck would limit her ability today, but that hadn't happened; these were spectacular shots. She should enlarge the best ones and have them framed for Joe. But maybe after getting one of Andrew first. That wasn't going to be easy ....

Shannon's gaze shifted from the camera lens. Her face lit up with joy. "Daddy!" Darby snapped the picture before turning to face her host.

"You've really got the bug," Joe MacKinnon called out, the husky sound of his voice falling in with sounds nature had assembled. It belonged. Looking up, Darby saw that he belonged. His feet were bare, pants rolled to mid-calf, exposing well-formed legs, deeply tanned and covered with golden hair. His shirt and shoes were tied around his middle, and again curled, golden hair covered his chest and torso in a v shape that disappeared at his waist. A tiny twinge reverberated low in her gut. Ignoring it, she focused her camera and took his picture. What she had previously thought as overly long hair now looked right, whipped back from his face by the wind.

"Carry me, Daddy. I'm tired."

He took in Shannon's pink pajamas, now wet to the knees and dragging in the sand. "I see you're dressed for bed already."

"Darby said we can have a Pajama Therapy Day."

"She did, did she?" Joe lifted Shannon to sit astride his shoulders, with a sideways glance at the words on Darby's T-shirt, *You Dim Sum, You Lose Sum.* "Is this a thing with you, the T-shirt thing?"

"I collect 'em," Darby replied, taking shots of father and daughter together before falling into step with him. "They make me happy. Are you back for lunch? Mrs. Russell threatened us with egg salad sandwiches earlier. This was before Shannon and I stepped outside in our pajamas, only for a moment, mind you. We haven't looked back since."

"So I noticed." He jogged in a circle with a delighted Shannon. Darby's camera whirred. Joe returned to walk beside Darby again. "Nice camera. You take it everywhere you go?"

"Yup. It's my life. Everywhere I go, I see people or objects or places in freeze-frame. I'm always setting up the shot in my head, planning the best light, the best angle."

"Always the observer, not the participant; on the outside looking in. A safe way to live," he concluded. "No personal involvement."

Darby pressed her lips together. She'd been unprepared for the criticism, and it was surprisingly hurtful. "I feel as much as anyone," she defended, regretting instantly that she'd said anything. Never let them see you sweat.

"I'm sorry, I shouldn't have said that. After what you did for Andrew and me yesterday, the last thing you are is uninvolved." He stopped and turned toward her. "I think after you've sand-blasted clean a man's fridge, we can safely assume you are totally involved. There can be no secrets now."

Darby laughed, forgetting her injured pride. Mucking out the fridge first thing this morning had been a gift really, allowing for that awkward transition from last night's strange agreement to her first day as a permanent guest at the MacKinnon ranch.

"The real reason I'm home is I need you to take Shannon in for some summer clothes when you go fill that gargantuan grocery list we made up this morning. Don't worry, the grocery store delivers, and Mrs. Russell will be here to accept it all when they do. It's the state of Shannon's clothes that's really alarming. I hadn't realized how fast she was growing out of her clothes. Everything is too small. I've arranged for you to charge at Claymores."

"I'm always up for spending someone else's money—so much more relaxing than spending my own."

"Andrew could use some decent jeans, too; minus the strategic holes, if you can manage it."

"And how will I get into town to do this?"

"A rental. It's being delivered here around one today. You'll need some kind of transportation while you're here. I don't want you to regret agreeing to help me out until the end of the summer."

"Thanks. It'll be good, as long as I get out with the camera every day." She reached up and gave one of Shannon's hands a squeeze. "And as long as this little one doesn't get tired of following me around."

"You can invite Laura over, or family, and have a good visit if you want. Consider our house your home."

"I'm way ahead of you. I called Laura this morning. She's going to swing by later in the week. As for my family, there is no family." She knew this information was disappointing, in light of their pending investigation into her connec-
⸺ith his family. Roberta's death shut the door on an important source of
ᴮut then, Roberta had never been forthcoming unless it suited her.
ᴺera away as they walked.
t your photography."

"Want me to bore you with all my lofty aspirations?"

"Go ahead, bore me to tears."

"Don't cry, Daddy." Shannon petted her father's head.

Darby laughed. "Don't worry, Honey, I won't make your daddy cry. It's not that exciting anyway."

"Ah come on, you're dying to tell us." Joe grinned down at her. A long dimple appeared in his yet-unshaven cheek, his unruly hair combed back by the breeze. The woman in her recognized that he was delicious.

"I heard the tourist bureau's promotional contract was coming due this fall through my friend, Maggie. She has a friend down in Victoria in the tourism branch, and he told her they weren't happy with their current guy and planned to send out for tenders this year. Maggie thought of me, and gave me the heads up, so I decided to give it my best shot. I had a bit of money left from a grant I earned in the last year of school and no one keeping me, so I gambled. I bought the old camper, packed up my equipment, some clothes, a sleeping bag, and each summer I've taken time off from the magazine where I worked to explore British Columbia like I never would have otherwise.

"I've been up north, in the interior and along the Kootenay and Rocky Mountains. All beautiful. I've hit hot spots, the out-of-the-way places, covering boutiques, restaurants, hotels, golf courses, would-be, could-be lucky fishing holes, campgrounds, old-growth forests, everything and anything. I've bumped down logging roads, abandoned roads, and hydro cuts, old oil and gas exploration roads, goat trails. Anywhere I thought I would find the unfindable. Now I'm concentrating along the coast."

"You did all this on a shoestring?"

"A mighty skinny one," she confirmed. She'd gotten it down to a science, in fact. She could break down or set up camp in less than ten minutes, and she could produce a decent meal in her camper from almost anything she had at hand. She smiled to herself; life's little triumphs. "I really want that contract."

"Good money?"

"Very good money. But it's not the money itself I want; it's the freedom it'll give me."

"Freedom from what?"

"I won't have to answer to anyone, for starters," she answered. "Deadlines, cranky editors. In the meantime I have to support myself. I want to become the best photographer I can be. And I want to preserve some of the beauty that's disappearing at an alarming rate. Maybe I can stop it somehow."

"Ah, a tree hugger." Joe said it like it explained everything. A lick of resentment flamed inside her chest.

"Not a tree hugger; an environmentalist."

He shrugged again. "Hey, I'm with you there."

She continued as if he hadn't spoken, wound up to defend herself. "I've lived out of my van for three summers now. I want unique pictures, strange pictures, something that will make people wake up and see what we've got right here in our own country for them to enjoy. I want them to see themselves. I want them to see what we risk losing if we don't protect it, and soon. And I want to be accepted in my own right, not as Roberta Walker's daughter."

She stopped, stunned that she'd said it. She could have cut out her tongue. This was absolutely not how she'd wanted to tell him about his wife's potential biological parent.

"Roberta Walker's daughter," he repeated, obviously picking up the nugget and turning it over in his head. "She was insanely talented. But she was …" He let the words lay unsaid between them. Everyone knew the brilliant Roberta Walker was bipolar. Being bipolar was not hereditary, but it did run in families, not good news for Nadine or her offspring.

When Darby was silent, he said, "Then you were out on your own at fifteen. You had it hard." She could see he was backing off from examining this information too closely, choosing instead to focus on her homeless status as a teen. Who'd have imagined teenage homelessness as being the lighter and preferred subject of conversation?

She said, "No harder than any of the thousands of homeless kids across this country. It's a tough, unforgiving life."

"Yet you made it, and here you are, trying to live up to your mother's reputation."

"Her work is unparalleled; it was her personal life that sucked." She turned to face him, walking backwards as she spoke. "All I want is to be accepted in my own right."

"Be careful what you wish for; you just may get it."

She turned back and walked beside him again. There was something behind his words. What had Joe wished for, only to be sorry later? What did he regret? Did it involve Nadine or maybe the recently departed Melody? When the silence stretched, she asked, "Got any more fatherly advice for a wandering photographer?"

He stopped, tossed a stick he'd been carrying out into the surf, watching it bob around for a while before answering. When he did look at her, his eyes darkened, and his expression was strange. "I'd never presume to offer you fatherly advice." She waited for him to continue. When he didn't, and his gaze dropped to her mouth instead, her heart flipped over in her chest and went zing, zing, zing.

"I'm glad we agree on that," she babbled, aware of a soft and warm feeling curling in the pit of her stomach. "I'd probably ignore it anyway—I'm notorious for going against the tide. Ask anyone."

He frowned briefly and looked away. "That's most likely for the best."

Again, she knew there was a double meaning in his reply, a meaning only he understood, and obviously one he was not about to share. Okay, enough of the double-speak. She decided to turn the conversation to something neutral that they both understood. "Did you pick up my package from town?"

"Yes. I put it on your dresser."

"Thanks." She couldn't help a little smirk.

Seeing her face, he asked, "What's going on?"

"Payback time for Andrew. If you want to witness my triumph, you should maybe hang out tomorrow morning and have breakfast with us before you head to the marina. Mrs. Russell has that kitchen shining. We can make waffles."

"I'm usually gone early, but I can hang out. I'll admit a morbid curiosity in seeing my wayward son taken down a notch or two by one of his victims. You pull it off, and you'll be the first." With his answer she could feel him relax and the tension recede. "In fact, I'll hang out every morning. Clint can open for a change."

"So what about breakfast? Do you cook your own, or should I include you when I prepare the children's?"

He smiled, white teeth flashed against his tan in a heart-wrenching combination. "Is that an offer?" he teased. "I haven't had breakfast made for me in years."

"Well, you won't be getting it in bed," she laughed, then, realizing what she'd just said, added, "Unfortunate choice of words."

"You blush, Miss Walker."

She turned to look at him straight on again. "That I do. It's the Walker curse."

"I see the war paint's back on."

"Time to project attitude. You do know it's all in your attitude?"

Abruptly, Joe changed the subject. "There's an important meeting at the town hall this afternoon. After you've gotten what you need in town, I'd like you to come. Bring the kids with you. I think it's important they be a part of what's happening here in Brennan's Point. It's their future that we're fighting to protect."

"All right."

"And about last night," he paused, squinting against the sun. "I'm sorry about the soap trick."

"Like I said, I'm taking care of it. You intervening will not help–it has to come from me. I'm not a delicate flower needing to be cared for; I'm tougher than I look."

His eyes slid toward her and away, staring down at the sand as they made their way back to the house. "You didn't look so tough last night."

"You shouldn't have seen how I looked last night."

She saw him raise an eyebrow, though he didn't return her gaze. "Nothing I haven't seen before."

"Not mine you haven't." Had she just said that in her out-loud voice? Darby closed her eyes and cringed. This was going to be a very long summer.

DISCLOSURE

DARBY NOSED the little rental into one of the last parking spots on the lot and shut it down. If they hurried, they'd make it just in time for Joe's speech. "Come on. Let's go inside and see what your daddy's up to."

Slipping her hand into Darby's, Shannon skipped up the sidewalk, head down and gaze locked to her feet. Her glossy-white shoes shone and clicked as they went. It would be so easy to fall in love with this little girl.

After grocery shopping, they'd spent an hour in Claymores, the local clothing store, and Darby was pleased with the results. Shannon was now set for the summer, complete with a pink backpack for trips to the beach. Andy had been pretty easy to get along with as well, maybe because his friend, Dougie, had grabbed a ride into town with them. She made no reference to the green soap incident, not wanting to give Andy the satisfaction. At the same time she wanted to show him she would always be consistent in her treatment of him. She could tell that he was puzzled by her lack of reaction to last night's prank.

Coming from the city and having a sense of what the style was for young people, she allowed Andy some latitude in his choice of jeans. Fourteen was an important age, and one did have to make a statement after all, she told him. His response had been a snort. Still, she knew he was pleased. He had even agreed to a haircut, and to meet them at the town hall by four o'clock. Darby felt it was important he knew she trusted him to get there on his own. Maybe it was wishful thinking on her part, but she thought he was relaxing. The battle was by no means over, but the start of a truce was evident.

Entering the town hall, she saw there was a lot of local interest. Already, the seats were filled, and people had crowded along the side and back walls. Fitting herself in between a doorway and table, she helped Shannon climb up to sit on a table then cast around for Andy. She spotted him with Dougie near the front of the gathering, both looking fresh from the barber. She was glad Dougie had made use of the twenty she'd pressed into his hand absentmindedly as she'd lectured them about the meeting before they'd left Claymores. These things had to be handled with care. Dougie had pride.

Andy saw her, nodded, then looked away. She was glad he'd kept his word to meet her here.

With a loud bang, the meeting was called to order. Talk died down to a hush and an occasional whisper. A portly man approached the microphone, tucked his thumbs into his belt loops, and began to speak. "Citizens of Brennan's Point, I am Mayor Bob Mayer."

Mayor Mayer? Darby could picture the election signs lining the streets now.

"We have assembled here today to meet with representatives from the Sperry Gas Company who will present their plan to develop methane gas extraction here in Brennan's Point. The future of Brennan's Point may very well be decided by you, our citizens, and with this in mind we want to present all the facts, have everything up front and out in the open. I and all the other members of your elected city council take our job seriously, and have been charged with making important decisions for Brennan's Point's future. With the facts, and I mean all the facts, we will do just that.

"In the interest of fair-handedness, the town council has agreed to hear from a local group headed by Mac MacKinnon as well. Mac and his supporters have a counter proposal to that of the Sperry group's, as we all know." Now Mayor Mayer looked grim.

Gee, I wonder whose side he's on? Darby thought peevishly. Politics!

People called out their opinions, some in agreement, some in opposition. It was evident that a very testy subject was being debated. Darby settled back in her chosen corner, her arm wrapped protectively around Shannon.

"Since we'll be covering a lot of ground this afternoon, we'll get to it without any delay." Mayor Mayer smiled and with a sweep of his hand drew two suited men from the audience. There was no doubt where his backing lay. "From Sperry Gas, may I introduce Mr. Larry Graham and Mr. David Ramsey."

"Sperry Gas has good news for the citizens of Brennan's Point," the man named Larry Graham proclaimed with the bravado of a circus crier, with the Ramsey character grinning and nodding like a bobble head at his side. Already she didn't like them. Tweedle Dee and Tweedle Dumb—heavy on the dumb.

Yes, apparently there was big money to be had here in Brennan's Point, big money with plenty to go around. The words "prosperity," "riches," "natural," and "easy" were featured pointedly and often in the Sperry presentation. A balloon payment of forty million dollars—a gasp from the audience—would pour much-needed funds into the town coffers to develop the downtown core and sweetened the deal.

Graham and Ramsey's presentation was slick, complete with diagrams of a new and modern Brennan's Point that featured strip malls, fast food restaurants, cobblestone streets with charming street lamps, all pictured through an artist's view of the modern Brennan's Point shopper. Graham talked of new jobs, new money flowing into the town, a bigger tax base to build the future on. He made Brennan's Point's prospects sound sure and thriving while Sperry pumped methane gases from the shale beneath the town. With Sperry in town, it would be Christmas Day, every day, so Graham and Ramsey claimed.

Confident, worldly, and witty at the mic, Graham's movements were over-the-top theatrical as he pointed out areas for development in and around Brennan's Point. Darby snorted. Where's the catch?

"When is my daddy going to tell his good idea?" Shannon wanted to know, pulling at Darby's shirt. "My daddy's the smartest."

Darby agreed with Shannon's childish assessment. Knowing what she'd seen in her travels of out-of-the-way locations, she knew exactly what companies like Sperry Gas could do to the environment. Trusting her instincts about Joe, she'd bet on Joe.

Ramsey and Graham moved off stage, the Sperry presentation finished. The crowd applauded with great enthusiasm.

They bought it, Darby realized in dismay. What could Joe say to convince the town that his plan was sounder? He came on the stage with an arm load of charts and papers, followed by a tall, almost rakishly handsome, dark-haired man and a flowery dress lady; an odd trio together, in sharp contrast to the sleekly turned out Ramsey and Graham duo.

Joe donned wire-rimmed glasses and began sorting through the papers as his partners set up. Wearing cotton chinos topped by a polo shirt and cardigan sweater, he looked scholarly; that cool, preoccupied college professor all the girls were gaga over.

The set up was complete. All three presenters stood at the podium, and most of the audience settled back to hear them out, though Darby could see many citizens were getting ready to leave, obviously feeling they had heard enough to satisfy their curiosity.

"Ladies and gentlemen of Brennan's Point," Joe began in his well-modulated voice, "thank you for your interest." He glanced pointedly at Ramsey and Graham, who nodded from the sidelines with placid smiles pasted to their faces, bobble heads the two of them. Joe's tone grew more forceful with his next words. "And deep concern for the future of our hometown."

People stopped their whispering; others heading quietly for the door stopped and looked back at Joe. Darby felt a thrill of pride. He had them.

"Yes. I said concern. Why concern?" He paused. A pin dropped in the hall would have been heard. "Concern because hot on the heels of the Sperry Gas's half-baked development plan will be the death rattle of a cold wind through empty streets and strip malls of the 'new' Brennan's Point."

Murmurs waved through the gathering. People shifted in their chairs uneasily. Others sat back down.

"So Sperry Gas wants to help us?" He raised his eyebrows and shoulders. "I say great! We could use the help. We could use more jobs, new money, a broader tax base." He shifted papers. "I have no argument with that. I want Brennan's Point to prosper. I want a thriving healthy community town for my kids to grow up in and," he paused significantly, "stay on in, and raise their families in. That's the Brennan's Point I envision." The crowd broke out in applause.

"So what do you say, Bob?" Joe addressed the grey-haired mayor, now seated in the front row. "You like this town. Born and raised here, have your family here. Am I right?" Mayor Mayer grinned and nodded. "So why, Bob, why would you vote to close out our downtown district?" Joe fired back. The mayor's jaw slackened.

"Because that's what you'd be doing, Bob, if you vote for this scheme. And I say 'scheme' in all seriousness. I simply cannot refer to it as a plan." Joe paused, his gaze sweeping the room. Darby smiled encouragingly at him, hoping that if he was able to pick Shannon and herself out, he would see they were supporting him. Did she imagine it? He sent them a wink.

Joe adjusted his glasses and slowly swept the audience with his penetrating gaze, seeming to look personally at each and every citizen with a sincere, troubled expression. "Has anyone here smelled a methane extraction site lately?" People began to murmur amongst themselves. "Times that by a hundred and you've got an idea of what Sperry has in mind for our Brennan's Point."

When the silence was beginning to stretch into something uncomfortable, he posed a second question. "And has anyone here actually looked at what land Sperry is asking to access to recover the methane gas they're so eager to get their hands on?" He walked away from the mic to retrieve a pointer, then revealed the Welcome to Brennan's Point sign that stood just at the edge of town. "Right at the entrance of our town, smack dab in the middle of old-growth forest."

People were becoming increasingly agitated. A general murmuring grew in volume with each passing minute. Darby could see that Joe was getting through in a big way.

"Great foot forward, don't you think? 'Come on in to Brennan's Point—if you can stand the stink.'" He let that sink in for a while before moving on.

"It's been my experience that the smell of methane gas is less than charming, and down-right off-putting, but hey, that's just me. 'Oh, it's natural.' Yeah—it's natural all right. 'Easy?' Not so much. And pretty, well, we won't even go there. Not a great tourist draw, if you get my drift, and let's face it: Our town lives on tourism." He handed the pointer to the dark-haired man standing at his side.

"Yes, we want to grow, but at what price? What are we willing to sacrifice?" The audience waited, hanging on his every word. "With me today is Mr. Samuel Morgan, a wind-turbine expert, who has agreed to come today to explain an alternate method for Brennan's Point to generate income. Mr. Morgan is the president of Morgan Eco-Adventures, a company that promotes natural interaction with our environment as well as respect and protection. Sam Morgan is a trusted member of several boards of directors for green-minded companies. He is also responsible for the self-sufficient system Laura Winthrop has out on Idle Island. Many of you are familiar with Miss Winthrop's ecologically sound innovations. Unfortunately, Miss Winthrop was unable to attend today as she had hoped."

Why wasn't Laura here? This was what she lived for.

"Mr. Morgan will now take over with the details of our counter proposal. He won't steer you wrong. You'll be surprised what we can do to enhance what we already have that works in Brennan's Point. Please welcome Mr. Sam Morgan."

A small wave of hand clapping came and went quickly. The people wanted to hear what Mr. Morgan had to say. Sam Morgan had a commanding voice, a piercing stare, and a real gift for public speaking. With charts and a pointer, he explained how wind generation worked, how it fit seamlessly into the natural environment of Brennan's Point, and how, if built on a large enough scale, it could not only entirely power Brennan's Point, but could pay for itself within three years by taking Brennan's Point off the provincial power grid as a consumer, making the town a power provider that could then sell its excess power back to the main grid. The pictured graphics of tall, slender, pure-white structures standing majestically out in the bay in a long, stately row parallel up the coast was beautiful. No mining, no burning fossil fuels, no disturbing fish-bearing streams.

Darby found herself excited at the prospect of Brennan's Point stepping into the future with such an environmentally sound proposal rather than live with methane gases blanketing the land. But how?

As if he'd heard her thoughts, Morgan delivered his secret weapon against Sperry. There was, right now, through the government, an opportunity for one coastal community to be awarded the funds needed to build a test wind generating system, and Brennan's Point was an ideal location. A successful proposal from Brennan's Point could see their own environmentally sound energy source up and running in two years. And that meant jobs—good jobs.

The excitement of the crowd was electric.

Ann Baker, the flowered dress lady, who turned out to be the librarian and local historian, ended the presentation with an impassioned plea for others to join their group and to work with them toward a common and secure future. What was unique about their town should be preserved, the environment protected and Brennan's Point's future made secure. The applause was deafening, with Mayor Mayer pumping the hands of each presenter, a broad grin of pride on his ruddy face as if he had personally championed the wind turbine proposal. Joe could do worse than have the mayor on his side, Darby decided, hugging Shannon fiercely. Joe MacKinnon, Sam Morgan, and Ann Baker had done it. They had taken on the 'big guys,' and it looked like they had won.

"And I was worried," Darby said under her breath. She should have known Joe was no pushover. If she could see he was head and shoulders above the likes of Ramsey and Graham, the people of Brennan's Point would too.

The meeting broke up, with people filtering out through the exits. Darby kept Shannon close to her in the crush, hanging back until the crowd thinned, to protect herself and Shannon from being jostled in the crowd, catching snatches of conversations for and against the Sperry proposal, or "Mac's" proposal. Whatever opinion each person carried away, there would be some heated debates around town over the next few weeks.

A round faced man with bristly, old-fashioned sideburns and white woolly hair stopped in front of her and read her T-shirt aloud, "I hate Tacos said no Juan–EVER!"

Darby smiled at him. "Yeah. I'm a fan."

"I like tacos too. In fact, I'm expanding my fish and chip stand to feature fish tacos–I hear they're all the rage in the city."

"Oooh, where's your bus? Truck?"

He looked regretful. "That's my problem–I can't keep a location, so I'm forced to move around a lot. I'm usually down by the welcome sign at the edge of town, so you can guess how badly I want Sperry to set up shop there. Come visit me; I'll let you test run my new fish tacos for free. Name's Carl–Carl's Catch of the Day."

"You use local fish?"

He grinned. "Is there any other kind?"

She laughed. "Guess not."

From the stage Joe caught her eye, waving for her to wait for him. She watched while he finished packing up the box, warmth filling her at his obvious pleasure at seeing her there. She was beginning to feel at home here at Brennan's Point, and it was a good feeling.

■ ■ ■

MRS. RUSSELL had left thick, slow-bubbling clam chowder in the slow cooker flanked by a cloth-draped basket filled with chocolate chip cookies for when they all arrived home from the town hall meeting. With Joe and Andrew tending to the horses, Darby and Shannon set up for supper.

Sunshine poured into the kitchen, turning everything bright and new. The appliances shone, the table was covered with a crisp white cloth. The scraggly bunch of flowers Shannon had picked this morning was proudly displayed in a mason jar at its center. Darby had music with a heavy back beat pulsating from her hooked-up iPod, and the rich aroma of cheese biscuits rose from the oven. She and Shannon danced playfully around the table with cutlery and napkins in hand, setting each place. Lost in the noise was the sound of coffee dripping and bacon sizzling, which Darby intended to add to the chowder. Clam chowder simply wasn't chowder without bacon.

Shannon caught sight of the men of her family first.

"Daddy," she cried out happily, "Darby taught me how to do 'the mermaid'! See?" She demonstrated by swinging her little bottom back and forth and flapping her arms.

Catching her up in a bear hug, Joe leaned over and turned the iPod down. "That's great, Honey. I was wondering who was listening to music so loud. I guess I know now." He looked balefully at Darby over Shannon's head.

"When did you get to be so damned old?" she stage-whispered at him and opened the oven door. Pulling out the muffin pan, she positioned it over a basket, and flipped it over. The cheese biscuits tumbled out. "Ah. I love it when a plan comes together," she sighed, nudging the oven door closed with her hip and placing the basket in the middle of the table.

She quickly chopped the bacon into small pieces, sprinkled them into the slow cooker, added a soup ladle and brought the whole thing to the table.

"Don't just stand there, sit down and dig in. Mrs. Russell worked hard on this supper and will want a full report first thing tomorrow morning." She poured a coffee for Joe, herself, and Andrew and sat down. Darby noticed that although Joe had raised his eyebrows at Andrew's cup of coffee, he was silent. He really was kind of a judgmental guy—or at least old-fashioned. He really should lighten up.

It was immediately apparent that Andrew did not drink coffee. He scooped a too generous helping of sugar into the mug and topped it to the brim with cream, and between spooning up chowder and inhaling biscuits, he grimaced through every last drop of his coffee. Darby had to give him points for pulling it off, hoping her gesture would be taken as she meant it. He was as important as his father.

However, she still had to deal with his soap stunt.

"This is good chowder," Darby said, breaking the silence that had descended upon the table. "You could sell this down at the marina for sure."

"I'm not in the restaurant business. I'm in the boat business. People want to eat, they should bring food."

Darby widened her eyes and pressed her lips together. O-kay. Silence descended once again.

Finally Shannon said, "Darby, my taste bugs don't like this soup." She glanced apprehensively at her father.

Darby frowned. "Your taste … what?"

"My taste bugs. They don't like this soup."

Darby bit back a laugh, glancing up at Joe and away. "That's okay, Hon. Finish up your cheese biscuit and drink all of your milk, and you'll be okay."

When Joe raised his eyebrows at Darby again, she shrugged her shoulders. "It's a half a cup of soup. Missing it won't kill her."

He muttered, "Are we playing good cop/bad cop here?"

"I've got to get in good with the kiddies somehow," she murmured, gazing back at him with a challenge in her eye. Did he really want to make an issue over a half bowl of soup with a five-year-old?

Shannon pushed her bowl away with obvious relief and bit into her biscuit. Then she said, "Daddy, why is Darby so mean?" A mischievous sparkle in her eyes took the sting out of her words.

"I don't know, Honey, why?"

"I mean, why is the cook so mean?"

"Why?" Joe smiled at Darby across the table, and tension between them disappeared.

"Because she beat the eggs!" she crowed in delight.

Clapping his hands to his heart, Joe laughed heartily at Shannon's joke. Her little face shone with pride.

Finished with his meal, Andrew picked up a tablet lying beside his empty coffee cup. "What's this for?" he grunted without looking directly at anyone in particular.

"A vitamin," Darby answered absently, beginning to clear the table. "It's chewable."

"Why doesn't Shannon have to take one?"

"She's too young for those." Darby opened the dish washer, stacked the dishes, and waited. She was not disappointed. Shannon screeched. Darby turned to see the little girl jumping up and down and pointing at her brother in delighted horror. Darby crossed her arms and relaxed against the counter.

Andrew looked blankly at each of them. "What?"

Joe rubbed his jaw to smother a grin, and looked at Darby. Barely perceptively, he shook his head. She shrugged back.

Shannon pulled at her brother's arm, "Look in the toaster, Andy. Look at your mouth."

Baffled, Andrew tried to remain cool. "What are you talking about?" He picked up the toaster and looked at his reflection. His eyes bugged in shock. His mouth, his gums, his teeth were blood red. Grasping the toaster with both hands he yelped, "I'm bleeding!"

At the burst of laughter that followed, he turned his panicked face to his father, then to Darby. Suspicion dawned across it. "Okay, what'd ya do?"

"Pretty nifty color there, Son."

Andrew rolled his eyes at his father, "Nifty?"

"Antiquated expression, I know, but it fits."

"What's going on?"

"A little eye for an eye," Darby chuckled. "Your red looks as good as my green."

Try as he might, Andrew couldn't keep a grin from his face. "Okay, you got me. What is it?"

"A disclosure tablet."

"The ones from the dentist?"

"Yup," Darby answered, handing him a glass of water. "Truce?"

He bared his teeth at her and leered. "Truce."

She grimaced at his mouth. "Good. Now, please, go brush your teeth. I can't stand it."

Growling playfully at Shannon, Andrew chased her from the kitchen. She screeched in delight ahead of him down the hallway.

Alone in the kitchen with Joe, Darby sighed, "He's wonderful with her." She shut the dishwasher and flipped it on.

"I thought you were going to even the score tomorrow at breakfast."

"Couldn't wait."

Joe reached for the last strip of bacon, sharing it with Buddy. "You handled it beautifully."

"Thanks."

"Always land on your feet?"

"Always."

"Nothing scares you?"

"Nothing," she answered. "Well, almost nothing. I don't much care for small, enclosed places. But that's not likely to happen here, is it? You have lots of wide open spaces."

He looked her up and down, his gaze lazy. "And you seem to be fitting right in."

She rinsed and dried her hands. "No path untraveled."

"That's your philosophy?"

"It is. Follow every path that's presented to you in life, and you'll find your true path. That way you'll have no regrets. Ever have that end-of-life conversation with people, you know, the one about what they regret?" She folded the dish towel and hung it over the towel rack, her thoughts skipping away to what this all meant, this time in Brennan's Point and the mystery of her connection with the MacKinnon family. Why was she here—really?

She looked up at him and said, "It's never about what they did in life they regret. It's always about what they didn't do."

PUPCAKES AND MINI-MEATS

"SO WHERE are we going?" Joe asked. They were traveling in Darby's tinny little rental, way under the speed limit. Why, why, why? He knew the answer without even asking her. She'd say something like, Why not? Life's too short to go fast, yada yada yada. She was so damned contrary.

The car, which looked like a roller skate and sounded like a sewing machine, was moving leisurely in and out of sun and shade and appeared to be headed out of town. He could see the back of the Welcome to Brennan's Point sign up the narrow and winding forest-hugged road. And Sperry wants to strip back this wild and gorgeous place to root around for stinking methane gas? *Not on my watch.*

"It's a surprise, Daddy," Shannon was informing him from the minuscule backseat, interrupting her latest exploration game currently being played out with her Barbie, now renamed Dora the Exploder after some television character and a raggedy stuffed cat name Lily Kitty. Ever since Darby had arrived, two weeks ago now, Shannon was obsessed with exploring, always humming a song about 'the map' that frankly, was beginning to drive him around the bend. *"It's the map, it's the map, it's the map, it's the map–IT'S THE MAP!"*

And as if on cue she launched into 'the map' song once again. Where was his iPod when he needed it? Bad enough the blood and DNA tests were still not back from the private lab in Vancouver, bad enough Darby's collar was long gone, leaving her slender neck bare and enticingly accessible–not!

He pressed his mouth into a thin line and shifted in his seat. Yeah, the collar was gone, no longer limiting Darby's physical activities and freeing her to barge headlong into every damned aspect of his formally laid-back life. Today was a perfect example. She'd basically railroaded him into this road trip when he was needed at the marina. Something was wrong there, something he couldn't put his finger on. He needed a sit-down with his staff to hash it out.

He glanced back at Shannon, saw her golden head bent over her latest Crayon rendition of their ranch, and recognized immediately that he was in a miserable mood and his daughter's joy in her little map song was a blessing. *Why am I being such a shit?*

Darby slowed the rental down and turned cautiously into the gravel parking area by the welcome sign. The only event of consequence here beyond a few split log benches nestled into the broad tree trunks and grassy areas and a set of waste and recycling bins was an old fish-and-chip truck decorated with hand-painted images of dancing French fries and shrimp. Apparently, these cheerful cartoon characters were very happy to be served up for lunch by …. He squinted at the sign over the awning. … By some guy named Carl. He glanced at Darby.

She turned off the car, smiled back at him, and announced, "Shannon and I are treating you to lunch."

"What's the occasion?"

"You'll see." Darby released her seatbelt and opened her door. "Come on, there's someone I want you to meet."

"I knew there was some sort of scheme in the works here."

"You do know you're being a giant poop, don't you?" Her tone was not accusatory; she was merely making an observation. This is what exasperated him about her so much–her assessments–her bang-on assessments, if he were in the mood to admit it, which he was not. She helped Shannon out of the car and waved gaily at the grinning man at the service window of the fish-and-chip truck. "Hey, Carl! How's business today?"

"Hey, Darby! Hey, Shannon! Back for more tacos? Got a beautiful fresh halibut off the Heartbeat first thing this morning."

"That's Bert Hadding's rig, isn't it?" Darby asked.

Joe looked at her. How did she know all this stuff?

"Yup." Carl leaned out the window on his elbows. "So what'll it be today, Little Ladies?"

Darby rooted around inside the pockets of her skinny jeans, producing a folded envelope and some crumpled bills. "Two fish tacos and a basket of shrimp for me, no hot sauce, one taco for Shannon, with a side of fries, also no hot sauce, and four tacos for Mac here, with lots of hot sauce, with two sides—fries and shrimp. Oh, and three bottles of water."

"Coming right up." Carl's rosy-cheeked face withdrew inside the truck. Darby turned and smiled up at Joe. "You're going to love these."

"I'll take your word for it. Who are we meeting?"

"First we eat, then we meet."

They strolled over to one of the benches, this one beside a sunny, grassy area where Shannon immediately set up shop with her map and dolls, humming her little song. From where she sat, Darby warned, "Don't let Dora the Exploder's hair get dirty." She chuckled and sent Joe an amused smile. "That is so cute." When he knit his brow in an expression of confusion, she leaned closer and murmured under her breath, "Dora the Exploder."

He looked back at her blankly.

She gaped at him. "You really don't get it, do you?"

"Oh, I get it all right, all damned day. "It's the map, it's the map ..." He rolled his eyes in a show of exasperation.

"Not that. How she hears and accidentally mispronounces things. It's so cute. Like Dora the Explorer has been transformed into Dora the Exploder. I simply cannot correct her, it's so delightful. Or her favorite breakfast cereal is Mini-Meats, not Mini-Wheats."

She watched him, expecting, he guessed, some sort of reaction that he wasn't able to give. She continued on more slowly, "The fact that she loves chocolate pupcakes best?"

He looked at her blankly. "Shannon says these things?"

Darby's expression changed to incredulous. "You don't know?"

"Pupcakes?"

Shannon's head popped up. "Does Carl have pupcakes too? I want a chocolate pupcake."

Joe turned to look at Shannon, hearing her version of cupcakes for the first time. How had he missed it? He felt a grin spread across his face, and a bubble of laughter travel up from his chest. Shannon's mispronounced words were innocent and unintentionally funny and sweet as hell. He glanced back to Darby and shook his head. "I didn't know. I didn't hear. I guess I haven't been listening to my own daughter."

Darby squeezed his hand. "You're hearing her now."

He nodded, his mood abruptly lightened. It was a beautiful day, they were seated in an almost park-like setting, surrounded by a rich and mysterious forest, and his little daughter was playing at his feet and singing. A swell of how good his life really was filled him.

"Order up!" Carl called from the fish-and-chip truck, his woolly head bobbing in the shadowed window.

Darby bounced up from the bench. "Let's eat." She hurried to the truck and returned with her arms loaded with three bagged lunches and three bottles of water, distributing them to Joe and Shannon first, then settling back onto the bench with her own. "Okay," she said, opening her bag and peeking inside. "Try this, then tell me what you think. If you love it–which I think you will–I have a proposal for you."

Oh man, not another one of her brilliant ideas, he groaned inwardly, but only half-heartedly. The food did smell good. In fact, he was suddenly very hungry. He opened up his bag, pulled out a fish taco, peeled back the wrapping, and took a bite. He looked up at Darby in surprise.

She nodded back, her mouth full. "I know!" she mumbled around the food, then swallowed and spoke again, more clearly and with obvious delight. "Isn't this awesome?"

He swallowed and took another bite, bobbing his head in agreement. Finishing off the taco, he declared with a groan, "Where has Carl been all my life?"

Darby's eyes were dancing. "Have some shrimp."

They quickly finished off their lunches, enjoying the crisp slaw and tender halibut in the soft taco, the sunny spot they were picnicking in, and frankly, for Joe, the escape from the marina. Now, if he had something like this down at the marina …

He looked over at Darby, suddenly suspicious. He emptied his water bottle, then asked, "Just exactly who am I supposed to meet down here?" She smiled guilelessly back at him and popped her last shrimp into her mouth, then bobbed her eyebrows and shrugged her shoulders. "Darby ..."

"What? A man can't have a nice lunch out with his daughter?"

Joe couldn't help a laugh. "My God, woman, you are slick. Is this where I wander over and introduce myself to Carl, or will he be heading over here?"

"That part's up to you."

He tossed his napkin into the bag and stood up. "Well, since he is exactly what I need down at the marina, I'll be heading over and having a talk with Carl. You're good on your own here?"

Darby's smile was huge. "Absolutely!"

With Darby reading a book and Shannon playing outside, Joe and Carl spent the afternoon together inside the fish-and-chip truck talking between customers, who, sadly, were too few. Joe found he liked Carl. The man was down to Earth, honest, funny, and sincere in his dealings with his customers and in his dedication to his business. He ran a clean little truck, his food was simple and tasty, with many of the ingredients gathered locally. This particularly impressed Joe, who believed in buying locally himself, and sealed the deal. By dinnertime, Joe and Carl had a handshake deal for Carl's Catch of the Day setting up shop permanently down at the marina. It was a win/win situation.

By the time Joe emerged from the truck, Shannon was asleep on a blanket on the grass and Darby was no longer reading, just sitting back on the bench with her eyes closed, soaking in the heat of the late day sun. Joe stopped for a moment, and drank in the sight. Today's T-shirt read *Happy is the New Black*. He chuckled. What a character she was. Her hair was still crazy, her eyes still over the top with black eyeliner, and her fingernails still black, but now, looking at her, he saw that she looked good, like herself. Different. Strong. Beautiful.

Whoa. That was a surprise. Yeah, she was sexy as hell–he'd give her that, and aggravating as hell when she was of a mind to push his buttons, which seemed to be almost every day the last few weeks, but beautiful? Then she opened her green eyes and looked back at him. Yeah. Darby Walker was one goddamned beautiful, off-the-wall woman.

She smiled. "Hey."

"Hey, yourself," he replied softly, surprised at the tone of his voice. This was no good, letting the world in on his suddenly discovered soft spot for Darby Walker. He'd have to do better at this.

Darby patted the seat beside her. "Come sit with me." He found himself complying. She pulled a folded envelope from her pocket. "Here's your second surprise."

He looked at the envelope then back at her, guessing it was the test results. He raised his eyebrows in question.

She nodded her reply and handed him the crushed envelope. "I'll let you do the honors."

He tapped the envelope against the palm of his hand and considered her face. "Should I? This could be a game-changer–your last chance at a simple, uncomplicated life."

"I love complicated."

"I generally lean toward simple myself."

She whispered, "Open it."

"All right." He tore it open, unfolded the single page inside, and scanned the text. When he was finished he raised his eyes to Darby's, recognizing the war of fear and eagerness mirroring his own. "Woo-hoo!" he yelled, tossing the paper over his shoulder and picking Darby up, swinging her around until her legs flew out in a circle around them. "You're a perfect match!"

"Oh, my God! Are they certain?" When he set her back onto her feet, she held tight to his arms. "The blood is a match with Andrew?"

"Yes!" he declared, relief and gratitude making him weak. "Yes, yes, yes. You can donate for him, and he'll be safe."

Her voice dropped to a whisper. "And the DNA?" Judging from her expression she was scared to hear his reply.

"Yes," he answered just as softly, the implications starting to trickle into the Wow, this really is Nadine's sister part of his brain. "You and Nadine are siblings."

The wonder and confusion that raced across her face softened his annoyance at her interference in his life. Everyone handled apprehension, worry, hope– whatever was on their minds–differently. Darby had chosen activity, bustling around the ranch "fixing" things. He'd been a bear with a thorn in his paw, grousing and complaining his way through each and every slow-as-glacial-ice day. And now here they were, with the answer they had both dreaded and longed for. Andrew would be safe, and Darby, well, Darby was his wife's sister, the fallout being that much of what she'd believed to be real in her life was now up for grabs.

He pulled her back onto the bench to sit beside him, keeping her hands inside his own. They were soft and warm, like small birds. "I know how this must be hitting you. Or maybe I don't know, but I can guess."

"This … this changes everything," she breathed, her eyes focused on some unknowable point in her past. He imagined he could trace her thoughts backwards, picking up pieces of her life to look at each with suspicion, then tossing it back down, knowing the truth of it at last.

He said, "You have a family now. We're family. If Nadine were alive, she'd have her arms locked around you and would never let you go."

Darby extracted her hands from his in stages, almost apologetically, her expression closed. "I guess we'll never know for sure, will we?"

"I know it for sure. I knew my wife. She was lonely as a kid; finding real family, finding a sister, finding you, would have made her insanely happy."

"You think?" Darby asked faintly.

"I do," Joe replied, then frowned at her. "Why aren't you happy? Are you forgetting the part where you could possibly save a life—your nephew's life?"

She pasted a smile on her face, for his benefit, he could see. "I know. I'm happy for Andrew and you. I know how worried you've been. We can see about stockpiling the blood right away, I promise."

"And, just as importantly, we have to tell the kids who you are to them, that you're not just the woman who helped us when Andrew ran his bike into the ground, but their aunt."

Darby didn't lift her gaze from her clenched hands. She muttered, "That'll be a conversation."

"You don't sound enthused."

"I am." She looked up at him, then quickly looked away, shivering. "I'm sorry. I guess I didn't really believe this was possible. The blood type, yes. People can have the same blood type. But the other … I'm still struggling with the other."

"We can wait on talking to the kids. In fact, maybe we should wait, let the summer play out, do the blood thing like we told them, and let them get used to you. It's only a couple of weeks more, and it could make the transition much easier for everyone involved."

"I guess, if you think so."

He watched her for a moment, then said, "Thanks for thinking about Carl for the marina."

She smiled wanly. "Yeah—good connection, huh? Since you didn't want to be in the restaurant business, and Carl's Catch of the Day needed a home, and the marina needs to offer some kind of food …." She faded off. "Sorry. I'm just not up to this."

"How about we head home?"

"Home," she repeated, strangely, as if the word was foreign on her tongue. She reached into her jeans, pulled out the keys to the car, and tossed them to him. "How 'bout you drive?"

They packed up Shannon's blanket and toys, waved goodbye to Carl, and headed back into town. Driving his family home—Joe's thoughts screeched to a stop.

His family? He looked over at Darby, who was gazing sightlessly out her window, her thoughts obviously a million miles away. Her profile was so achingly the same as Nadine's and Shannon's that his heart squeezed inside his chest.

THE BINGO DAUBER SOLUTION

DARBY THREW her arms around Laura, and they jumped up and down together laughing and hugging.

Laura was first to pull back. "Where's the collar?"

Darby gave Laura's thick dark braid a playful tug. "Oh, that came off weeks ago. I hated it. I'm so glad you're here. Come in, come in, we're baking." She linked her arm with Laura's and brought her into the fragrant kitchen. Mrs. Russell looked up from arranging cookie dough on a baking sheet with Shannon.

"Mrs. Russell, this is my friend, Laura, the one I was telling you about."

Mrs. Russell smiled her hello and said, "Ah, Idle Island. Love what you're doing over there for the young ones."

"Nice to meet you, Mrs. Russell," Laura answered. "And thanks. Having the kids there is the high point of my summer."

Darby turned to look at her friend, narrowing her eyes. Something was wrong with Laura, something in her voice and in her eyes, something she didn't want to talk about.

"Hi." Shannon's small voice diverted Darby's thoughts.

"And who is this?" Laura asked, smiling at Shannon. "A good little baker, I see. Did you make all these cookies by yourself?"

Shannon rubbed more flour across her cheek and nodded. "Mrs. Russell helped." Her explanation ended with a long yawn.

"Uh-oh. Time for a bit of a nap, I'm thinking," Mrs. Russell said, slipping two more trays of cookies into the oven and setting the timer. "Let's go, young lady."

"Thank you," Darby mouthed to the housekeeper.

Mrs. Russell nodded her understanding. "You girls have yourselves a nice little visit. It sounds like you have lots of catching up to do."

Once they were alone in the kitchen, Laura looked pointedly up at her tricolored hair. "Have you discovered your natural color yet?"

"Absolutely not. I will not capitulate!" She poured two glasses of ice tea and sat down.

Laura took a sip, then said, "Okay, explain why you're living in Brennan's Point with Mac MacKinnon of all people."

Darby gave Laura the Reader's Digest version of the accident and the circumstances of her staying on to help Joe and the kids and stockpiling blood for Andrew but left out the part about Nadine. That part she could hardly believe herself; it felt too fresh and too scary and personal to share–even with Laura. Besides, she and Joe hadn't spoken to anyone about it. They still hadn't come up with a way to tell the kids, and the kids deserved to be the first to know. All Andrew and Shannon knew so far was the fact that Darby's blood type was the same as Andrew's, rare and not easily obtained away from the city, and she was staying with them because she had agreed to provide a private supply for him in case of emergency in the future. In the meantime, she and Joe hoped the kids would grow accustomed to having her around, and when the time was right, accept her as their mother's sister.

Darby's thoughts skipped away from that hornet's nest of a problem and landed back on the good fortune of spending time with one of her most favorite people in the world. She said, "I'm telling you, it's a sign–both of us back here after four crazy years. I just wish we could all be here. Wouldn't Maggie and Hayley love it? Could I come over and take some pictures on the island?"

Laura laughed. "Oh Darby, you haven't changed a bit. Is it in the tides; in the stars? Is it all part of a master plan? I love that about you. And I have to say, Mac MacKinnon is not too hard on the eyes." She reached over and plucked at the errant tuft of hair at the crown of Darby's head. Joe really had chosen the very worst spot to snip away a sample. "What have you done to your hair?"

Darby smoothed the tuft. "Too much wine."

Laura looked at her balefully. "Oh, like I believe that."

"I could have taken up drinking."

"Uh-huh."

"Not this time, okay?"

"Okay." Laura let it go. "So, now that you're living with hunky Mac MacKinnon, maybe you'll be the first to wear the wedding dress."

Darby burst out laughing. "Now I know you're nuts. There is no way on Earth Joe MacKinnon is even remotely attracted to me. He hates how I look, the music I listen to, and how I talk–even my T-shirt collection."

Laura looked at her in mock horror. "How can he not love that?"

"I know! Right?" She grew quiet and narrowed her eyes. "But there's something going on with you, isn't there?"

"Nothing. There's nothing. I'm good." Laura's face grew taut with forced cheer.

"Laura, I know you, your face tells everything–you are physically unable to tell a lie." Darby raised her eyebrows in apology. "Sorry, Sweetie, that's just the way it is."

Laura stared back at her clear eyed and steady–for a few seconds before her shoulders slumped in defeat. "Damn it, Darby!"

"It's Saunders Industries, isn't it? That place is eating away at your soul."

"You know I promised Marion, for Holly. I have one more year." In a measured, dead tone she repeated, "One More Freaking Year," then dropped her chin into her hand. "God help me."

This was so not the Laura she knew. Laura Winthrop was cool and calm, the rock of their group.

Laura whispered, "I haven't completed a single piece in months. It's like I'm dead inside, Darb." Her face was a picture of despondence. "I'm freaking out about it. I've tried everything. Talk-your-head-off therapy, tai chi, yoga, meditation; anything, everything. This is just the way I am now. I can't change it. It's a nightmare."

"So, nothing? You look at a lump of clay, and that's it, nothing? Laura– it used to speak to you, call out to you what it wanted to be. It used to be you couldn't keep up with what it wanted you to reveal."

"It used to be." Laura dropped her eyes to the table top. "It's scary, Darb."

Darby studied her speculatively. "Have you tried getting mad at it? The clay, I mean?"

Laura barked a laugh. "You're a crazy woman."

"No—I'm serious. Do you have supplies over on the island?"

"I do."

"So here's your assignment. I want you to drag out a lump of ol' mister clay, and pound the hell out of him. Smack him, smash him, throw him, squish him, flatten him–do whatever horrible thing you need to kill that evil, soul-sucking piece of clay. Do it every day."

"That's it–that's your prescription, Dr. Walker?" Laura said with a nervous laugh. "Beat up clay?"

Darby reached over and squeezed her hands, focusing her eyes intently. "It is. I want you to beat it up every damned day. This could take weeks, maybe even months, but don't give up. You give it hell until whatever is holding you back slinks away and leaves you free. You're too talented to give up."

Laura stared back at her, her eyes suddenly glossy with unshed tears. "It's as good a suggestion than any other I've gotten."

"So you'll do it?"

"Yeah. Why not?"

"Good." Darby released her hands. "So what's up for your summer on the island?"

Laura blinked rapidly and swung her braid back over her shoulder. "I'm starting a breakwater, actually. I'm meeting up with a guy about starting it today; I'll be taking him over to the island with me." A genuine smile appeared on her face as she warmed to the subject. "It'll give me a protected beach and a place to moor the boats on the west side of the island. I'm hoping for some free fill. I hate paying ..."

Darby laughed. "No way! If it's something you need, like this for your summer camp kids, you'd never quibbled about the cost." The oven timer rang, and they both jumped in their seats. Darby got up and took out the cookies, slipped the last tray in, and reset the timer.

"Imagine it, Darb, all sandy and beach-y, the water smooth as glass inside the breakwater. We could teach snorkeling, diving, maybe even produce some budding marine biologists, people who'd make it their life's work to protect the environment. You never know."

"Maybe once I'm done here I should come and stay with you."

"You can't afford Idle Island."

"Who says I'm paying?"

Laura grinned. "Things never change, huh? Are you going to get yourself another camper?" Her cell phone rang. "Oh, that may be my breakwater guy."

Darby left the kitchen to look out at the horse corral while Laura spoke on her phone. *I knew something was wrong. Every e-mail full of nothing, full of subtext.*

"All done," Laura said, joining her at the window. "So I have to get back to Vancouver first thing tomorrow. No week off for me. All the board members at Saunders just got served over a valve that's supposed to be defective. Everyone's panicking, busy covering their ass. In case I haven't mentioned it yet, life at Saunders is shit. As far as I could see, the only difference between the pope and Richard is the pope only expects you to kiss his ring." She looked to the ceiling and wailed, "I want out!"

"And I want to be down some old logging road collecting chanterelle mushrooms for my dinner. I know: let's run away together."

"If only we could." They drifted back into the kitchen.

"Well, there's got to be a reason we're both ..."

"Please don't say it was meant to be."

"If you insist, but you have to admit ..."

"No, I don't!" Laura fell back into her chair with uncontrollable giggling. Darby couldn't help herself and joined in. God, it felt good to laugh with this woman, her sister of choice. Then she remembered that she had had a real sister, a secret sister— Nadine—who was dead, and whom she would never have the opportunity to laugh with about anything. Sadness stole into her heart and her laughter died.

The screen door slapped shut. Darby asked, "Is that you, Andrew?" They waited for an answer but heard none. "Andrew?"

More silence then reluctant shuffling. Finally Andrew and Dougie Brewer appeared at the kitchen door.

"Oh, my God, Andrew, Dougie, what have you done?" Both boys wore stricken expressions and mushroom-green/grey hair. Instead of achieving some sort of out-there attitude, their hair just looked sad. Something had gone terribly wrong. "W-whatever look you were going for, you missed."

The boys exchanged glances. Dougie said, "We need your help. Any help. We can't be seen like this. They'll kick our asses at summer school."

"I'll say," Darby agreed. "What do you want to do now?"

"Change it back?" Andrew suggested hopefully.

Darby shook her head. "Not going to happen, boys. The damage is done."

Dougie jammed a watch cap over his head. "Shit! I knew it was a waste of time coming here. What now? I can't wear this damned hat all summer."

"I told you it was a bad idea!" Andrew shot back. "Now look at us, a couple of losers!"

Dougie pointed to Darby's T-shirt that read, *Some Days You're the Bug, Some Days You're the Windshield*, and muttered, "It should say, 'Unless You're Fourteen, When You're Always the Bug.'"

"Hold on, guys. I might be able to help. But it won't be back to normal, that's for sure." Darby looked them over speculatively. "How far are you boys willing to go to save face?"

Andrew's eyes grew round. "Anything!"

The oven timer rang, this time no one batted an eye. Laura quietly removed the last of the cookies from the oven.

"Do you think you could carry off, say, a color like mine?"

Their eyes flicked to her hair and back. "Yes!"

"It'll take guts, confidence to pull it off."

"We'll do it."

Laura interjected. "I don't know, Darby. Mac isn't going to ..."

"Anything is better than what they've already done to themselves."

"But, you don't know Mac ..."

"But I do," Andrew interrupted, "my dad won't mind."

Mrs. Russell walked into the kitchen and gasped. "Oh, my Lord! What have you boys done?" Darby saw her eyes flicker over to her hair and away and fought the need to grin. Poor Mrs. Russell; the things she put up with in the MacKinnon household. "And I can most decidedly assure you that your father will mind." Her gaze flicked over to Darby's hair again, this time staying, apprehension etched in her face.

Darby said, "Mrs. Russell's right. He'll mind–big time. But, I know he'd want to fix this … travesty." Darby pulled her apron off and grabbed her purse. "I'll go into town and get some Bingo daubers."

"Bingo daubers? I have Bingo daubers," Mrs. Russell volunteered almost reluctantly. "A whole set."

Everyone in the room rounded on her and said in unison, "You do?" Silence followed, then they were all laughing, Mrs. Russell included.

"Okay," Darby agreed. "We'll set up in here, while you two boys go into my bathroom, find my hair conditioner, load it on your hair, and leave it there 'til we're ready for you."

Half an hour later, Andrew and Dougie were back in the kitchen draped in old bed sheets, convinced the road to their salvation was a fluorescent Bingo dauber, Andrew blue, Dougie purple, expertly administered by Darby. Shannon was a giggly, rapt audience. Laura just stood by trading out the daubers to Darby like a surgeon's assistant. Poor Mrs. Russell was speechless, no doubt regretting she was, in fact, their supplier.

Bonus–once Darby spied Dougie's pierced ears she pronounced he would one day be scooped up by some lucky girl because he had already experienced pain and purchased jewelry. He blushed so hard, his face almost matched his new hair, but his grin was ear to ear, something completely new for tough-guy Dougie Brewer. The rest of the afternoon passed with gales of laughter, loud music, and too many cookies to be considered responsible.

METAMORPHOSIS – PART A

"AND WHAT in God's name ..." Darby jumped in surprise at the sound of Joe's disembodied voice. "... led you to believe I would go along with this ridiculous Bingo dauber experiment!"

She staggered into the kitchen with a towering load of clean laundry. Uh-oh. She knew they would be "discussing" Andrew's new look, but she hadn't thought the discussion would be so damned quick. She dumped the laundry on the table and saw Joe was seated there, waiting. His expression did not suggest he was open to hearing new points of view.

Soothingly she answered, "Don't worry, you'll get used to it."

"This is bloody ridiculous!"

She selected a towel and folded it. "You said that already."

Joe slammed his palm down on the table and stood up. "What the hell?"

She folded a second towel then reached for another, pacing her response. "Ridiculous. You said ridiculous twice."

He grabbed the towel from her hand. "Your attitude is ridiculous!"

"You're helping?" She raised her eyebrows. "Thanks."

"No, I'm not helping, and neither are you. And why the hell are you doing laundry, anyway? Mrs. Russell is supposed to be doing this." He shook the towel for emphasis. "This whole situation is ridiculous. My son is not walking around town gussied up like some disco–."

"Disco?" She took the towel back and continued to fold. "Come on, Joe, even you know disco's dead. It's called clubbing these days. I think 'gang-banger is the expression you're looking for. And shhh, you'll wake Shannon; she's had a busy day."

"Gang-banger." Joe glowered at her. "How reassuring."

After stacking the towels neatly on the table, she crossed her arms and settled her gaze squarely on Joe's angry face. "It's like this, Joe MacKinnon. Kids have to express themselves, find a way to make themselves different from the rest of the crowd."

"Express themselves, yes; look like idiots, no."

"That would be your opinion, not theirs."

Joe glanced pointedly at Darby's multicolored hair, currently tied up off her neck to stay cool. "Or maybe yours?"

"Are you saying I look like an idiot?" she shot back. "You knew the color of my hair when you asked me to help you." When he didn't respond, she smiled. "At least you won't lose me in a crowd."

"How unfortunate."

She refused to be drawn in and began pairing socks. "Aren't we in a testy mood."

"Bingo-daubed hair tends to do that to a man."

Darby laughed. "My God, your problems could be so much worse! Would you rather Andrew express himself by experimenting with drugs or alcohol or by coloring his hair over his summer vacation?"

Joe snorted and picked up a sock, found its mate, and folded them together. At least he was willing to hear her out.

Darby continued, "Or is it Dougie you object to? If you don't accept Andrew's friends, you risk him staying away. He might not come home for help when he screws up, and I know that's not what you want." She could see she was getting through to him, though the struggle for such a straight-laced man to understand the inner workings of the teenage mind showed on his face.

She smiled softly. "I know this 'look' is hard to take, but try to understand what's behind it. Andrew's been going through a hard time this past year. Shannon tells me his best friend moved away, and I can see he's just now finding a new friend in Dougie."

Joe continued pairing socks, shaking his head. "You don't understand. Dougie Brewer is bad news. His father's the town drunk."

"All the more reason to include him in healthy family events."

"Okay, that's it." Joe fired a pair of socks at the table, knocking over the towels. "You call Bingo daubing my son's head a healthy family event?"

"I call saving your son's feelings and those of his new best friend a family event." Patiently Darby restacked the towels. "Joe, you didn't see those two boys drag their sorry selves home this afternoon. They were devastated by what they'd done. Their summer was ruined, their reputations about to be trashed."

Joe jammed his hands into his pockets and began pacing the kitchen. "I don't give a rat's ass about their summer being ruined."

"Well, you should. Has it been so long you can't remember what it was like to be fourteen years old, longing to be accepted?"

"I know that Dougie Brewer is a bad influence."

"Why is that your first thought? Why not approach it from another angle—maybe Andrew can be a good influence on Dougie? You say he's the son of the town drunk. What home life, what image, is Dougie trying to escape? I've lived Dougie's life, and it's not good. Fourteen is tough; believe me, Bingo daubed hair is the least of your worries."

"Shit, I know that. The kid's had a bum start." Joe leaned back against the door jamb and blew out a frustrated sigh. "You know I should fire you, right?"

"You can't afford to hire me in the first place." Darby picked up the stack of towels. "Besides, you need me for Part B of your son's metamorphosis." She walked past him with a smile.

"What metamorphosis?"

"Trust me, he'll go back to school with a look you'll be comfortable with. Think of this as a blip in his life."

"Some blip." Joe shook his head and laughed grimly. "And trust you? I must be crazy."

■ ■ ■

"GOT A safety pin?"

"I think so," Darby answered, puzzled as to how a safety pin was going to entertain Shannon for the afternoon. She rummaged around her pack for the travel sewing kit she carried.

Joe lay on his stomach across the dock, his jacket off, shirt sleeve rolled back and his arm plunged into the water almost to his shoulder. With a grunt, he pulled back holding a lump of mussels in his hand. "Here's our bait."

"What are we going to do, Daddy?"

"Catch a big fish for dinner of course."

"I can't wait." Shannon clapped her hands together and bounced up and down.

"No jumping on the dock," Joe cautioned her. "You might fall right in, and there goes Daddy's best suit when I jump in to get you."

Her eyes big, Shannon vowed solemnly not to wreck her daddy's best suit while fishing.

"Lying on the dock can't be great for Daddy's best suit either," Darby muttered under her breath, pulling out the safety pin.

"Got any thread in there?"

She looked at him incredulously. "What do you think I am? The local dollar store?"

He just looked at her expectantly.

"Yes," she admitted grudgingly, shoving the sewing kit into his hands. "I come equipped for all sporting events."

"I like your equipment." He pulled out a spool of button thread, unwound a length of it, and snapped it off with his fingers. Skillfully, he jury-rigged a hook and line with the pin and thread. With a pen knife, he pried open one of the mussels and scooped out the soft flesh inside. This he speared onto the bent tip of the "hook." He then wound the excess thread around a piece of wood that had been lying on the dock.

"There you go, Sweetie." He demonstrated for Shannon how to bob her line up and down in the water through a five-inch square hole cut out of the dock. "This way you stay away from the edge, and you can see if the little fishies come to nibble on your bait because it's shaded," he explained patiently. "If a fish takes a nice big bite for his lunch, you just pull up on your line to hook him then bring him up for supper."

"You're funny, Daddy. The fish comes for lunch, except it's supper."

"Only if Darby likes him," Joe winked over his daughter's head. "She's the one who has to cook him."

"And only if your daddy likes him," Darby countered. "He's the one who has to clean him."

"Oh, yeah?"

"Yeah."

"I'll arm wrestle you for it."

"Go away, you fool."

A pained expression on his face, Joe handed the sewing kit back to her, wagging his head sadly. "Calling me names now. No respect from the hired help these days."

"You keep calling me the hired help, and I'll start demanding a salary, Big Guy." Darby hauled a blanket and thermos from her backpack, then a pack of sandwiches. She spread the blanket and their picnic out on the dock. "You have such a great spot down here, Joe. Licence to print money." She bobbed her eyebrows at him. "I had a great idea today, after you'd left for the bank. I converted my little bathroom into a makeshift darkroom, and developed some shots I've taken around town over the last week."

"You don't take digital photos?"

"Oh, I do. But I like developing from film as well. I like the creative control."

"So, what was your great idea?" Joe sat down beside her, looking over the lunch. "Hey, this looks good. Are you two ladies here for the rest of the afternoon?"

"Yeah. A steady diet of fish and chips is hard on the waistline, much as I love it." Darby placed a sandwich and drink for Shannon by her fishing hole, then glanced over at Carl's Catch of the Day set up at the top of the string of docks. "Carl's doing good, huh?"

"Better than good. I've doubled my rentals since he's been here. Thanks to you."

She smiled and shrugged. "Just putting two nice people together."

Joe grinned wickedly. "So I'm a nice person, huh?"

"Not often, but occasionally."

He laughed and loosened his tie. "I hate wearing a suit."

"How did it go at the bank? They like your expansion ideas?"

"It's a go."

"That was fast."

"I only need bridge financing for about a year. I should be able to cover it by then."

"That's great; I'm glad for you. Anyway, like I started to say, I thought maybe some photos of Brennan's Point would look good in your proposal for the wind turbine funding. You might find some of the ones I developed today a good fit."

"Now there's an idea. A picture's worth a thousand words. Got enough lunch for a starving stranger?"

Shannon scoffed, "Oh, Daddy, you're not a stranger."

"Oh, yes he is," Darby said. "He's stranger than rhubarb. Stranger than belly button lint. Stranger than–."

Joe was on his feet and had her dangling over the water where she shrieked in laughing protest. He said, "Belly button lint, eh? Want to rethink that, Miss Walker?"

Still laughing, she clamped her arms around his neck and said, "Okay, okay, you're not stranger than belly-button lint! Now let me go, you creep!"

He held her farther over the end of the dock. "Let me go? You say 'let me go'?" he taunted with an evil grin and loosened his grip enough that she began to slip.

"No, no, don't let me go," she corrected hastily, tightening her grip.

"You creep?"

"You saint, you saint!" she gasped.

Still holding her over the water, he pondered her sincerity. "I guess I would only be teasing the fish. You're too small for an honest-to-goodness lunch anyway. And that hair–you'd probably scare all the fish away. Plus I'd just be wasting a perfectly good babysitter, right, Shannon?"

Shannon was peering down her fishing hole intently. "Daddy, a fish is nibbling my bait."

"She's blanked us out in her pursuit of dinner," Darby observed from her comfortable perch in Joe's arms.

"Not very interesting, are we?"

"Guess not."

"Then let's eat."

Darby nodded happily. "I could always Bingo daub your hair in the interest of father/son relations. We still have orange and green at home." When he growled at her, she tugged playfully at his hair. "Don't cut it."

He let her slide back to the deck. "My hair? I wasn't intending to."

She settled back on the blanket cross-legged and handed him a wrapped sandwich. "When I first met you, I thought it was too long, now I think it suits you."

He unwrapped the thick sandwich. "Didn't know you'd given my hair so much thought."

"You won't be needing someone following you around with a wind machine to maintain that windswept look, if that's where you're going."

"No?" he asked with mock surprise. "No wind machine, no director shouting, 'You're a tiger. Be a tiger. Roar, shake your head like a tiger.'"

"You are such an ass! Oops!" She glanced at Shannon and was relieved that she hadn't heard Darby's slip up. "I just meant long hair suits you." She bit her sandwich then waved it around in the air to encompass their surroundings. "Suits your lifestyle."

"It isn't a lifestyle decision. I just don't have the time or the interest to do the barber thing as often as when we lived in the city.

"What did you do there?"

"I was an advertising executive, vice president of marketing with Sandridge and Sloan."

Darby choked on her sandwich. "You what?" She grabbed a napkin and covered her mouth.

"It sounds more impressive than it really was, believe me."

"Sounds impressive and is impressive," Darby insisted, folding another napkin around the remains of her sandwich. "And here I am thinking you're going to be impressed with my little photos for your proposal. You're probably miles ahead of me on that score."

"No, I'm not, and yes, you're right—the pictures are a good idea."

"How did you ever get to Brennan's Point, running a marina?"

"Oh, it's an old story, pretty run-of-the-mill stuff. I just got sick of the phoniness, the petty office politics. Country living started to look pretty good."

"Still, it's a stretch, to say the least. You went from a Sandridge and Sloan executive to Brennan's Point marina owner."

Joe's face stilled. "It's a stretch, yes, and a step up in my opinion."

"Was it that bad at Sandridge and Sloan?"

He balled up the waxed paper that had wrapped his sandwich and dropped it into the backpack. "It wasn't Sandridge and Sloan, it was the whole industry. Got coffee in your thermos?"

She nodded and filled the cup with steaming liquid. "It has cream and sugar but only one cup; we'll have to share."

"Smells great."

"So quit stalling and tell me about your defection," she prodded, handing the cup over. "I've been here for weeks, and I still don't know what makes Joe MacKinnon tick."

With a wink and salute with the cup he said, "Great food and lazy afternoons with beautiful women."

"Guess I'll have to force it out of you. You like to arm wrestle. Let's arm wrestle for details of your sordid past." She flashed him a wicked grin and raised an eyebrow suggestively.

He laughed. "You think you can take me on?"

Eyes locked in challenge, they settled on their stomachs across from one another. Darby's hand disappeared into his when they clasped hands.

She began, "Now, the rules are–."

"Rules," he protested. "Hey, you didn't say anything about rules. Ya takes what ya gets, Lady."

She blinked back at him innocently. "No rules?"

Satisfied with her compliance, he grinned a confirmation. "Nope. All's fair–."

With lightning speed, she grasped his hand with both of hers and slammed it to the deck. Grinning into his astonished face she crowed with delight. "Okay, you fine specimen of the male gender–easily duped I might add–spill your guts."

"Oh, you're a mean one, Darby Walker," he said, rubbing his wrist ruefully. "You have no scruples at all. First, I have to check for broken bones." He examined his arm carefully, glancing up to see if he was getting any sympathy at all.

"Can it, MacKinnon. Pay up."

"Only if you agree to a rematch."

Darby sipped from the community coffee cup and purred, "After I hear about your exodus to Brennan's Point."

"All right, all right. Anyone ever tell you you're pushy?" Joe retrieved the cup and refilled it from the thermos. "Back in the day–I've always wanted to start a story with 'Back in the day,' by the way; yet another of life's targets met.

"Back in the day, I was your typical yuppie corporate bright guy, the 'rising star' of Sandridge and Sloan. I put in long hours, showing up at home just long enough to change clothes and kiss my wife goodbye." He sipped from the cup, the humorous light fading from his eyes as he focused inward. "I schmoozed with the best of them, and I did climb that ladder.

"Nadine understood, never complained, and always supported my career. I basically left her on her own to raise Andrew. I figured I was being a good stepfather by bringing in the bucks and providing for my new, ready-made family." Darby could feel the warmth of the sun drain from their little picnic site as Joe spoke. She bit her lip and listened.

"Nadine began to be tired a lot, not feeling up to snuff was how she put it. Still she wasn't a complainer, always there to listen to me go on and on about the office, or some big account." Joe's face was a study of regret, and it seemed as if he'd forgotten she was even there. He was back in time with Nadine and the ghosts that haunted his past.

"She became ill–very ill–and pregnant with Shannon against her doctor's advice." He shook his head. "But there I was, still racing on that treadmill, making a career. I was going to pay for the best doctors, the best medical care money could buy." He stopped and stared down into the coffee mug. "In short, I was a bloody fool.

"Then one day, a big client came to town. I was to do the usual wining and dining. I did it up in style, the best hotel, restaurant, tickets for the theater. He seemed to enjoy himself, but I could tell there was something more on his mind. I was eager to get home, Nadine was having a rough go right about then, and I didn't want to be away. So I came right out and asked what, in a nut shell, would it take for him to sign with Sandridge and Sloan." His eyes cleared, and he turned to her, "Do you know what that man said?"

She shook her head and waited.

His mouth pulled back in a humorless smile. "He wanted a woman, a 'companion,' for the evening." Joe's gaze shifted to Shannon's small figure kneeling over her fishing hole, then expelled a noisy grunt. Seconds ticked by, the air heavy with disgust. Joe turned back to Darby and continued, "So there it was, right in front of me, the sum total of what my so-called career had become." His eyes were rueful. "I was now pimping for Sandridge and Sloan."

He tossed the rest of his coffee into the water. "I had missed every special moment in my young son's life, my wife was dying, fighting to give our little girl life before she went, and I, the great provider, was asked to fix up this VIP with a prostitute—a pretty lofty assignment. I had thought I was doing something significant. What I was really doing was simply adding to the ugliness of the world. It was one hell of a moment of truth. I quit that night, and never went back."

Hearing Joe's bitter account of his experience with big business, Darby suddenly understood so much of what she had seen and heard since moving into the MacKinnon home.

Here was the reason for the messy housekeeping, the disjointed scheduling, Andrew's hostility at her arrival, the dozens of phone calls and hasty meetings to preserve the integrity of Brennan's Point, his leaving work to show Shannon how to fish with a safety pin instead of arriving with a new fishing rod with all the latest gear in hand, why he was a single parent and not out chasing women.

"Did Nadine live to see Shannon?"

His face softened watching Shannon bob her line, her little tongue stuck out of the corner of her mouth in concentration. "Yes, she did, and thank God for that. As I've already said, Nadine didn't have it too good while growing up. She was adopted when she was just a week old by an older couple, well past their child-raising years. Turned out they didn't know how to handle an active child. Once she became a curious toddler, they turned her over to a series of live-in nannies. Some were kind and loving toward her, some weren't. Much of her childhood was lonely. That's when she rushed into her first marriage, to get away, to be loved, and have a family of her own, the way she imagined it could be. It didn't work out.

"Then she and I met and married, and I took on Andrew. We agreed that Nadine would stay home so she could raise our son in a loving home with both parents. Having Andrew and Shannon meant the world to her. She lived to see

Shannon's first birthday, our home here being built, and her family having come together for the first time. I know she was happy that last year; happier than she had been throughout the rest of our marriage. At least I gave her that."

"Joe, you're a wonderful father," Darby said. "You really have succeeded in making a happy home for your children." She looked down and saw she was holding his hands in hers. "And I'm sorry I pushed you to tell me. I had no right to pry."

He looked at their clasped hands. "I've never told anyone about that client, or how his request made me feel, not even Nadine. I couldn't tell her what I'd traded our life together for; I was too ashamed. All she knew was I was sick of the city and wanted a simpler life for the kids."

"Maybe that was all she needed to know. I'm sure she knew you loved her. You said yourself she was happier here."

He didn't reply. Her breath hitched in her throat as she watched him bring her hand to his lips and press a kiss onto her wrist.

"Thanks for listening," he murmured against her hand before letting it go.

"Any time." She busied herself with picking up from their lunch. She couldn't help thinking about Nadine, and her wish to raise her children herself, with both parents present and not wanting to repeat the mistakes that were made during her own childhood, that of a series of nannies coming in and out of her life.

The irony of it touched Darby's heart. Joe didn't see it, but he had, in his efforts to juggle his family and the marina actually created Nadine's exact fear. Her children were, in fact, living with a series of nannies.

WARM MILK

DARBY WALKED dreamily into her room. She was tired, but it was a good tired—the kind that comes from a day of accomplishment. She kicked off her sandals and slumped across her bed with a happy sigh, stretching lazily, reaching her arms up to the metal rungs of the headboard and giving them a satisfying tug. She pointed her toes and rotated her feet. The cat stretch felt good. The cold-ham-and-salad supper she'd come up with to beat the heat had been good. Her long walk in the moonlight with Buddy and her camera had been good. The afternoon at the marina with Shannon and Joe had been really good. The pictures for Joe's proposal were also good. She laughed softly at herself. It had all been good.

Okay, Goody Two Shoes, have a quick bath then right into bed for a good night's sleep. Ah, but that would mean getting up off this comfy bed, and we wouldn't want that now, would we? No, we'd rather snuggle here and drift off.

Darned if she didn't catch her eyes sliding shut. It was so hot in here, it was making her sleepy. She pushed herself up and away from the tempting bed, trailed into the bathroom, and flipped on the light.

"No!" she gasped, taking in the sight of her Brennan's Point photos strewn around the room, slashed, torn, crumbled, tossed. Not trusting her legs, she sank to the edge of the tub, taking it all in.

She reached into the tub and picked up a scrap of picture. It looked to be part of a picture she had taken of the town hall. She retrieved more pieces, finding parts of the marina, the heads of two children playing in the surf, a corner of Brennan's Point's quaint library, the top half of a cappuccino bar by the beach, Carl's Catch of the Day surrounded by hungry customers.

She let them slide from her fingers. Ruined. All of them, ruined.

This could only be Andrew's work.

The picture Darby had taken of Joe on the beach caught her eye. It was still whole, but was pegged to the wall with the point of her nail file driven through the smile on Joe's face. Anger fairly permeated the room. She shook her head in stunned, sad disbelief. How could one boy be so angry? Hadn't they come to some understanding? The past few weeks had been without incident; in fact, she'd thought Andrew had accepted her. The hair disaster had felt like a turning point. He'd come to her for help, and she had helped him, she'd even gone to bat for him with his father.

How wrong she'd been.

What should she do now? Go to Joe? Show him how angry his son really is? This wasn't a mere prank, this was an attack. No. Joe had enough to deal with. You're an adult, Darby, take care of this yourself. But how?

Slumped over the remains of her pictures, she came up with nothing.

For now, she had to get out of this stifling room and away from Andrew's anger. She stood up and left the bathroom, closing the door firmly on the ruined pictures. Think, she commanded, stripping out of her clothes, and slipping into the lightest thing she owned, a thin cotton nightie. What was the best way to handle a disgruntled fourteen-year-old boy's vandalism? And it had to be something big—something just between her and Andrew, leaving his father out of it.

First off, she'd develop the pictures again, take the sting out of the attack. But wait, had he gotten to the negatives too? She hurried back into the bathroom, stepping over the strewn pieces, and pulling open the drawer where she'd placed the negatives, sagging with relief to find them inside, untouched. She shut the drawer, left the bathroom, closed the door again, and began pacing the small space from bed to dresser. Right, the negatives were okay. What should be her appropriate reaction? She had to be smart—smarter than Andrew.

Suddenly, she was ravenously hungry. She wanted toast, with lots of chunky peanut butter and a glass of icy cold milk, with a hint of vanilla and honey.

Because everyone else in the house was asleep, she slipped quietly out of her room, her bare feet noiseless on the hall runner. In the kitchen, she eased the door of the fridge open and brought out the milk. The quiet was vanquished by the sound of a sharp intake of breath. She whirled toward it. The fridge door swung wide, bathed the room with light and revealed Joe leaning against the wall beside an open window, smoking a cigarette.

"Geez, you scared me!"

Joe's answer was slow in coming, delivered with an uncharacteristic growl. "Sorry."

"I thought you didn't smoke?"

He stared at her without speaking for what seemed an eternity, than finally said, "I don't."

Darby stared back at him. "B-but ... you are ... smoking."

Here in the darkened kitchen, Joe looked different. She could see instantly that he was different. Dangerous. It was as if the smiling, laughing Joe from their afternoon picnic had never existed.

"You are smoking, now," she repeated, making her voice stronger.

"Yes." He took another drag of the cigarette but didn't exhale. He crushed the remains of the cigarette into a saucer and straightened. Again, he simply stared. When he did finally speak, he released the smoke from his lungs at a measured pace that matched his words. "You can't sleep either?"

Darby glanced down at the jug of milk in her hand. "I–I was going to make a cold vanilla milk. That usually relaxes me so I can sleep."

"Relaxes you," Joe repeated, a lazy smile spreading across his face. Darby recognized a hunger in his eyes, an answer to the hunger she'd been hiding from herself for days, maybe weeks. His body heat seemed to reach out to her from across the room, and she felt a coiling longing gather low in her stomach. Carefully, she placed the jug of milk on the counter, not trusting her grip.

She said, "It's better than smoking." Her eyes met his, preventing her from saying more.

"Much," Joe answered, closing the space between them leisurely

Should she turn around and run? It wasn't too late to run. But it was too late. She stood rooted; everything between them had been leading up to this moment. Did she want to cross that line with Joe MacKinnon, risk the balance they'd achieved? Her head said no while her body screamed a 'Hell yeah!'

She needed to say something, anything, to slow this thing down. "W-what are you doing sitting alone in the dark?"

"Looking at you."

"This is a regular thing with you?" She'd meant to sound flippant. Instead she sounded scared. She started to shake.

Joe's mouth turned up at the corners. "You're the photographer. You must be familiar with the term 'back lighting.'"

"Uh-huh."

"You make a delectable picture."

Darby looked down at her nightie, slow to catch his meaning. He was closer now—too close. His husky voice washed over her as he continued his appraisal, "… back lit by the light from the fridge." A heartbeat passed, then Darby gasped, realizing what he was saying. The light from the open fridge would silhouette her body as clearly as if she had stood before him naked. Instinctively, she stepped out of the revealing light to swing the door of the fridge closed and at the same time, in darkness, stepped into Joe's waiting arms.

She fought to speak, her limbs quaking. "I-I never meant …" She licked her lips. "I mean, I didn't realize …" Her voice caught in her throat when Joe slipped one arm around her, bringing her nightie around with his hand, so that it twisted, fitting tight to her body and exposing one breast, bare to the cool air and his heated magic hand. Her body celebrated his touch, her brain thrashed for someplace to hide.

"But what about the children …" she sighed, attempting to remain sane in an insane situation.

"They're asleep," he murmured, moving closer, covering her mouth with his—finally, at long, long last, he was kissing her. She sank into him with a moan, pressed the length of her body against his, relishing his hard warmth, his quiet strength, his instant response. She raised her hands to frame his face, savoring the roughness of his late-night stubble, drinking in the taste of him; even the lingering taste of the cigarette was welcome on her tongue. Her shoulder straps drifted down her arms to her elbows; his lips followed, feasting on her throat, her shoulders, her breasts. Wherever he touched her, she was on fire.

She pulled his shirt open and underneath its folds ran her hands over his warm skin and softly, springy triangle of hair on his chest, then passed her palm across the bulge behind the zipper of his jeans with a pressure he answered with a growl. He lifted her up, turned, and pressed her against the wall. Compelled to daring by desire, she wrapped her legs around him, her arms around him, and tunneling her fingers through his hair, guided his mouth to her breast. He drew her nipple swiftly, sweetly into his mouth, driving her beyond reason with every caress of his tongue, every tug of his lips, to a craving that shook her, a craving that demanded contact deep inside of her.

Suddenly he withdrew, her damp skin abruptly chilled at the loss. He pressed his forehead against her throat, his breath coming in short gasps. "Just a minute; let's just take a minute," he whispered, moving away from the wall. The Joe she knew was back. He was no longer standing, but was seated on a kitchen chair, and she was sitting astride him, still fitted warmly against him. She dropped her head to his shoulder and could feel his heart beating steady and strong where her cheek lay nestled to his neck. She felt him drop a kiss on her bare shoulder, and was suddenly aware of her near nakedness. She shivered.

"Cold?" Joe's voice was a rumbling vibration against her ear.

She nodded, reluctant to speak. He shrugged out of his shirt, and brought it around, draping it over her shoulders. The shirt was still deliciously warm from his body and smelled of him. She smiled into his neck and whispered, "Thanks."

"Here," he said, adjusting their position. Reluctantly, she raised her head from the warm nook she'd found at his neck and watched his face as he concentrated on the task at hand; his dear, stubbled, beautiful face.

With singular attention, Joe threaded first one of her arms, then the other into the sleeves of his shirt before patiently folding back the cuffs until her hands were visible. Finally, his eyes met hers, the aggressive, almost haunted expression she'd first seen in his shadowed face by the window replaced now by a softer, tenderer Joe. "Better?" he asked.

"Um-hum," she nodded.

"Sorry about scaring you–."

She stopped him by running her finger along his lower lip, then covering his mouth with her own, dipping her tongue inside his mouth in playful combat. Slowly, seductively, she rocked her pelvis against him. He groaned, wrapped both arms around her, flattening her breasts against his chest. His tongue matched her invitation with an urgent one of his own. Her skin burned from his unshaved face, and she didn't care. In a heartbeat, passion flared brightly again.

"I'm not scared. In fact, I'm the opposite of scared," Darby breathed against his mouth.

Joe's eyes lit up. He pulled her hard against him again. "How opposite?"

With an answering wiggle of her own she growled playfully, "About as opposite as a girl can get."

"Oh, Baby, have you come to the right place." Holding her close, he stood up suddenly, taking her with him. "But not here."

Darby laughed softly and then froze. Joe was still as a stone–listening. He'd heard something too. Suddenly, Darby realized what they were doing, where they were doing it; with two children in the house. She moved swiftly out of his arms; Joe made no protest and let her go.

"Daddy?" Shannon's little voice came from the direction of her room.

Darby panicked. "Oh, my God, Joe, she can't see me like this." She wrapped his shirt around her. "Go! Go to her–she can't come in here."

With barely a whisper, he was gone.

Darby was alone, in the dark, shaking in disbelief at the horrible chance they had taken. What if they hadn't heard Shannon? What if she'd come upon them in the kitchen, making love? It was too awful to think about. Darby listened again. Joe was taking Shannon back into her room. Now was the time for Darby to quickly return to hers. Swiftly, soundlessly, she sped down the hall and into the guest room. She closed the door softly, turned the lock, and collapsed against it. What had she been thinking?

■ ■ ■

"HEY THIS milk is yucky," Shannon announced at the breakfast table. She made a face and curled out her tongue with distaste. "It's all warm. Yuck!"

Joe glanced across the table at Darby. She quickly looked away and made a business of serving up fruit-explosion pancakes all around. Oh, dear God, get me through this nightmare, she prayed. Joe sighed loudly, but she refused to meet his eyes.

"What's wrong, Daddy? Did you drink some milk too?"

"No, Honey, I'm just thinking about something else, that's all." Shannon's obvious concern put a smile in Joe's voice when he answered. Darby could feel her face pink up.

"Well, take it from me," Shannon continued on wisely. "You're gonna hate the milk."

Swiftly, barely able to disguise her impatience, Darby removed Shannon's glass, replacing it with a tumbler of apple juice. "You don't have to have the milk, Sweetheart. Have this apple juice instead. Someone left the milk out on the counter overnight, that's all. Let's not talk about the milk anymore." She knew her face flushed even more.

Shannon sipped on her juice thoughtfully and then said. "We can give it to Buddy. He'll drink anything." She turned round eyes to Darby. "He even drinks out of the toilet." Her tongue curled out in disgust again.

Joe pretended to grab Shannon's tongue. "Keep that tongue out of sight, Young Lady, or you're going to lose it."

"Oh, Daddy," she giggled. "Everybody knows you can't lose your tongue."

"If you don't keep it zipped, it's gone." Joe cut into his stack of pancakes and took a generous bite. "Mmm." He bobbed his eye brows appreciatively at Darby. She pretended not to see, concentrating on her plate. What did he want from her, breezy nonchalance? It simply wasn't in her, not after last night. She passed her hand across her forehead and fought to remain seated.

Shannon chattered on between bites of pancake, unaware of the silence between Joe and Darby. "You have your tongue forever and ever." She chewed thoughtfully. "And it's good for lots of stuff, too." She looked briefly at Andrew. "Andrew wants to wear an earring in his."

Andrew glowered back at her. "Big mouth," he muttered darkly.

Joe's eyes flicked up at Andrew's hair. "We won't even go there, right, son?"

Andrew looked back with feigned innocence. "Did I say I was getting it pierced?"

"Just as long as we understand each other," Joe said, gathering up the last bit of syrup with a fork full of pancake.

Undeterred, Shannon went on, "Your tongue's good for tasting stuff, and licking stuff. And you can tell if someone likes you if they lick you."

Darby's knife clattered across her plate and onto the floor. Her gaze flew from Shannon to Joe in mortification. Shannon wrapped her arms around her tummy and giggled.

"W-what are you talking about, Shannon?" Darby asked.

"Buddy," Shannon said.

Andrew poked his sister. "Yeah, right after he drinks from the toilet– yummy, huh, Shannon?"

Darby sagged in her seat. She couldn't take it–it was torturous.

"That's it, guys," Joe interjected, "Darby and I need to talk about plans for today. You two clean up from breakfast. Come on, Darby, bring your coffee out to the deck."

Darby couldn't get out of the kitchen fast enough. Coffee mug in hand, she charged ahead of Joe to the deck. Once there, she dumped it out over the railing and dropped into a chair, covering her face with a loud groan. "I thought she'd never stop."

"Out of the mouths of babes," Joe said.

"Oh, shut up!" she said crossly. "You don't have to enjoy this so much. I'm dying of embarrassment, and you're encouraging her!"

"My, my, nasty temper you've got there, Miss Walker," Joe commented, sipping on his coffee with pleasure.

Darby jumped up and paced the length of the deck. "This is not funny. We took a terrible chance last night. My God, what were we thinking? It could have turned out differently, you know–then you wouldn't be sitting so smugly."

"But it didn't."

She stopped in front of him. "Only out of sheer luck, Joe, sheer luck." She jammed her hands into the pockets of her jeans. "This isn't what I had in mind when I moved in here, Joe. This is so terrible; I truly can't believe I really did that."

"First of all, we did it, not just you." He clasped her shoulders with both hands and gave her a gentle shake. "Calm down. It wasn't the end of the world. I got to her in time, got her back into bed with a little drink, and back to sleep in no time."

Darby looked beseechingly up into his face. "You don't seem to see how serious this is. I've been here a grand total of six weeks, and I ..." She covered her face with her hands again. "Oh, I can't even say it. It's too humiliating."

"Darby, Honey–." Joe tried to take her into his arms, and she jerked away.

"Do not 'Darby, Honey' me. This absolutely cannot happen again, Joe."

Finally, he saw she was deadly serious. He dropped his hands. "You're right, of course," he agreed easily, picking up his coffee cup, "and I totally agree with you. You have my word it'll never happen again."

"I do?"

"Absolutely," he nodded. "You're here to build up Andrew's safety net, and to be introduced as the children's aunt, and that's the sum total of your obligation to us. Consider the matter closed."

She looked at him in surprise, not knowing if she should be insulted he'd brushed their fateful meeting in the kitchen away so easily, or relieved the whole sordid mess was over. She hesitated for only a moment. "Fine, it's closed."

"So, can we move on to another subject?"

"Of course," she agreed.

"You mentioned you had some photos I could add to the proposal."

"I did." She hesitated again. "There's a problem with them, but, I think I can have them ready for you by this afternoon."

"A problem?"

"They didn't develop correctly. I'll have to do them over."

"All right. Since you brought up the idea, I think they could be pivotal to our proposal's chances with the Natural Resources Board. I'd appreciate if you'd get to them right away." Joe dumped the last of his coffee over the railing as she had done and added, "This will be a great help for the committee."

She looked at him, amazed and a little appalled at the sudden change. He'd switch off so cleanly and decisively, with no sign of a struggle or self-doubt. It was back to business as usual with Joe MacKinnon. How do people do that? It took her a moment to make herself speak. "That's good," she agreed.

He continued, "I could take the kids off your hands for the day, leaving you free to work."

"Okay to taking Shannon. I could use Andrew's help."

"Well, all right then. That's settled; Andrew's all yours for the day, and I'm in charge of Shannon. Her birthday is coming up soon. We'll pick up some birthday party invitations while we're out."

"Right," Darby agreed, squaring her shoulders to the task. "It seems we each have our assignments for the day."

They walked back into the kitchen as a united front, though now they were miles apart.

Once Darby waved Shannon and Joe out of sight along the bumpy, rutted road, she caught hold of Andrew and silently brought him through her bedroom to the bathroom. The expression on his face told her he was not expecting this reaction. What had he thought would happen? Had he anticipated tears, shouting, Darby moving out perhaps?

The thing was, she could easily have shed tears, only not for the torn photos, but for her torn heart. She was only six weeks in, and the MacKinnon family now lived under her skin, was part of every breath she took. After only six weeks.

BIG DEVELOPMENTS

BROOM IN hand, Darby stood in the doorway to her bathroom, which was still strewn with scattered and torn pictures; Andrew slouched next to her. Saying nothing, Darby let the room speak for itself. She could see Andrew give it his best shot, making a show of belligerence, but she knew he was completely put off balance by her silence. Seconds ticked by. He shifted his weight to his other foot and leaned against the door sill. He tried to look bored. Darby knew him enough by now; bored he was not. His face was unusually pale below the cocky blue of his hair; Andrew was scared.

Finally, he cracked. "Okay. So, why didn't you tell my Dad?"

Darby answered him carefully. "Because this is between you and me, Andrew–not you, me, and your dad."

He snorted. "Yeah, right. I suppose you expect me to clean it up now?"

"You're half-right. First you're going to clean it up, then you're going to reprint the pictures yourself."

"Are you crazy? I don't know anything about photography."

"You're about to learn."

Andrew's mouth hung open, and he shook his head in disbelief. "You can't make me do anything I don't want to do–and I don't want to learn about your stupid pictures."

"There's where you're wrong. I can, and I will." Darby shoved the broom into his hand. "You've got a lot to do, and not much time to do it in. Your dad is expecting these pictures by this afternoon, and you will not disappoint him." She nudged him into the room and added, "I'm even going to help you clean up, because, well, I'm just that nice." She smiled at him, and demonstrated by clearing off the counter top and sink. After a moment's hesitation, he caved and started sweeping. "Once we're done," she said, "we'll set up a temporary dark room in here." She took his silence for acquiescence.

With two of them working, the cleanup was swift. It wasn't long before they were both on their knees, arranging her enlarger, timer, and trays across the floor. Darby explained that they would need stability for the enlarger, and the floor was their best bet in such a small room with so little counter space.

"Okay, before we set up the trays, we'll tape over the window and door with duct tape and these black plastic bags." Andrew looked at her questioningly, but didn't ask why. She could see he was curious, but too proud to break his silence. That was okay. She explained the need for complete darkness as if he had asked her. Let the mountain come to Mohammad.

As they sealed off the window, Darby felt the familiar light sweat break out on her upper lip and her heart pick up its pace. The usual claustrophobic tension of closing herself inside a small dark space squeezed her chest. She took a deep breath and blew it out.

Andrew looked at her questioningly.

She smiled at him and said, "No worries. I'm just a little claustrophobic."

"Something happen to you?"

"You could say that."

Once the window and door were sealed to her satisfaction, Darcy showed him how to set up the safe light. "This is so we can see what we're doing in here. This kind of light won't interfere with the process." Andrew nodded, drinking in what she was saying. She could see he was beginning to relax.

"Next, we set up a hanging line in here, much like a mini clothes line. Once we're happy with each picture, we'll hang it up to dry with these tiny clips." Darby showed him the line and the clips.

"I can do that," he volunteered. Darby smiled her thanks, and turned to selecting the paper she wanted to use. Once Andrew was done, he knelt down beside her and asked, "What's next?"

"Chemicals," she said. "For this, we have to be careful. The good thing is, a little goes a long way."

"How much do we need?"

"This is the developer. It's called silver halide. We'll make up a 10-percent solution, using only about a third of a cup. That should do over a hundred prints."

"Cool," Andrew said. "Are we doing a hundred?"

"No. Not necessary. We'll do a couple dozen," Darby said. "Your dad will have plenty to choose from. He knows which pictures will suit his proposal; our job is to give him a variety of great pictures to choose from."

Andrew nodded thoughtfully. "Yeah, he really wants the town to go with his plan, not those other guy's."

"Maybe what we do here today will tip the scales his way. Who knows?"

"Why are we doing this here, anyway? Can't the one-hour photo shop do this?"

Darby shook her head. "No, sorry to say it, but we can do it better here. This way, we control the exposure. Plus, we're going to do these in black and white, then hand tint a focal point in each. It's a bit artsy and fussy, but it can be very effective." She reached for one of two old shirts she had draped over the tub and a pair of safety goggles. "Here, put this shirt on. It'll protect your clothes. And these will protect your eyes." Andrew quickly shrugged into the shirt and snugged the goggles to his head. He grinned at Darby.

She put on the other shirt and her own safety glasses then asked Andrew to turn on the safe light and flip off the main light. Instantly, they were bathed in an eerie red glow. Now she handed Andrew the silver halide.

"Pour enough of this to reach this line in the container, that'll be one part, then fill it up to here with water, that'll be nine parts. That makes a one-to-ten solution." She pointed out the markers. "Then pour it slowly into the tray."

Once he was done, she directed him in mixing and setting up the rest of the trays in sequence; after the developer came the stop solution, next the fixer, then into the sink for the water rinse. Finally, she demonstrated with the zoom knob how to use the enlarger, and how to use the timer for measuring exposure time.

Andrew was a quick learner. Once he'd seen the process with the first negative, he was eager to try the next one. Darby let him try his hand at it so he could to see the results of over-and underexposure, then try again with more accurate measures of exposure time. She wasn't surprised to find he had a gentle and steady hand with the tongs, slipping each print into and out of their sequenced baths smoothly. When it came to hand coloring each photograph with the small supply of photo tints she had on hand, Andrew proved to be a natural. Leaving the majority of the print black and white, he highlighted sparingly with the tints. She found she liked this new Andrew very much. Hours flew by unnoticed. The resulting prints were good.

When it was time to break down the makeshift darkroom, Andrew grew quiet. Regretfully, Darby watched his forgotten wall of defense returning with the natural light that poured back into the small room. Before he was lost to her entirely, she reached into one of her canvas bags, brought out one of her older cameras, and handed it to him.

"What's this for?" he asked, surprised.

"I thought you might like to try taking the pictures yourself. I think you might have a gift for it."

He looked at the camera for a long time, turning it over in his hands. Finally, he looked up and into her eyes squarely for the very first time since she had known him. "This is nice. And, I would like to have it, but ..." he trailed off for a moment. "I gotta be honest with you. This camera won't buy me."

Darby nodded slowly. "I know. It's not meant to."

He laid the camera on the counter top carefully, regretfully. "I can't take it. It wouldn't be right. And–I gotta say, I'm sorry for messing with your stuff. I shouldn't have done it."

Encouraged by his openness, Darby asked, "But why, Andy? Why are you so angry?"

"I saw you and my dad."

Darby blanched, catching herself by sitting down abruptly on the edge of the tub. This was so much worse than she'd thought. Shannon wasn't the only one she and Joe had so foolishly forgotten last night. Apparently, Andrew had gotten an eyeful. She blushed crimson. That explained ... but wait, that couldn't be. Andrew had torn up the pictures long before she'd met Joe in the darkened kitchen.

"What did you see, Andy?"

"You and my dad, fooling around down on the docks; laughing and rolling around." He looked away. "Geez; all out there for everyone to see–kissing."

Now Darby was confused. "But Andy, we weren't kissing."

His eyes shot back to hers. "Hey, I'm not an idiot. He was kissing your hand!"

"Oh, that."

"Yeah, that."

"That was a joke. Andy, I'm not chasing your father, and your father isn't chasing me. This arrangement is only for banking blood for you, nothing more." *Say that three times and see if you believe it.*

"Yeah—my dad has so much faith in me he's preparing for my next major screw-up, and everyone in town knows it."

"That's not what's happening here, and you know it!"

"What I do know is my dad's not chasing you. He doesn't have to chase women down. They just call themselves nannies and move right in."

Darby was shocked speechless.

Andrew continued, gathering steam as he vented. "You don't think you're the only babysitter trying to make time with my dad, do you? It's been a revolving door around here—with all these new 'mommies' getting all set to stay permanently. They pretend they care about Shannon and me, but it's all bull. I know they're thinking, 'Hey, great setup—rich guy, two stupid kids, easy street.' Well, with me around, they don't stay long. I make sure of it. This family is just fine the way it is." He stopped, glaring at her, daring her to argue his theory. Darby didn't have it in her to hurt this boy any more than he was already hurting. And Joe had no idea.

"Andy, I can't comment on the people who came before me. Probably you know better than I." She stopped him with her hand when he started to argue the point. "Hang on a minute there, let me finish. The way I see it, Andy, is what you've been doing is hurting your dad more than anyone else. He's working to build up the marina, he's trying to keep Brennan's Point a town that you and Shannon can grow up in safely, and be proud of, maybe raise your own families in one day. He's trying to be a good father. He's trying to keep his family together, cared for. And you've been tearing everything down here at the home front instead of helping him. When he and I met, he was at the end of his rope. I could see that, and I didn't know him from Adam."

She picked up the camera and pressed it into his hands. "Andy, please take this. It's a peace offering. Have fun with it. And trust that your dad knows what he's doing."

A strange look came over Andrew's face. "You just don't get it, do you? When I said my dad didn't have to chase women and that they just kept inviting themselves in here, I didn't say he wasn't up for it. You say he knows what he's doing. Yeah, he knows what he's doing, all right. Watch out, or he'll be doing you next."

ESCAPE

THE WHOLE town council loved Darby and Andrew's pictures. In fact, all ten council members squeezed into the MacKinnon dining room, bobbed their heads in unison, and wiped clean Mrs. Russell's tray of treats with the help of cup after cup of freshly brewed coffee. Joe's informal presentation of the finished proposal had been a rousing success. The black and whites, with their sparse tinting of appropriate color were well received, and Andy was complimented accordingly. From her safe place, flitting in the background, keeping things moving, Darby smiled and watched his confidence rise as the afternoon progressed. He was a different boy. If only this boy would stay, leaving the suspicious Andrew behind. She sighed.

She glanced up and found Joe's gaze on her, his expression vigilant, but still. So it wasn't just about the blood for him either. She averted her eyes, struggling to maintain the calm exterior she had chosen to masquerade under for the balance of her stay in the MacKinnon household.

Over the last several days, she, Andrew, and Joe had pored over the prints, deciding how they best supported Joe's case for building the wind power station. Darby had been amazed at the quality of Joe's work. But then, she shouldn't have been, knowing his corporate past. He knew all the buzz words that make decision makers' hearts race with joy. After hours of culling the prints, deciding where they should be placed within the text, they began the painstaking process of scanning each into the final document. Once a clean copy was put together, next came the make-it-look-pretty part– graphics, bullets, white space, headers, footers, tables of contents, references. It was all there, as required. Then painstaking proofing, making sure every 'T' was crossed, every 'I' dotted.

Darby hadn't known how she would handle working so closely with Joe, after their encounter in the kitchen. Now that she was aware of his history with the nannies that had come before, she was especially on guard. Surprisingly, they'd clicked as a team and seemed to anticipate one another's thoughts and instincts. When it came to business, they were on the same wavelength. The awkwardness that she'd felt before was gone, due to Joe's all-business attitude, which she'd come to appreciate.

Yesterday's final edit had been brutal. They'd worked through lunch and through dinner. By midnight, the final product was pumped out of her printer on forty-pound bond paper and bound together. Looking it over, careful not to crease the pages, Darby knew they had a winner. Only then had she quietly excused herself, and crawled gratefully into her bed.

Now the afternoon had finally ended, and the meeting was breaking up. Seeing all the hand-shaking and back-slapping going on, she knew they'd pulled it off. The mayor now had the proposal safely tucked under his arm, to be sent by overnight courier. It was close, but the proposal would be in the Natural Resources Board's hands before tomorrow's 4 p.m. cut-off. Everyone was all smiles. It looked like all of Sam and Joe's work had paid off. The council was on board.

■ ■ ■

DARBY'S SLEEP was not restful and filled with proposal jargon, oven mitts, and hot cookie trays, time-exposed pictures of Joe standing at the kitchen window, smoking a cigarette and asking when she intended to repair his truck. She woke with a start at the sound of a gavel coming down, the mayor having just sentenced her to three years at babysitting school–until she got it right!

She blinked and looked around, surprised to see her room filled with late morning sun. She'd slept in–lots. She scrambled from the bed, reaching for a clean T-shirt and jeans, then stopped and listened. The house was silent.

Emerging from her room, she could see she was alone. In the kitchen, there was a single note taped to the fridge. Joe had taken Andrew and Shannon on a cruise up the coast for a couple of days. Eric, their neighbor to the north, had the horses on his land and they'd feed there. Darby was free to pursue her own interests. It was signed Joe. Just Joe; nothing friendly, nothing to show he gave a damn what she did while they were away. There was nothing nice, like 'We let you sleep because you've been working so hard', or 'We'll miss you'.

Making a face, she snatched it off the fridge and tossed it away. So what if she wasn't off cruising with the MacKinnon clan. She could use a break from those three loonies anyway.

It was 9:30 by the time she was showered and dressed for the day. Deciding to hike over to the neighbors to take one of the horses out for a ride, she was caught at the front door by a courier carrying two large envelopes. She scribbled her signature on his board, excited to see one of the packages was from Tourism B.C. Here was her answer! She hurried inside to tear it open.

Grabbing scissors from the kitchen drawer, she made a beeline toward her package, stopping in shock when she caught sight of the address on the second package. The scissors clattered to the table when she seized the envelope, willing her eyes to be wrong. They weren't. It was the wind power proposal, covered with a large sticker that read, Return to Sender, Address Unknown. How could that be?

The address was wrong–she knew it by heart by now, and here it was, wrong, wrong, wrong. The single task left to the mayor's office, and they'd gotten it wrong!

Then a new thought, an ugly thought. Mayor Mayer had backed Sperry from the beginning. Was he still secretly backing Sperry? Was this sabotage?

Today was the deadline; today at 4 o'clock.

She glanced at her watch. It was 9:40. Could she do it? She yanked the kitchen drawer out so hard it dropped to the floor, spilling half its content across the tile. She seized up the ferry schedule, frantically searching for sailing times. The next sailing was 10:15. It would take her half an hour to get to the ferry terminal; the ferry would arrive in Vancouver at 11:45. The proposal acceptance offices were downtown. That gave her lots of time to get the proposal to them before the 4 o'clock deadline. What about Joe? Could he take it by boat? That would be better still. She ran to the phone and dialed his cell number. Voice mail. She slammed the receiver into its cradle. She'd have to take it herself.

She dialed Joe's cell again, this time leaving a hurried message, then ran to her room for her purse and keys. Seeing her reflection in her mirror, still wearing riding clothes, she yanked them off, pulling on nylons, a blouse, and her only dress suit, a blue jacket with matching pencil skirt. She stopped again and considered her hair. No.

Shoving her feet into a pair of heels, she grabbed up her purse and keys, sped into the kitchen, picked up the two envelopes, and dashed out the door to the little rental. Starting it up with a roar, she backed it out of its spot by the side of the house, with a jerking motion, and headed down the drive, leaving a dusty trail in her wake. "Whoa, Nelly," she said under her breath, easing her foot off the gas. "Let's get there in one piece, why don't we?"

Humming steadily, the little car ate up the miles, delivering Darby and the proposal to the ferry terminal in time for the 10:15 sailing. When she was safely on board and had turned off the car engine, she gratefully closed her eyes and let herself relax. She'd made it—the first part anyway. She prayed traffic would be light once she arrived in Vancouver, knowing very well it wouldn't be. She'd get a map and plot out her route, but first—caffeine. She locked the car and climbed the grated metal stairs along with the other passengers, all, it seemed, to be of like mind—caffeine.

Once armed with a large coffee, Darby bought a city map at the onboard gift shop, found a quiet corner in the passenger's lounge, and spread it out. She wasn't familiar with the area where the Natural Resources Board offices were located. She studied the streets, trying for the quickest route there without hitting the main thoroughfares.

A wave of excitement rippled through the lounge. Someone had spotted a pod of orcas swimming alongside the ferry. Passengers crowded the open decks on the leeward side, craning to see the whales. The captain cut the engines as was the custom and through the sound system directed the sightseers to the spectacle. As always, the magnificent animals struck the people on the crowded decks speechless, the only sound being the clicking and whirring of cameras. Through habit, Darby reached for her own camera and was surprised to find she'd left it behind. Huh. She never left home without it. She shook her head and smiled to herself. Her answer to months of work to get the tourism contract was sitting inside her little rental car on the lower deck, and she hadn't thought to open it yet either. What was wrong with her?

She'd gotten her invitation to submit last month, and this was her reply. If she won the contract, she would be free to travel wherever she liked from now on—no ties, no obligations. Just freedom. The sight of the whale pod blurred and faded, her heart suddenly a thousand miles away.

If she'd been awarded the contract.

If she opened the envelope.

She walked back to where she'd laid out the map, took a sip of her coffee, and put together a plan for the quickest route to the Natural Resources Board, with one important stop along the way. Then she folded the map away and tucked it into her purse, settling back to enjoy the passing view of the Gulf Islands, and then of open sea.

■ ■ ■

CLEVER GIRL! Darby congratulated herself, slipping into a tiny parking spot in front of the Natural Resources Board office. Little cars do have great advantages in the city. And here she was, with an hour and forty-five minutes to spare.

She took a moment to check her face in her compact mirror and applied lipstick. Presentation is everything. She heard Laura's favorite lecture as she ran a comb through her brand-new blonde wig. You're so right, Laura, she thought with a smile. She fished some coins out of her change purse to feed the parking meter, tucked the proposal under her arm, and headed into the lion's den.

Once inside the building, reflective surfaces, glass walls, mirrors, polished elevator doors—all showed her how good she looked in the blonde wig. So this is how she'd look if she stopped messing around with hair dye. The wig was still jaw length, but was styled and sophisticated. She felt like Queen Esther about to face the irate king to plea for the lives of her people. Joe wouldn't be embarrassed by having her deliver the proposal, he would be proud. It was so important that Brennan's Point's proposal be taken seriously, and that required serious hair. She stifled a nervous laugh and read the listings for which floor she needed.

She was soon carried to the top floor by elevator, and making inquiries of the man behind the receptionist's desk. As it turned out, he was not the receptionist, but the receptionist's boss, the minister himself, Frederick Trudeau, and he was in a magnanimous mood.

Darby quickly realized the minister expected her to speak to him about the proposal, not simply drop it into his lap. In a split second, she made her decision not to disappoint. She accepted his invitation to come into his office, to sit and to discuss the merits of the proposal. Thankfully, she'd paid close attention to everything Joe had told her. Almost before she could catch her breath, Darby found herself presenting the entire proposal personally.

When the impromptu meeting drew to a close and Darby's hand was heartily shaken by the Honorable Frederick Trudeau—Fred, as he insisted she address him—and two of his executives whom he had invited to join their meeting, Darby floated back to her car, completely unconcerned at finding a parking ticket tucked under the windshield wiper. She merely slipped it into her purse and got into the car. Once inside, however, all bets were off. She let out a whoop, hitting the steering wheel with the palms of her hands again and again. She'd pulled it off! Natural Resources loved the proposal! She couldn't wait to tell Joe the great news.

She glanced at her watch, surprised to see it was already well past six o'clock. She was in for a long ride back to the ferry terminal. This was rush hour in Vancouver, and it would take her two hours, at least, to get to the terminal, with no guarantee she'd get on a ferry.

Suddenly, she was exhausted, simply wrung dry, and knew for certain that she would be a danger to herself and everyone around her if she elected to battle the roads. She needed downtime. It would be wiser for her to stay here in the city and return to Brennan's Point on the first ferry tomorrow morning.

If she took side streets, she could be at Walker House in forty minutes. She'd stop at her favorite Thai restaurant for takeout and call Joe from her mother's place, since her cell phone was currently lying on the kitchen counter back at the ranch where she'd left it this morning.

When she finally climbed up the steep stairs to the tiny attic loft she kept for herself in the huge house, she was completely drained, her joy about the proposal a distant memory, crowded out by the ghosts of this house. The truth was she hated coming here, endlessly surprised, it seemed, at the place's ability to deaden her spirit whenever she came back.

She'd simply have to stop coming here.

Closing her door against the noisy floors below, she locked it and pulled the dust covers from the bed, sofa, coffee table, and television. Positioning the table close to the sofa, she set up her takeout dinner and with the remote turned on the television. Thankfully, her tiny room still had cable, and she was able to watch the local news while she ate. It seemed in her absence that Vancouver's petty crimes and bottlenecked traffic had not changed, the incidents reported tonight all holding a familiar ring. Still, Vancouver was considered clean and safe by worldwide standards.

The house phone rang. "Hello?" she answered.

"Darby." Joe sounded angry.

"Joe. How did you get this number?"

"I found it in your drawer in your room."

"You went through my stuff?"

Joe said, "You left me no alternative. Your message was hardly enlightening, when I finally got it. Who's there with you?"

"What? Oh—you mean the TV."

"I thought you were homeless."

"I thought you were gone for a few days."

"Homeless?" he repeated grimly.

"I thought you'd be happy I came."

"I trusted you, and the first chance you get you're out of here? Yeah—that makes a man happy."

"Why are you so angry?"

"I trusted you with all the details of the wind turbine proposal, and now I learn from the courier company they didn't deliver it in time; in fact, they have no idea where it is. What did you do, deliberately change the address? So we're screwed before we even get out of the gate. I've been a bloody fool—trusting a complete stranger with my children, my home, my personal business. What the hell was I thinking?"

"What, so your first thought was me? You seriously think I'd deliberately sabotage the proposal? You do know it was the mayor's office who couriered the stupid thing, don't you? And guess who has been backing the Sperry Group from the beginning?"

Someone was banging on her door. What now?

Into the phone, she said, "You obviously don't understand. Just wait a minute while I ..." She grabbed the remote and shut off the TV.

The banging continued. "Miss Walker? Miss Walker."

"Just a minute." Darby hurried to the door. It was Gibson, the very last person she wanted to see at the moment. "Oh, Miss Walker!" He gushed. "We're all so happy to see you–it's been so long–too long."

"That's–I mean, hello, Gibson, thank you. But as you can see, I'm talking on the phone."

"Oh my, yes. So sorry." Gibson bobbed his shiny head several times as she unceremoniously closed the door in his face. She'd be apologizing for that, for sure.

"There! He's gone." She hissed into the receiver. "Happy now?"

"Look, I don't give a rat's a–."

"Don't you dare speak to me like that! I didn't invite him here–he does that, just shows up. I'm here because I couldn't make the ferry to get back in time."

"Don't bother." Joe countered. "We can do without you."

"What are you talking about?" Darby was incredulous at Joe's attitude. "I came here for you–."

"Yeah, right!" Joe's laugh was harsh. "And now you're sitting on the corner with all the other homeless victims of Vancouver, licking your wounds, grateful to have escaped your unfortunate commitment to your sister's family."

"What are you talking about? I didn't escape, I came here to–."

"I've heard enough."

"Obviously, you haven't," Darby defended. "Didn't you even listen to my message?" When he didn't speak, she rushed on. "You're going to be so sorry when you hear–."

He cut her off. "I'm sorry already. I don't want to hear anything you have to say, Miss Walker. I've heard plenty." The phone went dead.

Darby looked at the receiver in disbelief. Furiously, she dialed the MacKinnon number. It went unanswered, ringing and ringing. Her chest constricted, her breathing quick and shallow. She was bursting to explain, with no one interested enough to listen. She hung up and dialed, again to no avail. Had he turned off his phone?

Abruptly, the fight went out of her, like wind out from a sail, leaving her dead in the water. Softly, she placed the receiver into its cradle. There was nothing left for her to do.

WALKER HOUSE

THE FOLLOWING day, the clothes and photography equipment Darby had left at the MacKinnon's arrived at Walker House by courier. Joe had wasted no time erasing her presence from his home. Darby bit her lip hard when signing for the boxes, and even managed to give the delivery man a tip without falling apart.

Too bad the delivery of the Brennan's Point wind power proposal hadn't gone as well. If it had, she wouldn't be accepting delivery of her non-life with Joe, Shannon, and Andrew.

Andrew must be thrilled to pieces I'm gone. Mechanically, she dragged the boxes into the foyer, then into the elevator, and finally up into her little attic room where they sat, unopened. She crawled under the covers of her bed. So it was just that easy for him to cut her out of his life. Good to know.

When she couldn't blank the world out any longer, she threw off the covers and groaned out loud. "Enough already." It was seven in the evening. She'd managed to sleep her day away. Trailing into the bathroom, she had a long shower, changed into sweats, then went downstairs to apologize to Gibson and show a happy, shining face to all the tenants. Then it was back upstairs to search through the trunk that held her mother's journals, a set of slim, black, hardbound volumes she'd steadfastly avoided opening but now had good reason to do so. Joe MacKinnon may be angry at her, but she was Andrew and Shannon's aunt, and the thought of never seeing them again was heartbreaking. Did she have the right to see them? Would they want to see her? Would Joe even tell them?

The journals were near the bottom of the trunk where she'd left them, and she could see that they dated back to before she was born. She wondered, did she want to understand her mother's thought process? Roberta Walker had been intensely private about her personal life. Darby knew that she'd had the reputation of being the black sheep of the family, with much of her early young adult life a mystery. She'd always been the wild one, something Darby had obviously inherited, though she loathed to admit it.

But Darby did remember the one time, in an unguarded moment when her mother had called Darby her second chance. What she'd meant, Darby could only guess. Was it a case of her mother regretting her wild days, or because Darby was her second child, the one she refused to give up? It would have been so much better for all concerned if she had.

Looking at the journals, Darby decided if her mother had wanted her secrets kept, she'd have destroyed the journals. Instead she'd left them for Darby. She opened the first journal and began to read.

It wasn't until after midnight that Darby–exhausted from the disturbing insight into her mother's tortured mind–looked up from the last journal. *God, I need to leave this place and never come back here.*

The good thing–the very good thing was–she herself had never even remotely experienced these kinds of thoughts herself. She closed the last journal and looked around. Her single task light cast the little attic room into a shadowing, lonely place. *I really need to leave,* she thought again, then remembered the envelope from Tourism B.C., lying unopened in the rental car, a testament to her true feelings about the contract. Suddenly, she needed to know her future, needed a place to direct all this pent up energy. Anywhere else was better than this toxic place and these feelings.

She crept downstairs so as not to alarm the tenants and hurried to the car, retrieved the envelope, and hurried back inside. One in the morning in this neighborhood was not a good choice.

Back in her room she laid the envelope on the table, afraid of what she would find inside. What if the answer was no? Where would she go then? What would she do? Return to the magazine with her tail between her legs? Her whole life for the last three years had been focused on this moment, and she'd left it sitting in the car? What the hell was going on with her anyway?

She opened a package of stale Scottish tea biscuits, prepared and poured a cup of Earl Grey tea. She dipped a biscuit into the cup and bit off the warm, sodden end, a habit she'd acquired from Laura back in their college days. Comfort food.

Eight biscuits and two cups of tea later, she finally opened the couriered package, tipping it so its contents spilled out onto the table. She saw a cover letter on government letterhead. She saw a thick contract. She saw a cashier's check. She's won the contract.

She poured a third cup of tea and rustled in the cookie package for another biscuit. A month ago, she would have been dancing on the table.

Suddenly, she was sobbing, loud, gulping sounds from deep in her chest. Reaching for a dish towel to stifle her cries, she knocked over her cup, spilling cold tea across the contract, and soaking the check. Pressing the cloth to her mouth, she laid her forehead to the little Formica table and cried harder than she'd ever cried in her life. She was never going to see Joe MacKinnon again. Not Shannon either. Or Andy, and he was just starting to come around. Everything was left unfinished. She needed to be with them. God help her, she was in love with Joe and in love with his family. They had become her family; they *were* her family. Somewhere along the way, they'd snuck into her heart and taken up permanent residence there. Without them, she was alone again; lost like she hadn't in years, proof positive that letting people into your heart was dangerous.

After a time, the rage of tears ended, but the hurt did not. Finally spent and without another tear to shed, Darby raised her head and stared at the check. She had to accept that there was another path for her to follow, and the MacKinnons weren't it.

She was back to her old dream: old, she realized, because it had somehow been replaced by the new dream she dreamt of in Brennan's Point.

Now she was back to the old one, which, sadly, now seemed dusty and a little worse for wear. It had been her dream to become a professional photographer. It wasn't a bad thing. And now, she had the assignment she fought so hard for and had all the time in the world to do it in. Isn't that what she'd always wanted? Of course it was.

Only now that she had it, she was crying like a baby. Over something she had no control over. She scrubbed at her face with the cloth, inhaled deeply, and blew it out. She'd done her best, and damn it if her best wasn't good enough for Joe McKinnon, well too damned bad. His loss.

She tossed the dish towel into the sink and turned her attention back to the check. Was it salvageable? She peeled it carefully off the table, trying not to rip it. Yes, it was still legible.

She rattled around inside a kitchen drawer and found a pair of tongs with long handles. She turned on the gas stove, gripped the wet check with the tongs, and held it over the flame, waving it gently back and forth. Very quickly it crisped up and started to brown at the edges. Hastily, she removed it from the flame, and lay on the counter to cool. She studied the impressive numbers printed on it. Well, apparently, she didn't have any more money worries.

And just like that, she made her decision—she would spend only one more night in this house—her very last. She would hit the road tomorrow. No one would be able to get to her for months, and that was just how she liked it. It never pays to leave yourself open. She wouldn't be making that mistake again.

She turned her attention to the cover letter. Okay, what did it say?

■ ■ ■

JOE LOADED up his trunk with groceries, aware of how short his time was. Shannon was due from playgroup and would get off the bus in less than an hour. They'd have peanut-butter-and-honey sandwiches for lunch; he'd take her to the marina with him for the afternoon, pressing Regina, his new afternoon bait shop hire, into babysitting duty until Andrew came by at four. With Andrew watching Shannon, he'd get the receipts in order for his accountant, and get started on the plan for this year's Polar Bear Swim. Then he and the kids could all head for home together by seven, tops, and eat the meal Mrs. Russell had promised to leave for them. They were not going back to takeout. Mrs. Russell had the meals covered, at least. He grinned mirthlessly and settled his sunglasses firmly on the bridge of his nose. He had it all under control.

"Mac, you ol' dog!" Joe recognized Mayor Mayer's voice and turned toward him. "Your gal pulled it off!"

At a loss, Joe's raised his eyes brows in question. "My 'gal'? Pulled what off?"

"The minister, Frederick Trudeau from Natural Resources, just called me himself; they loved the presentation," Mayor Mayer gasped out as he careened to a stop at Joe's car, huffing and puffing over his considerable belly. "The address problem and mix-up with the courier notwithstanding, your young Darby must have wowed them. Walked in there, with only minutes to spare, bold as brass and presented it to them personally, right there, on the spot."

Speechless, Joe looked at Mayor Mayer through his sunglasses.

Taking Joe's silence for an invitation for more accolades, the mayor went on. "We just got the call this very afternoon. Apparently, Minister Trudeau called an emergency meeting of the Natural Resources Board, and your proposal passed with flying colors. They're sending out a representative before week's end to finalize the deal. They couldn't say enough good things about the plan, and about Darby Walker—called her our ace in the hole. I gotta say, Mac, you know how to pick 'em."

Joe's mind whirled with this new information, suddenly recalling Darby's angry voice over the phone saying "You're going to be so sorry when you hear–." He hadn't let her finish. He recognized that she hadn't been angry, she'd been hurt–by him. And he'd deliberately ignored her subsequent phone calls.

He hadn't counted on Darby's absence leaving such a hole in their lives.

When he and the children had returned from the boat early–he'd known almost at once he shouldn't have left Darby behind–and found she wasn't there, desolation dropped him like a linebacker. Searching through her belongings for clues, he'd gone from hurt to hostile. Calling and finding her at her mother's home and hearing that not only was she not homeless, as she'd led him to believe, but that she was obviously with another man had sent him out of orbit. The sheer power of his reaction had shaken him. He'd felt so betrayed that he'd refused to listen to another word the woman said.

"Well, don't stand there with your mouth hanging open, man; time to celebrate." Mayor Mayer grasped his hand and pumped it up and down. "We've got to get the town council together, and set up a–."

Galvanized to action, Joe interrupted Mayor Mayer, pulling his hand away and yanking open the door of his car. "Yeah, you do that, Bob. Right now, I've got something very important to do."

"What could possibly be more important than the future of Brennan's Point?" Mayor Mayer blustered, unaccustomed to being cut off so abruptly.

Joe jumped into the car and brought it roaring to life. "Trust me, it's the most important part of this whole thing." The car lurched forward. Joe waved, and yelled over his shoulder, "We'll talk later, Bob."

■ ■ ■

DARBY JAMMED the envelope with her signed copy of the tourism photo contract into an outside pouch of her now bulging backpack. It was a squeaker, but she got it in. She blew her bangs out of her eyes, and swung the pack onto her back.

She was set, self-sufficient once again. She'd contacted the car rental agency and arranged for someone to pick up the rental Joe had gotten for her. She was happy to see it being driven away, though was devastated when a sudden lump formed in her throat. No. No way was she going to tear up over Joe MacKinnon.

Now she would walk downtown to an RV dealership, and buy a brand-new camperized van with all the bells and whistles, right off the lot. Then she was going to go anywhere her little heart led her. She pasted a smile onto her face. Maybe soon, if she acted the part, she would be happy again.

She backed out of the house, wrestling the heavy old door shut. Spying Miss Hager from next door, she waved a cheery good morning she didn't feel.

She walked to the sidewalk, and stopped for one last look. Already, it was no longer hers. Truthfully, it never was. She turned and walked away.

■ ■ ■

SPRINTING LIGHTLY up the stairs, Joe knocked on the door and waited for the sound of footfall on the other side of the door. He paced the front porch of the house like a caged animal, examined the small plaque on the door that declared this to be The Walker House, then peered up and down the empty street, searching for—what? What did he expect to find?

"Are you looking for Darby?" A thin, reedy voice floated from behind the wall of shrubbery that grew between Darby's house and her neighbors.

"Yes! Yes, I am." Joe leapt down the steps three at a time and rounded the hedge toward the voice. A tiny, white-haired woman, bent almost double over a glossy, hardwood cane was struggling to pour bird seed into a feeder. She was getting more seed on her lumpy, crab-grassy lawn than in the feeder.

"Here, let me help you with that." Joe took the bag of seed from her unresisting hand, and filled the feeder. "You know where Darby is?" he asked.

"Oh, you young people don't know how lucky you have it," the woman wagged her head slowly. "You just did in less than a minute what would take me twenty. Enjoy your youth, young man."

Awkwardly, she turned away, took tiny, unsteady steps across the lumpy lawn, and headed toward a narrow sidewalk that led around the side of her house. Joe followed her.

"You mentioned Darby just now. You wouldn't know where she is?"

"Heaven's no. No one can keep up with that girl. She's a wild one, that one. Never in one place long enough to sprout roots."

Joe persisted. "But, she was here?"

"Only for a few days, enough time to settle everything with the house, I imagine, before she's off again, on another adventure. That's what Mr. Gibson said anyway."

"Mr. Gibson?"

"He runs the Walker House kitchen."

"Runs?"

"Like a tight ship. Those kids are lucky to have him. That Bloomberg fellow is pretty scary. But then, that's his job … and Darby said so, of course, but you must know that."

"You spoke to her?"

"Only a 'good day' today, after she handed over the car keys and all." The woman stopped to rest both hands on her cane and catch her breath. Joe pushed down the urge to hurry her story along, letting her tell it at her own pace. "All packed up, she was. How that girl can get so much stuff up and onto her back I'll never know. She'll end up like me, no doubt." Alarm bells sounded in Joe's head. Packed up? Off on another adventure?

"You said you spoke to her today? Before she went," Joe prodded gently. "Went where? When?"

"Who knows where she's off to now?" The lady resumed her shuffle into her backyard, drawing Joe with her.

"And when was this? When did she say good day?"

"Why, just before you arrived, I'd say." The woman looked at him in astonishment. "I just told you she said good day, then just started walking toward town. Not five minutes ago."

A zing of hope shot through him. Maybe there was still a chance for him to find her. Maybe it wasn't too late to get her back. Joe fought to keep his voice calm. "Which way did she go?"

The woman raised a shaky hand and pointed, "I told you, young man, she started toward town. You young people must learn to listen–."

"Thanks, Mrs.," Joe called over his shoulder and sprinted to the car. He did a U-turn, and headed in the direction Darby's neighbor had indicated, driving slowly and checking each side street for Darby. It just couldn't be too late. She had to be nearby.

His car ate up the blocks, but there was no sign of Darby.

■ ■ ■

DARBY HAD that creepy sensation someone was watching her. The hair on the back of her neck rose. Warily, she looked around and quickened her steps; her intuition was never wrong. Suddenly, she was jerked backward, pulled up and off her feet. She saw a flash of metal from the corner of her eye. A knife? Fear seized her, then the weight of her backpack was inexplicably gone, and she was thrown to the ground. She heard a gasp and thud behind her, followed by running feet that quickly faded down the dusty back lane she'd just passed. She scrambled to her feet and turned to find Joe on one knee, holding her backpack.

"Joe! How did you …? Joe, you're hurt!" She could see a slash through his clothes and a dark stain quickly spread across the left side of his chest. She fell to her knees in front of him and gingerly spread apart the new opening in his shirt to see the wound. "It's long, about eight inches, but it isn't deep." She scanned his face. "Are you hurt anywhere else?"

He shook his head. "No, he got me with a box cutter, just a wild swing to get away. He was after your backpack, not you."

Darby could see one of the straps of her backpack was cut clean through. "I must be losing my edge. I'd never have been caught like that when ... never mind." She parted the fabric of his shirt again and examined his chest more closely. "We're lucky this is superficial. It could have been so much worse." A tremor ran through her when the image of Joe lying in a dark pool of blood planted itself into her brain before she could stop it, a repeat of too many she'd seen in her young life on the streets. "Just zip your vest closed for now," she said thickly. "Let's go back to my room. I can clean and bandage it up for you there."

"So you're not homeless?" he asked, his expression more sad than angry. She knew he was sad because he believed she'd lied to him.

She sighed. "It's a really long story. How about I tell you all about it after we bandage you up?"

IN THE ATTIC

BY THE time they had walked through Walker House and Joe had seen the main dining room, and the counseling room, plus the half-dozen kids who were currently residing there, the hard lump in his chest—one he hadn't even been aware he'd been holding onto—suddenly gave way, and he was able to breathe freely again. Darby hadn't lied.

This was a shelter for homeless kids. Yeah, this was her mother's house, and yeah, apparently she had a room somewhere here, but it was obvious she was merely a visitor, an outsider. The relief he felt knowing this, knowing it hadn't all been a lie was huge. Huge. He said nothing and simply followed her through the space, nodding and grasping the hands offered at the brief introductions she made with the program leader, a tough-looking guy named Ed Bloomberg he'd never want to meet in a dark alley and the timid and affable Gibson McAleer. This—his imagined rival.

Regret washed through him, both for his anger toward Darby and her imagined liaison with the always smiling, shiny-headed Gibson who was obviously and joyfully gay, and his own preposterous claims on Darby herself. She wasn't his. She was her own person, the person who had dropped into his life and set it, finally, on the right course. She was free to go where she pleased. Could he convince her Brennan's Point was her most "pleasing" option? He sure as hell hoped he could.

Necessary introductions done, Darby took him up in a retro-fitted elevator to the third floor, then up a narrow, crooked stairway into a tiny attic room. After closing the door behind them, she leaned back against it and observed him as he surveyed the space. There was a double bed under the eaves at the far end, with a chipped, white-metal headboard that was piled with time-worn quilts beside an old-style wardrobe. A small love seat sat before a narrow fifties-style coffee table and maybe a seventeen-inch drum of a TV. A turquoise Formica table with two chrome chairs was pushed up against the wall of a tiny galley kitchen that featured an ancient gas stove and an iron-stained porcelain sink. Other than two big steamer trucks and a door that likely lead to a bathroom, there were the boxes he'd shipped back to her, piled high beside the entrance. He grimaced at seeing them here, mute testimony to his temper. Yes, I am an asshole.

Finished with his assessment, he turned to Darby, who looked back at him without expression. Today's T-shirt, a purple one, declared, *Happiness is an Inside Job*. Was she trying to convince the world, or herself?

He'd treated her badly.

"Darby." His eyes locked with hers. A pregnant silence ticked by interminably, stretching the agony of recognizing the woman he was hopelessly in love with, and who he was still unwilling to risk baring his soul to. The price he could pay was too high. If he got any deeper into this, and she left again, the last few days would seem like child's play. Yet here he was, ever hopeful.

"Joe." Good. That sounded okay, normal even. Then she added, "Fancy meeting you here."

"I won't say it's a small world." His reply was slow, testing the waters, waiting for her to—what? Fall into his arms? Slap him silly? Patch him up and kick him out of her life for good?

She crossed her arms and tilted her head. "So, what is it you want to say?"

"How about, I'm an ass? I'm sorry? Can you forgive me?"

"It's a mouthful."

"It's a start."

She relaxed a little. "You do make it hard to stay mad at you. And what an entrance—'enter hero, stage left.'"

"A little more drama than I was going for," he admitted.

She considered his apologetic face with a bleak expression. "You give up shaving?"

He scrubbed at his jaw, guessing he did look pretty scruffy. "Didn't seem worth the effort." There—a little exposure, admitting how her absence had affected him. Surely that wouldn't come back and bite him in the ass.

"You cut me out of your life so easily," she said, her voice barely a whisper. "You were swift, clean, and cold."

He took a step toward her, reached out to touch her, but stopped at the warning he saw in her eyes, suddenly glossy with unshed tears. He said, "Not so easily."

A noisy clock somewhere in the stuffy room ticked off the long moments she simply stared at him, considering his face and what he'd said. Which way she'd go, he had no clue. Then she wiped at her eyes with the backs of her hands and pushed away from the door. "Right. Let's get you looked at. That's why you're here."

He started to protest, then thought better of it. She was talking to him, and at least willing to help him. He unzipped his vest to examine the slashed shirt and skin beneath. "It's not too bad."

"I'll be the judge of that." Her words were firm, authoritative, but her voice was thready. She retrieved first aid supplies from the bathroom and set them on the Formica table. "Let's take a look," she murmured, pulling his clothes aside, her attention pointedly centered on his wound. It was better than being shown the door. "Okay. We'll need to use Steri-Strips, and that means we have to shave your chest, at least around the cut." She glanced up at him, and abruptly her eyes crinkled. "You're a furry kinda guy."

He shrugged, trying hard and not quite succeeding in hiding his joy and relief at seeing her smile. "Okay by me."

With a short nod, she put together a few supplies then set about shaving his chest with a pink lady's razor. Then she mopped up the wound, covered it with antibiotic cream, and drew it closed with the Steri-Strips. Finally, she taped a long non-adherent pad along the wound, then patted his arm in satisfaction, her gaze finally rising up to his and staying there. "You're good to go."

"I'm good? Or do I go?"

She rolled her eyes. "You're good. And you're impossible." She gathered up the supplies and returned them to the bathroom. "How did you happen to find me anyway?"

"Your neighbor. She told me you were off on another one of your adventures, and that you'll probably never settle down and grow roots. Scared the shit out of me. I thought I was too late. Then she said you left just five minutes before I'd arrived, and you'd headed "that a way." I'd been scouring the streets ever since, taking a chance I'd find you. You walk fast, by the way. I'm impressed."

Back in the main room, she crossed her arms again and prodded her backpack with the toe of her shoe, seeming to consider. Then she sighed, her decision obviously made and said, "Apparently, not fast enough. So, why does it sound like you're a man with a mission, scouring the streets of Vancouver, looking for a woman? The question is would any woman do?"

She smiled at the baleful look on his face. "I'm kidding. So, you've been looking for me. What exactly were you going to do once you found me?"

"Prostrate myself before you, beg your forgiveness, and convince you to return with me to Brennan's Point. We need you."

"Oh?"

"Well, actually, Shannon needs you. Her birthday is just around the corner. I promised her I'd bring you back."

"Oh?"

"And if that didn't work, I was going to blackmail you."

Now she rested her hands on her hips. "Is that so?"

"You do owe me two more pints of blood."

Darby considered his words for a moment. "So, let me get this straight. You promised your daughter a babysitter for a birthday present. And you're still all about the blood. Two pints isn't good enough for you; you want it all?"

"Aw, Darby, you have to know you're more than just a babysitter to Shannon. And Andrew. And me." When she remained quiet, he pushed on. "Plus, if today is any indication, you shouldn't be wandering the streets alone. That could have been ugly."

"First of all," Darby started patiently, "I wasn't 'wandering,' I was on my way–."

He caught her in his arms and kissed her with all the longing and tenderness he possessed, his lips soft against hers, gentle, caressing. She sighed and leaned into him, forgetting his chest–hell, he didn't care–wrapped her arms around his neck, ran her fingers up the back of his head, opened her mouth and invited him in ….

He picked her up and strode to the bed, fell onto it with her. Their clothes came away, leaving heated skin against skin, hard against soft, rough against smooth. Weeks and weeks of holding back gave way to freedom to touch, to explore, to love. She was beautiful, more beautiful than he'd imagined, her slender limbs made just for him, the passion in her hitched breath coming only for him. "Darby, I've wanted this for so long–wanted to touch you, to love you."

Her eyes opened, focused on his. "This is why I've been so afraid–there's a history here, one where I wasn't even there, and … that's scary."

He kissed her, needing to stop her from saying too much. He didn't want to talk about the baggage, the complications. He only wanted to feel her skin against his, her heat surrounding him, her softness giving way to him, enveloping him, taking him in. He ran his hand down the length of her body, pulling her up against him. She closed her eyes and pressed close with a low moan, as responsive as he'd imagined, quickening his blood.

"Just a minute." He drew away, the air cooling his skin instantly as he rummaging around for his wallet.

"You came prepared," she said.

"Be prepared, I always say," he grunted, his angle awkward. "Better than the alternative, isn't it?"

"Well, yeah. I don't have anything around here."

After a moment he came up with the condom package and settled back beside her. She watched him tear open the package before seizing the foil wrapper from him and reading the expiration date out loud. She frowned and sat up. "How long have you been prepared?"

He barked a laugh. "A while."

She slated her green-eyed gaze at him. "A very long while. This is older than Shannon."

"Oops!"

"Oops?" She fell back onto the bed with a groan of frustration.

He lay back beside her. "So we're basically screwed."

She began to giggle, the sound joyous to his ears. Darby happy was a very good thing. She drew her knees up to her chest and rolled away from him, helpless to stop. "We ... we have to go shopping. Like right now!" she gasped, wiping her tearing eyes.

He pulled her back toward him. "Screw that."

"No, screw me!"

"I'm trying." He nuzzled her damp neck, knowing it wasn't going to happen, but was grateful for her laughter. "You're being bad, you know."

"No, I'm being encouraging."

"You're a team player."

"That I am." She rolled away from him and got up. Stretched out on her bed with his hands behind his head and his legs crossed at the ankles, he watched her dress. The artless and unaffected way she moved in front of him filled him with happiness. He noticed she had long silvery scars tracing along her ribcage and wondered what had happened.

After pulling on black leggings that showed off her behind (to heart-stopping perfection), she reached inside the wardrobe for a different shirt, this one black. It read, *Warning–Explicit Adult Content*. She asked, "When do you need to be home?"

"Tomorrow is soon enough."

"Then get dressed. We're going out."

He did as he was told, and hand in hand they left Walker House and strolled downtown like they did it every day. And it was a great day, filled with binging on street bus food, searching the drugstore for the perfect shade of condoms, finding and buying him a new shirt and that all important razor, in light of Darby's whisker-burned face. They hiked over to Stanley Park, rented a bicycle built for two, and rode it along the seawall, wobbly at first, but quick to fall into sync. Once they were in the cover of the woods, they dropped the bike, hurried into the woods and made out like teenagers behind a huge chestnut tree.

When they emerged, Darby was pink-faced, and he was grinning from ear to ear. Time to head back to the attic and get serious.

It took some time to get back, they'd strayed farther than he'd realized. By the time they reached Walker House, he was dead on his feet and very glad of the elevator. Inside, he pushed the button for the third floor and leaned back, waiting for the doors to slide closed.

"Not that I'm complaining, but isn't this a bit of overkill for a three-story house?"

She tightened her grip of his arm and leaned her head against his shoulder. "The elevator?"

He kissed the top of her head. "Yeah. Did your mother put it in, or did you put it in for the kids?"

"I put it in for the kids, but really it was for myself. There used to be a closet here, a closet I didn't want to see anymore."

He frowned. "What does that mean?"

"No worries. It's all taken care of." The door opened onto the third floor. They stepped out and climbed the narrow staircase to her attic room. Reaching the door, Darby inserted her key and unlocked it. Before she could step inside, he picked her up, kicked the door closed behind them, and headed straight for the bed. Enough waiting.

Off came her T-shirt and bra, revealing all that lovely explicit content he'd seen but barely been able to touch. Off came leggings, panties. Off came his vest, sliced shirt, jeans, and boxers. They came together instantly, naturally, the condom sparkling new from its package and doing its job very well indeed. Darby came quickly, easily, and he followed not far behind. Then they burrowed into the covers and fell asleep tucked together in her cramped little bed, Joe sleeping better than he had since before he could remember.

■ ■ ■

WHEN HE opened his eyes, it was hours later and dark, save for a pale slice of moonlight coming in the window on which the headboard was backed. He heard muted voices coming from below them, several high pitched and excited, one very low and coming in measured segments. The teens? Ed Bloomberg? He glanced over at Darby, and was startled to see her watching him.

"Hey," he murmured, taking her into his arms and kissing her mouth. She tasted good. "You been awake long?" She ran her hand up his back, then lightly raked her nails back down. His voice gruff, he warned, "That'll get you into all kinds of trouble."

"I'm counting on it," she said, smiling against his mouth and biting his lower lip playfully. "I heard you turn into a pumpkin tomorrow morning, so I have to get while the getting's good."

"Oh yeah?" He pulled her under him and set to work on her breasts, sucking each nipple into a peak, strumming it with his tongue until she purred and stretched in his arms. He looked up at her face. "I love you, you know."

She stilled, then whispered, "I kind of figured that out," stroking his face gently, her eyes wide. "The expired condom was kind of a giveaway."

He smiled ruefully. "I'm that transparent, am I?"

She hitched herself up onto an elbow, doing lovely things to her breasts in the moonlight. "I'm … just not as brave as you."

He could see she was trying hard to tell him the truth. He waited her out.

"I want to say I love you too, but that's my heart out there … A scary place to be. I'm scared you have feelings for me because of the age of that condom, and because … well, because of Nadine and I being so alike. And if that's true, it's going to hurt like hell. So … I don't want to tell you … that I love you."

"You couldn't be more unlike Nadine if you tried."

"Just so you know—I'm officially undeclared."

"I get it."

"How will we really know?"

He pulled himself up so that his back was against the headboard and brought her into his arms. "We try? We love each other and try?"

"And what about the kids? What if we ask them to accept this, our new relationship, and the fact that I'm their aunt, and then it doesn't work out? What will that do to them?"

"What will it do if we don't try? They love you already."

"Shannon, yes. Andrew, not so much."

"He's fourteen," Joe scoffed. "What does he know?"

They were silent for a long time, each lost in their thoughts.

Then she surprised him. "I found my mother's journals and read them."

"And, what did you find?"

"What you'd expect from a secretive bipolar wing nut."

"Anything about babies?"

"Yeah. Nadine was her oh-my-God-what-have-I-done baby. I was her I-will-be-the-best-mother-on-this-planet-dammit baby. Nadine got the better deal."

"Nadine never thought so. She'd developed some pretty romantic ideas about her birth mother. She envisioned a misunderstood, desperate teen with no other choice, who lived to regret giving her away. She dreamed they'd be reunited one day, and grow close, make up for lost time. Nothing could dissuade her."

"She was so much better off where she was."

"What finally made you leave?"

"Oh," she sighed. "So many things."

"What was the main thing—the one thing that made you finally go, then?"

She rolled over and tucked her back up against his side, held his arm across her body, and gazed up into the darkness. "There was this thing our mother liked to do when I wasn't 'behaving,'" she hedged, so obviously uncomfortable where this was heading. "I never talk about this—with anyone. Not even to the girls at school, and they're the closest thing to family I've got. No one knows this about me except Laura."

He settled a pillow against the iron headboard and leaned into it, bringing her more securely into his side. "I'm not going anywhere. Shoot."

She looked up over her shoulder at him uncertainly. "Are we really going to do this?"

He wanted to know, but more importantly, he knew she needed to tell him. Not wanting to push, he tilted his head to one side and shrugged, letting her decide for herself.

She blew out her cheeks then twisted her lips to the side, her eyes growing distracted. Finally she said, "With my mother, you could do nothing right. Everything was a conspiracy. When I didn't agree fast enough—I must be lying. Or if I agreed too fast—for sure I was lying. If I knew the answer—I was a smart mouth. If I didn't know the answer—I was lazy, or obtuse.

"Obtuse," she repeated, the word rolling off her tongue. "One of her favorite words, that—obtuse. 'Don't be so obtuse, Darby!'" she recited in a loose rendition of what must have been her mother's voice, her head wagging from side to side with in-your-face attitude. Joe could almost see her mother in action. "'How can you be so obtuse!'"

She sighed, dropping the imitation. "The weatherman, bank teller, checkout clerk, teacher, magazine editor, flight attendant, meter reader, tinker, tailor, soldier, spy …. What were they, boys and girls?" She raised her hands as if she were conducting a choir. "All together now. Obtuse! Very good, boys and girls!"

She tucked the blankets around herself with quick stabbing motions. He saw she was struggling to bring her emotions back in check. She looked up at him, pressed her lips together, and shrugged a silent apology.

"Take your time," he murmured.

After a moment, she began again, this time her tone was controlled. "If she'd misplaced something—I'd stolen it. If I had a friend—I was telling family secrets. If a boy from school called—I was a slut. You get the idea."

"And 'that thing she liked to do' for these infractions?"

She didn't answer him right away, then finally said, "Isn't it enough Nadine was spared? Do we really have to drag this all out?"

"I want to understand you."

"My mother doesn't define me."

"No, but surviving her made you who you are, and I happen to like who you are very much."

"What doesn't kill you makes you stronger?" Darby laughed bitterly. "I wouldn't have minded a chance to be weak."

"Tell me about the closet."

She jerked away from him, then tried to cover it up by rearranging the covers around her once again. He wasn't fooled. He'd hit very close to the mark. Facing him now, she said, "I don't want to talk about the closet. I've said more than I wanted to already."

"And that's why we should talk about it."

"You are such a man! You can't fix this, you know."

"Everything you tell me stays here when we leave. We will never speak of this again. Say it once then walk away from it, from the experience, from this house, and from carrying the secret."

She looked across the darkened space between them, her eyes vulnerable. "Are we walking away from here, together?"

"We are." He gathered her back into his arms. "I did rescue you, and got slashed for my efforts." He stroked her soft hair, his fingers finding and petting the nub of hair left after he'd chopped out his sample. (And she'd let him!) If possible, his heart melted a little more recalling her complete and unqualified investment in his blood supply plan for Andrew. Darby Walker was the same girl from top to bottom–no games played, no agendas followed. When she was in it, she was in it 100 percent. He added, "The least you can do is come back with me and help out until I'm healed."

She had softened against him, tucking her hand under her chin and was now laughing against the uninjured part of his chest. "You have no shame."

His grin widened. "You're right, I'll take you anyway I can get you. You have a family now, and we need to get to know one another. That's a lot to walk toward."

"Promise me you'll never ask again."

"I promise."

She was silent again, thinking it over. "Okay–the punishment. At first, she would ground me from school. I missed a lot of school, so kind of home schooled myself there for a few years. After a time, when the authorities began questioning why I wasn't in school as I should be, she'd let me go but would lock me in my room when I was home. There was no laptop, no Internet connection for me, just whatever library books I could schlep home by the pound. Thank God for libraries; I'd have gone crazy without books. It wasn't so bad–at least I got to go to school."

He tightened his arms around her. "You do know that this goes way beyond bipolar, don't you?"

"Oh, she was a piece of work, all right, but a famous and talented one. People fawned over her. She had a fabulous public face. I could never fight that."

"Ah, Darby. What a life."

"Have you had enough, or are you ready for more?"

"Go ahead."

"So locking me in my room lasted a while, a few years, but then the shine was off the prize, and she needed a newer, better way to deal with me. I was a teen by now, and starting to push back. That's when she came up with the perfect solution: locking me in the closet. She was way bigger than I, and I always lost, no matter how I fought. There. You happy?"

"No, I'm not happy." He was freaking furious was what he was. Roberta Walker was a goddamned Amazon compared to Darby. Picturing the struggle between the two made him want to break something, preferably Roberta Walker's neck.

"Ouch," Darby complained softly, flexing her shoulder, reminding him just exactly where he was. His fingers were digging into her arm.

He made himself slack off. Struggling to keep his tone neutral, he asked, "It was that closet?"

"That closet."

"What changed when you were fifteen?"

There was another silence, this one long. So long he began to have doubts about pressing Darby about the closet. If it was this painful, what right did he have to grill her about it?

"She locked me in the closet," Darby started, her voice very low this time. "She left me there, alone, in the dark, then went on a trip to calm her nerves."

"A trip?" This was not going to turn out well.

"She left me there for days, forgot all about me, I imagine. I don't really know how much time passed before I realized she wasn't coming back." She paused, maybe gathering enough nerve to continue? "I'm pretty sure it was three days, but it was hard to tell. By then I was all screamed out. That's when I knew I had to get myself out or die trying."

"Jesus!"

"I couldn't break down the door, so I broke through the wall by scraping at it with a metal hanger until I had a hole big enough to squeeze through. I've always been small, so it only took me two days; a regular person would have had to work at it longer. This is an old house, and it was built to last, none of this wimpy drywall construction back then. I got stuck partway through and passed out for a while, maybe a few hours, maybe the better part of a day? It doesn't matter. When I came to, I knew if I didn't get out I was going to die."

He stroked her side tenderly. "Is ... that how you got these scars?"

She stopped his hand by covering it with her own. "There was blood; it was messy; let's just leave it there."

"I am so sorry you went through that."

She laughed then, surprising the hell out of him. "Spoiler alert! I'm here, talking to you, so I did make it out."

"You don't have to act so tough."

"How do you think I've survived my life? Through the kindness of strangers? You have to be tough to survive out there. It's a cold, hard world."

"Don't be tough around me, then. I know what fifteen looks like."

"Yeah, well … maybe what it should look like. The thing is, I did make it out. Once I was free I was so weak I had to crawl for water. That forty-foot crawl was the longest journey of my entire life." Another surprise—this time her voice cracked. "I-I didn't think I'd make it. I knew next time I wouldn't be so lucky. I never went back."

SEXUAL HEALING

DARBY LOOKED back at Joe, who seemed to be seeing her for the first time, his face a mask of shock and horror and ... pity.

It was the pity that did her in. She hated being pitiable. She had been through hell, long ago, and had built a life for herself, one she was damned proud of, and Joe MacKinnon, the man who made her heart skip in her chest with just a look, now pitied her.

For the first time, she felt naked.

Holding the blankets to her chest, she sat up and twisted round to see his face full on. "Well, you don't have to look at me like that!" Then she scooted away from him. "See–this is why I don't tell people about this. They can't wrap their brain around it, can't make themselves believe that I'm fine now, that I'm over it."

"How? How can anyone be over that?"

"Necessity."

"It's that simple?"

"Yes. I could let that define my life or make my own life. I made a bargain with God in that closet. I promised that if he would help me escape I would be brave, I'd be open to life, I'd welcome everything he sent me. I promised I'd live my life the best and the bravest way I knew how. And then–something in the wall simply collapsed, the hanger broke through, and I saw light for the first time in days, and I believed. Oh, I believed so hard."

Joe sat up and reached for her, his expression softer now, and not pitying as she'd first thought. "Come here, my brave girl." She narrowed her eyes a moment, then relented. He pulled the sheet from her, brought her naked body against his, tucked her securely into his hard, smooth side, and held her tight. The heat from his body felt good, slowly seeping into hers until she, too, softened and found herself wrapped around him like a second skin.

He murmured against her hair. "Here's a thought. How about we make a new ending?" When she didn't protest, he continued, "Here's the ending I want. I want to somehow know about that little girl in that dark closet, and I want to find that closet, break down the door, reach inside, and pick that little girl up in my arms. I'll keep her warm and close, and safe, and carry her away, far, far away from everything in that house, in that life, to a place where she's happy, and loved, and valued, as any little girl should be, and deserves to be. In her new place, she runs free and laughs and plays, and stays in the sunlight all day long. She only comes in when she's tired and only if she wants to."

Unknowingly, he'd stumbled exactly upon the sort of story she told herself every night, those many years ago, and Darby found that there were tears leaking from her eyes as he told it—the rescue, the carrying away to a sunny, happy, and safe place—a place of free will.

He pulled away from her, slid down on the bed, and turned to face her, bringing her back into his arms, his blue eyes close to hers, filled with what could only be love, and she believed for the first time that Joe MacKinnon might actually love her for herself, and not because he could be looking into Nadine's face right now. Looking back at him, she believed that he was seeing Darby Walker.

He pulled her closer. She closed her eyes and felt him press his lips tenderly on each eyelid in turn, before brushing each damp cheek with his mouth, then finding and claiming her mouth, kissing her softly, stroking her open lips softly with his tongue, until she gave him entrance, then mating his tongue leisurely and unhurriedly with hers, drinking her in, kissing her forever. As if she were floating down a slow-moving river, he led her into liquid warmth, his hand petting her body with light strokes, almost as if to soothe a skittish animal. Each soothing stroke went from the top of her head, along her shoulder, along the length of her arm, ending with her hand, where he entwined their fingers for a moment, a promise of connection, before moving on. He did this again and again, almost hypnotically, and she was surprised to find it was soothing, calming.

After a time, he stroked down her back, again and again until she felt her muscles loosen, soften, give way to his touch. Then his hand ran down her back, and beyond, along her bottom and down the back of her leg until she almost moaned with pleasure. She melted into the bed, coming away from him, allowing access to her front, which he stroked as he had her back, trailing his fingers teasingly up her thigh, lingering at her hip bone, but, sadly, not staying there....

The softening that occurred from the back massage had the opposite effect on her front. Her breathing was coming in little rushes now. He stroked her stomach, which quivered at his hand's passing. Finally, he covered her breast with his big warm hand. Heaven.

He stroked, kneaded, squeezed, rotated, dragged his palm across her nipples until she almost lost her mind from wanting him. Her back arched as if it had a will of its own, and her toes stretched and flexed and pointed. This was not the same effect of the back massage, not at all. Now everything, every little thing, was different.

He stopped kneading her breasts and pinched her nipples, —an electric current rocked hard to her pelvis, and this time she did moan. She could not stop herself. Then his mouth replaced his fingers, drawing her nipples into warmth and wetness, drawing, pulling, strumming. Oh God, she never wanted him to stop. Molten heat flooded between her legs, then his hand was there, his fingers parting her, and moving inside her and oh ... the heel of his hand pressed against her as his fingers delved deep, and she couldn't help rocking against him. It was too much, too much, and she couldn't stop ... could not stop ... her back arched .... She shattered around him, her whole body quivering, concentric circles of sensation bursting from her core, wave upon wave of pure sensation, hot and pulsating, bringing her with it to a distant place she had never been before, leaving her on its hazy shore to slowly, gradually, and languidly come back to herself.

The darkened room made itself known to her, and when it did she smiled and curled up like a leaf, drawing her legs up to her chest, burrowing against Joe, feeling impossibly soft and liquid and pliable. Boneless. Formless. A puddle.

"Sleep now," he whispered, enveloping her in his arms. She slept.

They stayed together in Darby's attic room for the next four days.

■ ■ ■

HEADING AWAY from Walker House for the last time, Darby said, "This is a new day, with new possibilities."

Joe gave her hand a quick squeeze. "That it is, my Darling, that it is." Was it her imagination, or did the sunshine just get brighter, the late summer air crisper? For now, she felt she was just where she was supposed to be—following her path.

She found she wanted more of Joe's low-timbered voice, so she asked, "Tell me all about the marina expansion." With that, she kept him talking for most of their trip back to Brennan's Point, mostly about real-life stuff—not the private, secret things they'd shared in the attic. She did pay some attention to what he said, like the part about doubling the width of the first two hundred feet of the main marina peer to accommodate the new bait shop and Carl's setup, which was now hogging all the space. Joe was excited about it, and she found herself drawn into his excitement. He really was creating a wonderful tourist spot that would benefit all of Brennan's Point. But mostly, she wanted to be free to watch the man she loved in action, and was gambling they could make a go of it in spite of the mountain of circumstances against them.

Her thoughts flitted away around the time Joe described the dry dock expansion. She noticed instead Joe's rolled-back shirt sleeves, exposed strong, tanned forearms, and broad, capable hands that handled the wheel effortlessly through traffic and up onto the ferry ramp. She noticed the deep tone of his voice, and how sexy he sounded when he spoke to the ticket agent at the ferry terminal and how the saleswoman seemed to sit up when she saw him.

She noticed the tingling sensation on the small of her back, where he placed his large, warm hand to guide her through the crowd of passengers, and up into the on-board café for a late lunch. She nodded in the appropriate places and watched him stir his coffee, run his fingers through his hair in an effort to clear it back from his forehead. She saw how his eyes crinkled when he laughed or smiled, and that his teeth were big and white, and flashed often in a grin. She heard his habit of jingling the change in his pocket while he waited in line for another coffee, not out of impatience, but the satisfaction of the sound and the movement. She liked that he "gave a penny" at the checkout.

She liked how he had a friendly nod for many aboard the ferry, and how he seemed pleased to introduce her as his friend to those he knew. It felt good to be known as his friend. And when they left the ferry she was glad he drove, that he knew his way home by heart, and she could close her eyes and let herself slip into a light sleep until they arrived, safe and sound.

Someone was shaking her awake. "Wake up, Darby. We're almost there."

She opened her eyes and blinked, surprised she'd fallen into such a deep sleep. She stretched, sat up in her seat, and saw they were on the ranch road.

"We're almost home," he said, handing her a bottle of water.

"Thanks," she said and drank deeply. He'd said "home." Now there was a term she was unaccustomed to hearing. Her stomach flipped over with nerves. She always got like this when she was scared, and suddenly she was scared, knowing that this time everything would be different. Being here like this with Joe, their connection so new and still wobbly on its feet, about to face his children with news that would change their world–who wouldn't be scared? What if, once Shannon and Andrew learned that she was actually their aunt, not just the woman who stumbled into their lives at the start of summer because of Andrew's fateful joy ride, they decided they didn't like her? Once they learned that their father and Darby had crossed that invisible line and were now a couple, would they feel tricked and hate her? Would Andrew's resentment rise, the pranks escalate?

Come on, now you're being silly. Andrew is rebellious, yes, but he's not evil, and Shannon is a sweet girl who accepts everyone at face value.

"So it's decided then," Joe said, glanced at her and back to the road ahead. The ranch house had just come into view. "We'll tell Shannon and Andrew after the birthday party."

Yeah. That's what they'd been talking about before she dozed off. Wasn't she a piece of work falling asleep partway through the discussion? She glanced at the backpack at her feet, considering the contract that peeked out of it and wondered again if she should have told him she'd won it. Joe brought the car to a stop and shut off the motor. There was no going back now.

"You okay?"

"Sorry. Yes. After the party," she confirmed, patting his thigh.

He covered her hand with his, holding it in place. "Your hand's cold."

She gripped his convulsively. "This is going to be a lot for them to absorb."

"They're smart kids. They'll get it. And you've already been here most of the summer. That's in our favor—you're a known quantity."

Normally, Darby would have teased him about labeling her a known quantity but couldn't be flippant, not now, when so much was riding on them getting this right. "Andrew already knows he and I are a blood match. This won't be too much of a stretch."

"Oh, it'll still be a stretch," Joe cautioned. "But he'll get it. There's been some talk around town about how much you look like his mother."

"Yeah, Kelly-Anne down at Crazy Plates filled me in."

"You do look like his mother. You can't change that." He glanced at her hair and grinned. "No matter how you try."

"You're smiling now, but you should have seen me in my blonde wig pitching to the Natural Resources Board. I looked good!"

He raised her hand and kissed it. "I absolutely have no doubt you looked good. You always look good to me."

She fingered her hair, surprised. "Even with …?"

"Even with. Which reminds me, everyone in town knows you're responsible for Brennan's Point being awarded the pilot turbine project, so be prepared to be semi-famous for a week or so. I should have told you earlier."

"We had other things on our minds." She smiled, linking her fingers with his.

"Yeah." They exchanged a long look before Joe gave his head a shake. "Okay. Head in the game. What I meant to tell you is Mayor Mayer will be out glad-handing around town and letting it be known you and he had it in the bag all along. Fair warning."

"Me and good ol' Bob, huh?"

"Be kind. Bob's harmless."

"You think the proposal going astray was an innocent mistake?"

"For now, I'm choosing to believe it was an innocent mistake. I have more important matters on my mind at the moment."

The way he looked at her turned her insides to mush. "Thanks for the warning, MacKinnon."

He looked at the house then at her. "You ready?"

"As I'll ever be."

"The really hard part will be staying away from you—not reaching out and touching you."

"I feel the same way."

This was a dangerous road she'd chosen. She was risking everything to come back here with him: her heart, her career. Remembering how swiftly her belongings had been returned to her in Vancouver, she wavered; remembering how Joe made love to her, her uncertainty fell away. All she could do now was put one foot in front of the other, live her life as honestly as she could manage, and see what fate had in store for her. It really was that simple. Give it a clear chance. Be here, 100 percent.

The front door opened, and they jumped apart. Shannon shot across the deck and down the stairs. "Daddy! Darby!!" The joy in her face filled Darby with hope.

SCHOOL'S OUT FOR SUMMER!

BECAUSE ANDREW had missed summer school the previous week to help with Shannon while Joe was in Vancouver, first thing Monday morning Darby drove him to the school. She wanted to speak to the teacher, to make excuses and request some make-up work. Together with Shannon whispering about one day going to a real school just like this one, they walked the quiet halls that smelled like paint and soap and floor wax–all things that tugged good memories from Darby's subconscious.

School had been her sanctuary. Where would she be if there had been no school to escape to?

They passed empty classrooms, their footfalls muted echoes against the rows of beaten-up lockers and freshly repainted classroom doors, scrubbed dark-green blackboards, neatly aligned student desks, all waiting for the kids' noisy return in three weeks.

When they reached Andrew's classroom, the door was slightly ajar, and Darby could hear the instructor, Mr. Pringle, speaking to the class. She raised her finger to her lips to shush Shannon. They would wait patiently until Mr. Pringle was finished before interrupting.

It wasn't long before Darby found herself listening in on what Mr. Pringle was saying to the class, or more accurately, to one poor, hapless student. Apparently, the boy's father had failed to attend an appointment with Mr. Pringle the previous Friday. She risked a peek at Mr. Pringle through the narrow window in the door and saw a short, pear-shaped man at the head of the class, tapping his temple with a stubby forefinger. He held a fistful of drawings in his other hand and shook them for emphasis.

"So, what is it, boy? When it comes to school work, the old wheels are turning in there, but the hamster is definitely dead. Am I right?"

Darby gasped. What in the world? She craned her neck to see it was Dougie Brewer who was Mr. Pringle's target, sitting miserably in a too-small desk at the front of the row, his face flushed scarlet beneath his purple hair. The other ten or twelve students didn't look any happier.

Her gaze snapped back at the teacher, her jaw clenched.

Mr. Pringle, obviously unaware he was being observed, felt free to continue his verbal abuse. "I'll send one more note home this afternoon, in an effort to interest your father in your studies." He threw the drawings to the floor, purely for dramatic effect, she was certain. Dougie jumped in reaction, his hand reaching reflexively out for the drawings, but remained in his seat.

Mr. Pringle scribbled across a notebook, reciting as he wrote, "Mr. Brewer, since my last report, your child has reached rock bottom and has started to dig. Please meet me after school on Tuesday, in order that this matter be rectified." He finished with a flourish, tore off the page, and slapped it down in front of Dougie. "After what I've seen in your work today, I'm sorely tempted to inform him that his son is depriving a village somewhere of an idiot."

She wrenched the door open and flew across the room toward Mr. Pringle. "How dare you call yourself a teacher! I heard every despicable word that has fallen from your disgusting mouth!"

Mr. Pringle looked startled, then offended.

Darby stabbed a finger at him. "What happened, you read a few clever lines surfing the net, because you have no life, which I highly suspect, hearing how you speak, or did you spend some quality time in your underwear with a couple of cold ones watching the comedy network last night, and now you're trying them out on this poor boy?" A few of the students snickered then fell silent.

Mr. Pringle's nostrils flared as he drew his five-foot nothing into a chest-thrusting pose of indignation. "You have no right to question my authority here. This is my classroom, and I will conduct it as I see fit." His pale eyes flickered down to her T-shirt of the day, *I Think, Therefore I am Single*, then up again, his expression shifting to patronizing.

She narrowed her eyes, took another step toward him, and softly asked, "Do you really want to go a couple of rounds with me, Mr. Pringle?"

Seconds ticked by. Mr. Pringle opened and closed his mouth like a cod fish, she saw with satisfaction.

She swept the classroom with her arm, encompassing the silent, watchful students. "You're sole purpose here appears to be perfecting your skills of humiliating people in public."

Mr. Pringle blinked, then shook himself, like a dog, she noted in disgust. "And who exactly are you?" he blustered, readying his pen to record her answer, as if by recording her name it would re-establish himself as the controller of the class. Yeah–like she was going to let that happen.

"I am the woman who will make it my mission in life to see that you are fired from this school, and any other school I hear of that has the bad luck or poor judgment to even consider hiring you in the future. You are abusing this child, and I will not allow it to go on one more minute." She turned to Dougie, who sat with his mouth sagging in surprised disbelief. "Dougie, you will come with me, right now."

The flood of relief in Dougie's eyes made Darby's prick with tears. He needed no coaching but was instantly on his feet, gathering up his books from the desk and the crushed drawings from the floor.

Once he had them all together, she held out her hand and asked, "May I see your work, Dougie?"

He flushed, and handed them over, prepared, no doubt, for more grief from yet another adult.

She stood silently at the head of the classroom, studying each drawing in its turn before looking up at Dougie. "These are really good. You have a true talent that will take you somewhere in life if you choose. Keep on trying." Mr. Pringle gaped at her.

To the students, she said, "I don't know what's been going on here, but this," she circled her finger in the air. "This is not how you should be treated. Never tolerate abuse, in any form. You are better than that. Always."

She whirled away and marched from the room with Dougie close behind. Mr. Pringle followed as well, catching up and passing her in the hallway, fear in his eyes, his short legs scissoring, blubbering words falling from his mouth. Darby blocked him out.

At the entrance door, she reached up and hugged Dougie fiercely then let him go. She sent the three children out to wait for her in the car then marched straight into the school office where Mr. Pringle was already whining an indignant protest to a startled principal.

A half hour later, Darby climbed wearily into the car. Dougie and Andrew were eager for details; Shannon had fallen asleep. "Don't worry about Mr. Pringle. He won't be teaching here anymore. It's—it's a bit of a mess, actually."

"All right!" Andrew and Dougie high-fived one another in the backseat.

She watched them with a sinking heart. She'd have to track Joe down at once and confess that she'd caused a huge scene at the school and had dragged both Dougie and his son out of class. And this was only her third day back in Brennan's Point. She'd do it again, of course, but how could this be fixed? The Brennan's Point summer school kids no longer had a teacher.

He was no teacher.

Darby looked at the boys with what she hoped was a stern expression. "This does not mean you don't have to work. You have to save my ass now. You have your books. You'll have to hit them, and hard. You still have to pull off some good marks to advance into the next grade—Mr. Pringle or no Mr. Pringle."

The boys grinned. "We will."

She grimaced. "But first we have to go tell your dad what I've done." Her eyes met Andrew's briefly, and she could see sympathy in his. They both knew this would not go down well with Joe.

∎ ∎ ∎

"YOU WHAT?"

"I know it sounds bad."

"Closing down the entire summer school program?" Joe parroted back, his face flushed. "What's bad about that? Andrew's good to repeat tenth-grade math, right son? Second time's a charm."

"Calm down. I'm sure something can be arranged to cover the last few weeks of summer school," Darby soothed, though even she found it hard to have faith in Principal Leary's assurance. "You'd have done the same if you'd been there."

"That I strongly doubt. There are always ways around these things. You're not going to get along with every teacher you run into, that's a fact of life. Sometimes you just have to suck it up. And it's summer school! Shit, Darby, they only had three more weeks. Couldn't you have let it go?"

She pressed her lips together and gazed out the window and across to Idle Island. Laura did these things way better than she ever did. Where was Laura's finesse when you needed it?

She had kind of exploded into the classroom, but dammit, that man had to be stopped. She watched Joe snatch up the marina telephone and punch in a number, watched him turn away from her and the boys and speak quietly into the mouthpiece. She really did hope he could make things right. She hadn't exactly had a plan when she'd effectively had Mr. Pringle fired. Even she knew finding a replacement this late in the summer was going to be next to impossible.

She glanced at the boys, then at Shannon, who was spying on everything in the office with her new magnifying glass, searching for treasure. Dora the Exploder had found diamonds in a cave on this morning's show, and Shannon was all about the diamonds now, complaining loudly that the boys got to have all the fun. "Yeah—summer school's awesome," Andrew had retorted.

The two boys were leaning nonchalantly against the ancient oak front counter, but their eyes were large and wary, waiting, no doubt, for the other shoe to fall. She pulled a twenty out of her jeans pocket and handed it over. "Hey, you go get sodas and fries at Carl's while your father and I work this problem out." Together with Shannon, they fled like rats leaving a sinking ship. She watched their exit with longing, not wanting to face Joe after the call.

She filled the time by rearranging the brochure display case, tossing out outdated folders, placing the new, more attractive ones in their place, front and center. When she was finished and Joe wasn't, she took to staring out the window again, this time watching Andrew, Shannon, and Dougie eat their fries at one of the picnic tables beside Carl's and the open, empty grassy boulevard and parkland beyond. Kind of a waste, that. It was actually a lovely space, with no apparent purpose.

Joe dropped the phone back onto its cradle with a sigh and turned on his heel to look at her. "There's going to be an emergency meeting at the school tonight. All the parents are up in arms, apparently. I have to go."

"Should I come too–to apologize?"

"No. I think you've done quite enough."

She pursed her lips again in an effort to stem further comment.

He came around the counter to look out the window with her. "Kids having a snack?"

"Yeah. You mad about that too?"

He scooped her into his arms with a whoop and pulled her back into his office. "Then we'll have to move fast."

He slammed and locked the door, pressed her up against it and ran his hands up her body, rasping his palms across her breasts, up her throat until he framed her face, kissing her deeply, his tongue invading her mouth like a starving man. She grasped his forearms and pressed against him, matching him kiss for kiss, her body on fire for him. Between kisses, he groaned, "These last few days have been torture! I can't stand being so close to you and unable to even touch you."

She trailed her hands downward and molded them against the bulge in his jeans. "Do we have time?" she whispered.

"Hell yeah," he groaned. They parted long enough to scramble out of their clothes. Out came one of the new condom packages–they snickered quietly at their fortuitous purchase of the large economy box back in Vancouver–then Joe lifted her up. She wrapped her legs around him, and he sank into her with a grunt of satisfaction that she could feel down to her toes. She closed her eyes and thought only about the sensation of being completely filled with Joe MacKinnon's lovely, hot, hard sex.

"Did I ever tell you how much I like you being so small?" he ground out, his jaw set with the oh-so-delicious job at hand, each thrust driving her further off the edge of reason. "It makes for many interesting possibilities. I've spent the last couple of nights imagining several of them as a matter of fact."

"Well, there's ... your ... problem then," she moaned in his ear. "You ... should, oh God ... You should be ... God. Joe. God ..."

"Shhh …" He captured her mouth with his, pounding into her until she felt nothing but the world according to Joe. It was a beautiful, beautiful place to be …

A thumping sound brought her back to the office. She tore her mouth away from his, gasping, "The door, we're banging … the–."

"Frigg the door," he groaned, slamming into her hard, and staying, grinding against her, then hard again. Her body tightened, frozen on the precipice. Going. Going. She shattered into a thousand sparkling shards of light, all floating, drifting, wave upon wave of lightness until gravity did its terrible duty and brought her back down to Earth, where Joe was breathing hard, as quietly as he could, and Shannon was calling from the other side of the door, "Daddy? Darby? Andy wants to know if you're still fighting, or can we go home now?"

Joe pressed his damp forehead against Darby's throat and shook with laughter.

"Shh–she'll hear you!" Darby hissed before breaking out in giggles herself.

"You are a very, very bad influence, Miss Walker," he murmured fervently, before capturing her mouth again and stopping her giggles with a kiss that reached down into her soul. Then he released her and let her slip safely down until her feet touched the floor. Still holding her close, he cleared his throat and answered Shannon, his voice only a little hoarse, "We're still talking, Honey. You go tell Andy we'll be another ten minutes."

"Okay, Daddy."

They remained locked together and stock still, following the sounds of her progress back out to the front office and the outside door closing behind her before breaking into laughter once again.

Darby was first to manage to speak. "You know we cannot do this again. We've got to be good and stay away from one another. I mean it this time."

Joe looked at her with his blue eyes alive with laughter. "And you know that's never going to happen."

■ ■ ■

"I SEE–."

Darby jerked awake with a frightened gasp.

"Oh, sorry." Joe sat beside her on the couch and took her book from her hands. "I didn't know you were sleeping. You looked like you were reading."

Darby sat up and stretched. "I was. I guess I fell asleep." She closed her eReader and focused on his tired face. "So how did it go? Are all the parents furious at me?"

"You should have told me what an idiot that guy was. Or Andrew should have come to me."

"You believe me now?"

"Oh, I believed you already, I just didn't get how bloody bad it was. One of the kids recorded the whole thing on his cell phone and played it for his parents. They brought his phone to the meeting and let all the parents watch it. I'm telling you, if I'd been there, that man would have been flat on his ass."

"So I can safely show my face around town?"

"You absolutely can, and be in danger of being hugged by perfect strangers. You are a bona fide hero in Brennan's Point now. First, we were awarded the turbine project because you hauled our proposal out of the fire, and now the scourge of our education system has been kicked to the curb because of you."

"So what about the summer school kids?"

"The parents took a vote and decided not to hire a new summer teacher. They got together, and divided up the grades amongst themselves. They'll take turns leading the groups of students who are making up grades in classes they have some expertise in. Some are strong in math, others in language arts. Looks like the students will be getting a marked improvement in any case. I have a feeling those kids are going to work harder in the next three weeks than they have all summer. Their own parents will see to it."

"Was Dougie's father there?"

"He was a no-show. I heard from Dave Albom that he got paid last week and he's been on a bender ever since." They were silent for a moment, each lost in their own thoughts. Then Joe asked, "Did Dougie stay over?"

"Yes. He's in the nanny's old room. I kind of told him ... to consider it his from now on." She raised her eyebrows and smiled hopefully at Joe.

He drew her into his arms with a sigh. "And that's why I keep you around."

"Because you need more moody teenagers in your house?"

"Because you make me do the right thing, even when it's messy."

"And I keep you around because my life does tend to get messy, and you seem to have a wonderful talent for straightening things out. You are a terribly practical man, Mr. MacKinnon."

"Good to know. A man needs to feel useful. I saw your trunks were delivered today. What's in them that's so important, anyway?"

"Hey, I think having all my important worldly goods distilled down to two trunks is pretty damned good. At least I'm not a hoarder."

"This is true."

Joe startled when Darby jumped to her feet. "So, I guess I'll turn in now, Joe. Good to know things worked out well at the school."

Shannon stumbled groggily into the living room, rubbing her fist into her eye. Comprehension replaced the questioning look in Joe's face. They had forgotten to remain apart once again. How were they going to manage at least a month of this? Shannon said, "Daddy, I can't sleep. Lily Kitty won't stop talking about our map plan."

BIRTHDAY PARTY

DARBY WALKED a tightrope at Brennan's Point; concerned nanny to the children, heroic project presenter to the council, defender of innocent summer school students to parents, donator of blood to the hospital staff, strange lady with the camera to the residents, and secret lover to Joe MacKinnon. It was hard to keep her head in the act. Her only respite from the stage was time spent with Shannon. The child was loving with her affection, open in her view of the world, and honest with her observations of it. With Shannon, you knew where you stood. It was such a relief.

The day of Shannon's birthday party, Joe was tied up down at the marina, going over preliminary expansion sketches with an architect, leaving Darby on her own with Shannon and Andrew. She pressed Mrs. Russell into duty for the morning while she ran errands, promising to take over the preparations herself by noon. She was planning a beach party, complete with roasted hot dogs and s'mores, birthday cake and ice cream, campfire songs, and popcorn, age-appropriate ghost stories and sleeping under the stars in sleeping bags.

Mother Nature had other plans.

After a hectic morning in town shopping for gifts and tote bag treasures for Shannon's little guests to take away from the party and a quick trip to the bakery to pick up the cake she'd ordered for the occasion, Darby couldn't help a tiny thread of foreboding when she glanced at the ominous, dark sky overhead. It promised a rained-out birthday. By the time she was home again with her purchases, that promise was kept. Heavy rain thundered to the earth, setting aside any plans for a cookout-sleepover birthday celebration.

"That's all right," she told Shannon, whose crestfallen little face, pressed against the window when Darby arrived home, spoke volumes. "We're just going to have to move everything inside."

Shannon stared back doubtfully. "But that's an ordinary birthday. I'm six now. That means I'm old enough for a campfire party," she explained sadly. She dropped her eyes from Darby's and watched the toe of her shoe as she pushed one of Buddy's scruffy tennis balls back and forth across the dining room floor. Her voice dropped to a wistful whisper. "That means cooking hot dogs and telling scary stories, the real scary ones, not baby stories—fun stuff like that."

"Oh, Honey, we can still do all that," Darby said, dropping down to give her a hug. "We'll make a nice big fire in the fireplace, and we'll cook all the hot dogs and marshmallows you can eat. And we'll turn out all the lights and tell the scariest stories ever."

Shannon's eyes shone with excitement now.

"And we'll push all the furniture out of the way, and you and all your friends can lay your sleeping bags out on the floor in front of the fire."

Andrew slouched into the room. "Dad said I should help you," he said, scrolling through his iPod play list.

Ignoring his show of indifference, Darby said brightly, "I'm sure you'd want to make your sister's sixth birthday a wonderful day for her. You don't need your Dad to tell you that." Andrew's eyes lifted to hers, skipped over to Shannon then back to his play list.

"Where's Dougie? I heard him leave early this morning."

"Trying to get his dad dried out. Again."

She grimaced. Poor Dougie. Of course he wouldn't have wanted Andy around to see his father like that, so now Andy was feeling left out, thus the sulky mood. Sometimes life was too damned complicated.

She said, "What you can do first is push all the living room furniture back against the walls, and away from the fireplace. Shannon's going to have her sleepover indoors."

Without a word, he turned on his heel and left the room. Darby waited then relaxed when she heard the sound of furniture being moved across the floor in the living room. It was a start.

"Shannon, you have an important job too," Darby said, smiling at Shannon's eager face and shining eyes. "I need you to make up the loot bags for all your friends to take home with them after the party. I'll set you up in the kitchen with the bags and all the stuff that needs to be put inside. Think you can handle that?"

Shannon nodded her head, a smile from ear to ear. Darby hugged her again and teased, "Oh, you're just too cute."

Once both children were occupied with their assigned duties, Darby made a quick call to the marina to let Joe know the change in plans, then called the parents of Shannon's young guests, confirming that the party was a go but now would be moved indoors. Once off the phone, she went into the living room to see how everything looked. Andrew was finished clearing out the space needed for the sleeping bags and was now draped across the arm of one of the couches, playing a video game, his face a picture of concentration.

"Thanks, Andy," Darby said, sorry to see the expression of his face change. What did she have to do to turn him around?

"Anything else?"

"You could bring the birthday cake inside from the car and put Shannon's gifts into the barn for me. I left them in the car too. They're already wrapped, so we won't need them until later, after the cookout," she corrected herself with a laugh, "Cook in I mean."

Nothing. No response. Andrew dropped the control and left the room. She followed him, and when she saw him go outside decided he'd heard her and was doing as she asked. First thing after this party, she intended on having a talk with Andrew.

It was hours later, and the party was in full swing, when she first noticed that Andrew was no longer there. Damn. She needed him to retrieve the birthday gifts from the barn. It was time.

She would simply have to go get them herself. The hot dogs and s'mores had all been cooked and devoured, followed by cake and ice cream. The fire had died down somewhat and was safely screened away from the children. Everyone seemed happy, eager to get on with the opening of gifts. Satisfied that the children would be okay for the few minutes she was away, Darby slipped on one of Joe's rain slickers and made a dash through the torrent of rain and fading daylight to the hay barn. Once inside, she threw her weight into closing the huge, hinged door against the rain. Drawing back her hood, she pulled on the rope that turned on the light overhead, revealing a massive tiered structure of hundreds of bales of newly curing hay. She loved the sweet, clean smell of the hay and fought the sudden impulse to climb up them and swing from the knotted rope that hung from the rafters high overhead. It would be so fun! Maybe that could be next year's party—if she was here next year.

Remembering Andrew's face, she worried. Recalling Joe's quick kiss in the hallway this morning, she stopped. She had reason to believe she would be here next year, and the year after that ….

But she had a party to get back to, with a dozen little guests waiting. She glanced around, searching for the gifts she'd bought. She didn't see them, but did spy an open trap door that lead somewhere beneath the hay-strewn barn floor. A root cellar? Had Andrew put the gifts down there? Thinking it was a bit excessive, she walked in hushed footsteps to the opening.

Everything was so quiet, so muffled by the stacks of hay. Almost unreal. Almost claustrophobic. Goosebumps skittered up her spine, but she shook them off. Not now; not today.

She peered down into the hole and saw a steep set of steps leading down to—yes, it appeared to be a root cellar. And there, at the bottom of the stairs, were two shopping bags, filled with wrapped gifts. Really, Andrew? In the root cellar?

She chewed at her lip and considered how far down the steps went and how quickly she could get down to the gifts and back up again. She really didn't want to go down there. Already, just considering it, her heart had kicked up tempo, drumming against her ribs at scared-rabbit speed.

She glanced back at the main door. The kids were waiting. She couldn't very well haul them out here to go and get the gifts now, could she? Or could she? Twelve little girls in their pajamas and raincoats, trooping out to the barn. It could be a birthday present treasure hunt.

Stop being a baby, she told herself, wiping her damp palms down her leggings. The gifts are there, just down at the bottom of the stairs. It would take her one minute to lower herself down, snag them, and bring them back up. Less than a minute.

She looked over the open hatch. It looked sturdy enough and wasn't going anywhere. She'd be fine. Down and back up in just a jiffy. Running her fingers across her forehead, Darby readied herself for the plunge. You can do this. She grasped the edge of the hatch firmly with both hands and gingerly tested the first step with one foot. It was as advertised–solid as a rock. She put her weight on the lead foot on the step, and brought the second foot onto the second step. Okay, so far so good.

Slowly, she inched her way down the steps, reminding herself to take deep breaths and remain calm. After what seemed an interminably long amount of time, she arrived within reach of the bags. Loosening her death grip from the risers of the steps, she groped down into the darkness with one hand for the bags.

Success! Her hand located and grasped up one string handle. With controlled panic, she scurried up the steps, the rustling sound of the paper bag chasing after her. While she knew in her head the sound was from the bag, somewhere deep inside of her–someplace basic to her survival–it screamed for her to run. She scrambled out of the hatch, threw down the bag, landing face down on the loose hay that covered the floor of the barn. Panting hard, she nudged the bag away from her face.

God, could she be more pathetic? She'd faced down knife-wielding crack addicts and hardly broken a sweat, yet couldn't bear a set of stairs into an innocent cellar.

Waiting for cooling air to fill her lungs and for her heart beat to return to normal, she thought she heard a sound. A mouse? It wouldn't last long with the two tomcats Joe had patrolling the barnyard. Just don't run over to me, little mouse, she said silently, closing her eyes for a moment. That's all I'd need. A mouse attack. The attempt at humor gave no relief; she still felt as if she'd just run a marathon. She muttered, "Okay, Girl, do that one more time, and you're all set."

Getting back to her feet, she turned to face the hatch opening in the floor and made herself start down the stairs once again. This time she shot down to the bottom to grasp the bag in record time. With a thunderous clap from above, she was suddenly buried alive in suffocating, deadly darkness.

Clutching the risers, she opened her mouth and screamed. Paralyzed in the complete absence of light, Darby's real nightmare began.

■■■

JOE WAS tired when he opened the front door. It had finally stopped raining, and everything felt and smelled fresh and new. He did not. It was late, he'd skipped dinner, and all he wanted was a hot shower, a good stiff drink, and some quiet time with Darby. He had a lot to share with her and needed her feedback before he gave the architect the go-ahead.

"Daddy's home!" Shannon screeched, running into the dark foyer and throwing herself into his arms. She was followed by a screaming riot of little girls, all jumping up and down with excitement. There would be no quiet time.

With her face buried into his neck, Shannon wailed, "Andrew's telling scary stories, Daddy. Make him stop."

"Okay, okay, calm down, girls," Joe said, robot-walking his body, complete with a dozen little arms wrapped around his legs, back into the living room. It was dark, except for the dying fire's dim light that cast gloomily over the furnishings, creating shadows that marched across the walls and surrounded the little circle of sleeping bags. There was evidence of party games and snack food strewn amongst the sleeping bags that lay in an untidy pile before the hearth. Andrew was making an attempt to straighten them out when Joe arrived with the party girl and her guests on board.

"Where's Darby?" Joe asked his son.

Andrew shrugged. "I dunno. She just left. I've been here looking after all these kids by myself for hours."

"What do you mean, 'She just left'? How could she just leave?"

Andrew looked patiently at his father. "Now, how would I know that? One minute she was here, the next she was gone. I couldn't very well go looking for her. Someone had to look after Shannon and rest of the kids."

Joe looked around, as if a clue would appear. "Darby wouldn't just leave ..."

"She has before, Dad," Andrew reminded him.

"That was different," Joe said.

"How?"

Joe pursed his lips. Something had gone wrong; he knew Darby wouldn't have just walked out. "Hey, it's way after you girls' bedtime. Time to hit the sleeping bags."

"But we didn't open my birthday presents from you and Andy and Darby yet," Shannon said. Joe looked inquiringly at his son.

"They're out in the hay barn, in the cellar," Andrew said.

Alarm bells went off in Joe's head. "And how did they end up out there?"

"Darby told me to hide them out there," Andrew answered. "I'll go get them, now that you're home."

"We'll both go," Joe said, "Girls, you straighten this all out, and take turns in the bathroom brushing your teeth. We'll be right back." He hurried out the door, and strode to the hay barn with Andrew trailing behind.

"Geez, Dad, where's the fire?" Andrew complained, picking up the pace to keep up with his dad.

Joe asked, "Why down in the cellar, Son?"

"I don't know, so no one would see them? It seemed like a good idea at the time."

"You know that hatch isn't reliable."

"So what?" Andrew answered with a shrug. "It's not like you can get locked in."

"Maybe we can't, but someone who's claustrophobic–." Joe trailed off and began to run. "How long has she been gone?" he yelled over his shoulder.

Andrew was running with him now, alarm written on his face. "Two, three hours."

Joe pulled back the barn door. The light was on, the hatch to the cellar closed. Beside it lay a brown shopping bag, trailing gaily wrapped gifts across the hay. "Oh no." He sprinted to the hatch and yanked it open.

There below, with arms wrapped around the risers of the stairs was Darby, frozen with fear. She made no movement in response to the hatch opening or the light pouring down the stairs.

Joe called her name and climbed down toward her. She showed no sign of recognition. Carefully stepping around her death grip, Joe saw her eyes were shut tight, her breathing shallow and rapid. He brought his body around hers, enveloping her in his embrace. She was cold and clammy to the touch. He placed his hands over her icy ones and gently pried her fingers from the risers, all the while whispering, "Darby. I'm here, Darby. It's okay now. We're going to get you out of here now." He turned her wooden little body toward him, forcing her arms around his waist. "Open your eyes, Darby, its Joe. Andrew's here too. We're going to get you out now. Just hang on to me, and I'll get you out."

She gripped the back of his shirt and pressed her face into his chest, saying nothing. There was nothing more he could do beyond getting her out of her nightmare as quickly as possible.

He wrapped one arm around her and with the other hauled them both up the stairs and out onto the floor of the hay barn. Once there, Joe shook Darby gently, whispering, "It's okay, Darby. You can open your eyes now." She gave no response beyond her fierce grip on his shirt.

"Go call Doc Turner," he instructed Andrew, who immediately raced ahead of him to the phone.

Lifting her easily, Joe carried her from the barn, across the yard, up the steps, and into the house.

Andrew met him at the door. "Doc Turner is on his way. He says to keep her warm and quiet."

Joe jerked his head toward his bedroom. "We'll put her in my room. I don't want Shannon seeing her like this. You keep curious eyes away from here and let Doc Turner in when he gets here." Joe swept into his bedroom, kicking the door closed behind him. Nudging on the light switch, he strode to his bed. With one motion, he peeled back the bedding, and attempted to lay Darby down. She refused to release her hold on him. Forced to lie down with her, he rested on his side with one leg off the bed. With his foot anchored to the floor for stability he pulled the covers over the both of them and wrapped his arms around Darby's now-quaking body. Soon she was shaking so much it seemed the whole bed was vibrating. He could hear her teeth chattering. She was going into shock.

"Andrew!" Joe shouted for his son. The door opened immediately– the boy had to have been waiting in the hallway. His eyes darkened momentarily at seeing his father in bed with Darby, then cleared at once. "Warm a cup of water with a teaspoon of sugar in the microwave and bring it in here right away. We have to heat her up now. It won't wait for Doc Turner."

Andrew sped from the room, returning swiftly with the cup of warm, sweetened water. In spite of Darby's frozen grip on Joe's shirt, together he and Andrew were able to sit her up somewhat. Joe raised the cup to her lips. With her teeth rattling against the cup, Darby managed to get the warm drink down. Still, she kept her eyes shut tight.

"Go get the electric heating pad, Son, and an extension cord. That should get her temperature up in a hurry."

Andrew nodded and worked quickly, preparing the heating pad and handing it over to his father, who tucked it under the blankets against Darby's body. Joe began to rub her back and arms vigorously. Andrew remained silent, watching and waiting. Joe could see he was sick with worry. He spoke to him quietly. "Son, she'll be okay."

"I should have gone out and looked for her sooner. I didn't because I was mad at her."

"You couldn't have known. You were right to stay and watch the kids. You were responsible."

Andrew shook his head. "No, I wasn't. I was mean to her. I was mad at her for leaving us, so I was mean."

Joe asked, "Did you set up the hatch to close on her?"

His son's eyes flew up to his. "No, Dad. I'd never do that!"

"I know that, Son. This was an accident, pure and simple. The hatch door has been slipping out of the open notch for months now. What seemed to be a small thing turned out not to be so small after all. It's certainly not your fault."

Darby's hoarse whisper startled them both. "More water," she croaked faintly.

Joe nodded to Andrew, who grabbed up the cup and hurried from the room. Joe brushed her hair back from her forehead, searching her now-open eyes for signs of recognition. "Darby, you're safe now. You're safe in the house, in bed."

Her focus seemed slightly off center, as if she had come a great distance to see him. "Darby, do you know who I am? Do you know where you are?"

Andrew came back in the room, this time accompanied by Doc Turner. By now, Darby allowed Joe to extract himself from her grip somewhat, but she held fast to his hand. Doc looked her over quickly, nodded in approval at her drinking a second warm glass of sweetened water, then gave her a shot. Within a few minutes she was asleep.

"What's wrong with her voice?" Andrew asked.

"Well, you say she's been missing for a few hours, she was trapped down in your old root cellar, and she's claustrophobic." Doc Turner grimaced. "I'd have to guess she's hoarse from screaming her lungs out, fellas. I know it ain't pretty, but, there's a good chance that's why."

Joe felt sick at the thought of Darby's hours alone down in the black cellar, frozen to the steps in fear. Looking at Andrew's face, he could see the same thoughts had passed through his mind as well. "Could you go check on the girls, Andy?" he murmured before turning to stare down at Darby again. He should have been here, at the party, not working late–again.

"Mac!" Doc Turner's voice filtered through Joe's thoughts. "Did ya hear that?"

"Oh, yeah, sorry–don't know where my head was. Bed all day tomorrow, no excitement," he repeated, then reached for the older man's hand. "Thanks, Doc, for coming so quickly."

The doctor nodded slowly, gripping Joe's hand with both of his. "I have an idea what you're going through Mac, her looking so much like Nadine and all. Be very careful, will you? You've got two young ones who could get mighty mixed up if you make the wrong move."

"I think about it every day, Stuart, every day."

Doc Turner gazed down at the sleeping Darby and murmured, "She could be Nadine's sister, couldn't she?"

Joe closed his eyes for a moment, torn, overwhelmed. They had to start somewhere with the truth–why not the family doctor? He might have some advice about how to approach the kids about it. But that wasn't the reason. The reason was he needed to tell someone. He opened his eyes and stared back at Stuart Turner. "That's just it, Stuart. She is Nadine's sister."

A choking sound from near the bedroom door made him swing around, already knowing what he would find–Andrew, standing in the doorway, his face pale with shock, his eyes huge and accusing. Joe took a step toward his son. Andrew turned and fled.

Doc Turner reached out and caught Joe by the arm, stopping him before he could follow his distraught son. "No, let him go. Let him pull himself together first."

"Jesus, Stuart," was all Joe could think to say.

"Pray to Jesus, Joe."

Joe blinked at his old friend in surprise. Stuart was a by-the-book medical doctor who believed in God; that he knew from their time together during Nadine's cancer, but never before had he spoken of his religious beliefs to Joe. They talked sports scores and fishing tales and local politics. Stuart Turner squeezed his arm in assurance, then began packing up his medical bag. Joe watched him, wordlessly. What more was there to say?

Joe saw Stuart to the door and thanked him again for making a house call. Then he checked on the birthday party. The living room was quiet with worn-out party guests literally sprinkled across the floor, arranged in strange and oddly peaceful positions, some in and some out of their sleeping bags. Joe grimaced at the irony of the calm room. If they only knew how close they'd come to disaster.

He moved to the bottom of the stairs next and gazed up into the darkness, wanting to go up to Andrew's room and talk to his son, but deciding that Stuart was right–let the boy be for tonight. He'd had a hell of a shock, and it would take him time to absorb it. He needed his privacy. Tomorrow would be soon enough to get into all the details. And he and Darby had agreed to tell the children about her connection to their family together. He'd wait until she was stronger and Andrew had pulled himself together.

He padded back down the hall to his darkened room, went inside, and quietly shut the door. A distant yard light filtered light through his window, providing just enough illumination that he could see Darby hadn't moved. Doc Turner had said she'd be out for the night. He settled into a chair by the bed and drank in her now-peaceful countenance.

She looked like an angel. With crazy hair. Who never met a challenge she didn't like. He leaned forward and stroked her small, silky head. A spontaneous lover, a generous friend, with an Achilles' heel that left her dead in the water.

He shook his head sadly, picturing Darby as a young girl desperately scratching her way out of a dark, locked closet with a metal coat hanger. She'd escaped her own personal hell and brought lightness into his life, possibilities, hope, and whimsy. With Darby, life was fun again, something he realized now had been missing for a very long time, and with it she'd shown him a better way to connect with his children beyond food, shelter, and structure. When had fun left him?

He settled back into his chair and put his feet up on the edge of the bed, prepared to stay the night.

Had she been sent to them by Nadine? Is that why she touched his heart? The troubling thought kept him awake for hours.

AUNTY DARBY

WHEN DARBY woke, she had the sensation of returning from a place very far away. Her surroundings were strange; the light was wrong, the sounds were wrong. Then she remembered, and she stiffened and sat upright, her chest constricting. But of course, she wasn't in the closet, she was ….

She looked around, saw she was tangled in Joe's bedding, was in Joe's bed. Brilliant sunlight flooded the room. How had she gotten here? God, the children mustn't find her here! She yanked off the covers and swung her feet to the floor, saw she was wearing the same grey leggings and T-shirt that she'd been wearing for the party. The room spun, and she almost fell to the floor.

Mistake—too fast.

She leaned drunkenly back and hitched herself against a pillow, grateful for the cool feel of the cotton against her heated skin. God. She was so nauseated.

The door opened. She turned her head to see who it was, mindful of the dizziness sudden movement caused. It was Joe, backing into the room, carrying a tray. He turned, saw she was up, and smiled a welcome. "Hey, she's awake," he called out into the hall. Shannon bolted past his legs, across the room toward the bed. "Whoa, whoa! Let Darby get her bearings at least."

Shannon landed in her arms, and they fell back into the bed together. Darby couldn't help laughing in the face of such enthusiasm, though her stomach was in her throat.

"Aunty Darby!" Shannon crowed.

Darby shot an alarmed expression at Joe. He shrugged in apology. "Sorry, cat's out of the bag. Apparently, Andy can't keep a secret very well."

"Andy? How does Andy know?"

Joe nudged Shannon over and placed the tray before Darby. "Two toast. Peach jam. One poached egg. One chai tea. Mrs. Russell assures me these are all your favorites."

Darby looked the tray over, surprised to find she was hungry, then up at his wonderful face. She was so glad to see him she could almost weep. She tried for light and brisk. "And Mrs. Russell would be right."

He settled on the edge of the bed and further confused her by stroking her face in front of Shannon. What had happened while she'd slept? "I'm just so damned glad you're okay," he murmured. His eyes told her he wanted to kiss her, but would be satisfied with touching her cheek for the moment. "We were very worried about you last night."

She looked down at the egg and flushed, remembering snippets of Joe and Andy getting her out of the cellar, the sensation of Joe's shirt against her skin, the blessed, rock-solid feeling of his arms around her body, of Doc Turner's concerned expression. And a needle …?

What a spectacle last night had been. "Sorry."

He raised her face up, and she saw his expression was bewildered. "For what? You have nothing to apologize for. Get that out of your head right now. I am so sorry you went through that. Andy's devastated. He's waiting out in the hallway wearing out the rug, waiting to be forgiven."

"No," she protested, making to get out of the bed. "This is not Andy's fault."

He gripped her shoulders gently but firmly. "Doctor's orders, in bed today, no excitement." She relaxed back into the bed, grateful, actually, since she was so lightheaded. "A little woozy?" he asked.

"A little. What did the doctor give me?"

His gaze not leaving her face, he called over his shoulder, "It's okay, Andy. You can come in."

Andy stuck his head into the room, his eyes searching for and finding hers. The expression in his, of wonder and expectancy, worry, held-back hope, regret, and not a little curiosity washed over her. Andy's world had just been turned upside down. She raised her arms, and he walked into them. They hugged for a very long time, Darby fighting back tears at the feeling of his gangly arms clutching her so fervently. Then, abruptly, it was over, and Andy was back, looking all nonchalant.

She followed his lead, seized up a butter knife, and spread peach jam on one of the slices of toast. "So," she said, directing her attention to Shannon, "how'd the party turn out? Sounds like I missed the best part: opening all your presents."

She slowly made her way through her breakfast with Shannon bubbling over with party news. All her friends had said Shannon's party had been the best one ever—the s'mores in the fireplace, the sleeping bags in the living room, the scary stories Drew had told, the terrible storm outside! Joe and Darby exchanged grime glances; Andrew adjusted the "ear bugs" strung from his iPod.

It seemed that to Shannon, saying "Aunty Darby" was a bonus birthday present, to be used as often as possible. This Darby loved. For the first time in her entire life she actually was part of a family. She had to make herself stop thinking about it because if she did she would be overwhelmed by it all and unable to function. She'd save this new thing, this family connection and acceptance, for a private moment, for a time she could safely take it out, turn it over in her hands, and marvel at it. But for now, hearing Aunty Darby was like a magic salve for her wounded soul.

She looked over at Joe with thanks in her eyes. He said. "We have another surprise for you. She's waiting in the kitchen."

"She?"

"I called Laura last night. Late. She picked up." He bobbed his eyebrows. "Good friends always pick up. Anyway, she's here, waiting in the wings for an audience with the queen."

"Go get her, please."

Darby's family left, and Laura came in, peeling back the covers and climbing in beside Darby, pulling her into her arms and hugging her fiercely. Then, ever the practical one, she helped Darby into the bathroom before settling her back into the bed and climbing in herself once again. They stayed together for most of the morning, with Darby slipping in and out of sleep.

At 1:30, Carl showed up with an armload of flowers for Darby and a fresh salmon for Mrs. Russell, having heard down at the marina that Miss Darby was under the weather. He was ushered into the master bedroom and was soon lounging across the end of the bed, entertaining the ladies with tall fish tales while Joe and Andy played checkers hunched over the night stand, Shannon examined everything under her new birthday microscope, and Dougie did pencil sketches of them all. At two, Kelly-Anne from Crazy Plates showed up with a quart of hand-packed banana chocolate mint ice cream, which she, Laura, and Shannon made short work of. Mayor Mayer was there by three, his mayoral paunch swaying breezily as he advanced into the room, glad-handing both the voting and soon-to-be voting public as he neared Darby who sat perched in a nest of blankets in the center of the bed, clutching a glass of ice tea. Faye Crabtree dropped by with one of her famous apple pies shortly after, which the mayor dug into with unbridled enthusiasm.

When Faye hugged Darby goodbye she whispered she'd bake a second pie and drop it by the following day. Mrs. Russell shooed them all out at four, claiming she needed a rest from all Darby's visitors while winking at Darby, who sent her a thank-you wink of her own. While it was heartwarming to be so cared about, she was exhausted. She fell back into a deep sleep.

■ ■ ■

WAVING MRS. Russell and the kids off for the evening was a relief. His suggestion that they all go into town for an early movie and pizza had been a stroke of genius, born of desperation. Mrs. Russell's offer to have them stay the night at her farm afterward had been a big red ribbon on the package, one he wouldn't soon forget.

The kids needed something other than crowding around their new aunt to occupy their time, and judging by Dougie's reaction, he was as excited about Darby's connection to the MacKinnon family as the rest of them.

Joe caught himself. When had Dougie leaked into the family? He chuckled and turned back to the house. Thanks to Darby, Dougie Brewer was firmly ensconced now, complete with Mrs. Russell setting a plate for him every night, claiming "one more potato in the pot, Mr. M," and Joe was glad of it. Dougie deserved a shot at a decent life, same as any other kid. Darby had opened his eyes to that fact pretty clearly. And, truth be told, now that he'd spent some time with Dougie he found that he liked the boy.

Back at his bedroom door, he hesitated a moment, reluctant to disturb Darby. He opened the door quietly and peered in the darkening room. She was propped up against the pillows, awake, her eyes unnaturally glossy in her pale face. Her T-shirt read a shadowy *I just want to do bad things with carbs*. How he wished she had that old fire in her now. He'd find her all the carbs she wanted.

"Hey," he greeted softly, easing past the door and moving toward her.

"Hey," she replied with a tired smile.

"We have the place to ourselves until tomorrow."

"So I heard."

"You look better."

"No, I don't. I've looked in the mirror–I'm a horror show."

"Mirrors lie. You look better."

"Mirrors don't lie," she insisted faintly, combing her hair–which was in major bed head mode–back with her fingers. "Lucky for me they don't laugh either."

He let it go, glad she was at least attempting to give him attitude.

When he sat on the edge of the bed, she reached for his hand. "How did Andrew find out?"

"He overheard me tell Stuart. He was shocked, ran off. I started to go after him, but Stuart said to let him be. Good advice, as it turned out. I'm guessing Andy was up much of the night processing it. By morning, he seemed okay. We talked. I explained about the adoption, and how we didn't know ourselves until the DNA tests and the journals. So, yeah–he's okay." He smiled wryly. "Okay enough to inform Shannon, who took to the news like a fish to water, no need to go into detail. She has an aunty, who just happens to be her favorite person on the planet at the moment." He made a thumbs-up sign. "Score!"

Darby flushed.

He said, "She's thrilled, as you well know."

"I picked a pretty dramatic way to get out of it, huh?"

"Oh, and Mrs. Russell knows too. It seemed the right thing to do, since everyone else in the house is in the know. She took it in stride, said she wasn't surprised, what with the resemblance and the blood donation and all."

"Dougie?"

"Well, yeah, him too. This just gets bigger and bigger, doesn't it?"

"About you and me though. You didn't …?"

"No. That's a whole other bridge to cross."

She pressed her lips together and nodded her head. She looked beaten up.

"It's not that I don't want to tell them," he said cautiously. "You know that, right? I want the world to know how I feel about you."

She glanced back at him, her eyes vulnerable.

Enough, he decided. "You've been cooped up in this room too damned long. How about a little fresh air? It's mild out."

"I would love some fresh air." She pushed away the blankets, but before she could get out of bed he scooped her up in his arms. "Hey, I can walk," she protested.

Taking her out of the room and through the house, he looked down at her and grinned. "I know. I like this better."

"I could get used to it," she replied. He could tell she'd tried for perky but settled for grateful.

Out on the deck, overlooking the beach, he sat back into an Adirondack chair with her safely tucked against his chest. Her expression was calm, though the wounded look he'd seen in her eyes all day was still present. He wondered how long before it would disappear.

"Thank you for bringing Laura. It was kind of perfect."

"I know she's your best friend; your 'family,' her and the other girls."

"She is." She pushed her hair away from her forehead and stared out at the surf. "She's the only one who knows ... you know, about ..."

"So I was right to call her?"

"You were."

"Brownie points for me."

"Ah, it's the brownie points you're after, is it, Mr. MacKinnon?"

"I'm a man. We gather brownie points. It's what we do."

She laughed, and the sound washed over him like a balm. Thank God. After last night, he'd wondered if he'd ever hear her laugh again. He wanted to kill Roberta Walker, send her away from this world all over again. He would never look at one of her "brilliant" photographs the same way; her brilliance, it seemed to him, had been built upon the very soul of an innocent child.

He gazed down at Darby's face, grateful beyond measure to be holding her in his arms, that she had somehow managed to survive Roberta Walker and become the loving woman he knew her to be. Loving, precious, and now, he knew: fragile.

They sat together and watched the ever-changing sky with its bruised purples and blues bleeding into streaks of magenta over a glowing halo of gold that surrounded the brilliant white of the setting sun. That brilliant white gradually grew dim, and after a time, suddenly, in a blink, it was gone and they were enveloped in soothing darkness, left with only a faint line of light tracing the horizon.

METAMORPHOSIS – PART B

THE FRONT screen door slapped shut as Andrew came into the house. In spite of the blistering heat, he had a knitted cap pulled over his fluorescent-blue hair. Darby watched him head straight for the fridge. "Shit, it's hot out there."

"Gee, it's hot out there," Darby corrected smoothly while flipping idly through the Claymores flier. "Have lemonade instead of pop."

He looked at her balefully then parroted, "GEE, it's hot out there." When his traitorous voice cracked, he grinned. Andrew was softening, finally.

"Better." She stopped flipping, leaned over a cluster of ads. "Hey, this is what I need." She pointed out images of various exercise equipment, all of which were being demonstrated by impossibly slim models.

Mrs. Russell dropped her knitting needles into her lap and peered over. "What, the treadmill or the elliptical?"

"Someone to come home and exercise for me," Darby chuckled, flipping the flier closed. Mrs. Russell was babysitting her, she knew, on Joe's instructions. Apparently, they believed she was made of sugar and was about to melt away at the first sign of rain. Sheesh! She picked up her crochet-hooked snarl of yarn and exchanged smiles with Mrs. Russell, who was teaching her how to crochet. Poor woman. To Andy, she said, "That hat's gotta be hot."

"I'd take it off, but I'd scare the damned horses."

"Good one," Darby snorted, turning her work like Mrs. Russell had shown her and struggling onto yet another row. Yes, this was only a dishcloth, but it was going to be the best damned dishcloth in Brennan's Point, unscheduled holes and volunteer bumps notwithstanding. Either that, or she was going to run screaming from the kitchen and take some pictures of something–fast. She glanced at Andrew. "We could always shave your head and start fresh."

Andrew's face grew still as he considered her suggestion. Darby knew Bingo-daubed hair would grow old quickly, even going so far as to promise Joe it would be over by the time school began, which was just around the corner. Andrew had hung on to the color for far longer than she'd imagined.

He'd been into town a few times with Dougie, but for the most part he'd stuck around home lately, hitting the books pretty hard in preparation for next week's test. Darby wasn't sure if his newfound attachment to home was the result of his hair color being a little too wild to carry off or if maybe he wasn't so anxious to leave home as he once was. The second option was very appealing.

"Could you shave my head this afternoon?"

"Sure."

"How about Dougie; he'd probably go for it too."

"That's fine."

Andrew poured himself a tall glass of lemonade and shoved the pitcher back inside the fridge. "I'll call him right now."

Darby let air escape from her lungs in a long, silent release. Thank you, God. She and Mrs. Russell exchanged tiny smiles before focusing on their projects once again. She loved it when a plan came together. She called after Andrew, "I have something I need you to do first."

■ ■ ■

THE MUSIC coming from the kitchen was deafening. Joe grimaced and poked his head in the doorway. Andrew was perched on a kitchen stool, wrapped in a bed sheet, with his head partially shaved and sporting a wild blue Mohawk, his naked ears sticking out at a comical angle. His face was split wide with a grin. Dougie Brewer was looking on, his head bald as an egg and looking equally as happy. Darby was manning the razor–of course–wearing her *Come Over to the Dark Side. We have Cookies ... T-shirt*.

The real disappointment was Mrs. Russell, who was seated at the table, hunched over and painting her toenails dark purple! Shannon appeared to be examining scraps of Andy's hair under her microscope.

Joe stepped into the room and snapped off the music. Startled, everyone looked up.

Darby said, "Hey, you're home early. We were going to surprise you."

"No kidding."

"How do you like it, Dad?" Andy blurted, his eyes sparkling with excitement. "I'm thinking this'll be my new look for school this year."

Joe took a moment before opening his mouth, but nothing diplomatic seemed to be available to him. He rocked his jaw and looked to Darby for some help—any kind of help. Then he was going to string her up once he had her alone. Or maybe some other interesting punishment might present itself to him by then. Seeing her face, so happy and relaxed, the haunted expression finally gone, he couldn't bring himself to be mad at her.

Andy burst out laughing. "Gotcha!" He and Dougie high-fived one another, then high-fived Darby ... then high-fived Mrs. Russell?

"Mrs. Russell!" Joe protested. "I thought I could at least count on you to keep sanity in this house."

Winding the top back on the nail polish, she grinned at him and said, "I couldn't fight 'em, so I joined 'em. And I have to say, it's a lot more fun on this side of the fence."

"I'll bet."

Darby made another pass with the razor, this time mowing down the Mohawk. Joe dropped into a chair beside Mrs. Russell, noticing for the first time that the table was littered with cancer pledge sheets and homemade posters. He picked up a pledge sheet, read it, then looked over at Dougie. "You earned five hundred dollars for cancer research by shaving your head?"

"Sure did, Mr. M. Darby wouldn't do the deed until we had it filled. Me and Drew worked the phones all afternoon. He beat me by twenty-two dollars."

"Drew?"

Darby answered him. "That's what Andy prefers we call him from now on, if it isn't too much trouble to remember." There was a warning in her expression for him not to laugh.

I can't keep up.

He looked at his son. "Andrew? Is this true?"

"Yeah, Dad. Andy's kind of lame."

"Your mother didn't think so." When Darby sent him a second warning he started backpedaling. "But it's your choice. Just don't call you late for dinner, right?"

Both boys looked at him incomprehensively. He shrugged his shoulders and gave up. Some days he felt very old. "Well, boys, I'm proud of you. That's over a thousand dollars to a good cause. Great way to turn lemons into lemonade."

Dougie cleared his throat, looking around to see if everyone was listening. "While we're at it, I–ah–would like everyone to stop calling me Dougie, if that's all right. I prefer Doug or Douglas. Dougie is my father's name."

This request was huge in meaning on so many levels; where he was asking, who he was asking, and especially why he was asking. The MacKinnon household really had become Dougie's safe place.

"Then that's what we'll do, Doug," Joe answered for them all. "From now on. Just give us a few days to get used to it, and I'm sure everyone will follow suit."

"That's what I'm counting on, Mr. M."

The faith Dougie–no, Doug–had in them was humbling. It was at this very moment that Joe vowed he'd see this boy safely through life no matter what occurred. And if his father caused problems, Joe would take him on as well. Unable to hide how the boy had affected him, Joe turned away and focused on one of the homemade posters.

It read, BRENNAN'S POINT FIRST ANNUAL GARDEN MARKET, CRAFT & BAKE SALE. THIS SATURDAY, 9 A.M. AT MACKINNON'S MARINA. COME! HAVE FUN. BRING YOUR FRIENDS. BRING YOUR MONEY!

And the surprises just keep on coming.

Joe turned to face Darby. She smiled brightly back at him. "Great idea, huh? Mrs. Russell has tons of tomatoes, Leo Crabtree is drowning in Granny Smith apples, and his wife has more eggs than she knows what to do with. I'm going to put together and sell s'mores kits. They're always fun."

She pulled the sheet away from Andy and brushed off his neck and shoulders. "There, all ready to face the world."

Andy ran his palms over the slick surface of his head and exchanged grins with Doug. "I like it," he said. "Thanks, Darb."

Joe leveled Darby a stare. "You think I haven't thought of this before?"

"Then why haven't you done it?"

"The logistics. It's a huge undertaking. It just isn't that easy."

"Why not?"

"Because it's a commitment I can't make right now."

"We aren't asking you–."

"You aren't asking at all," he interjected.

Darby pursed her lips momentarily, waited a beat then began again. "We aren't asking you to take on this task. We know you're very busy with the expansion, and we're not claiming this will be weekly. We thought just a one-off for now. See how it goes. It could be huge, or it could be a flop. In any case, it should be fun. We have … well, you have the space."

"And just who'll run this little shindig?"

"The boys are taking it on."

Joe turned surprised eyes toward the boys again. "You'll run it?"

This time Drew answered him. "We thought we'd do a bit of a fundraiser. Mr. Crabtree's going to help us get the tables down there. We do the setup, of course. We'll donate all the proceeds along with the cancer pledges."

Joe couldn't help himself, he was impressed. Up until now, the sum total of Andy's philanthropic efforts were limited to sharing excess Halloween candy with his little sister–when pressed. He asked, "Where will you get the tables?"

"Mrs. Russell made a call. The church is lending us the tables, we'll rent them out at twenty bucks a table, ten for the church, ten for the fundraiser."

Joe surveyed the little group, their faces expectantly waiting for his approval. There really was so much more to this than they realized. Permits for one. Pubic washrooms for another. Parking. Where was everyone going to park? Along the highway? Not good, so that meant parking attendants. Garbage containers, recycling containers, shaded seating areas for seniors to stop and rest. He really hated to burst their bubble.

Darby added, "Carl's on board. He'll introduce a new fish burger with 'secret sauce.' He's ordered in twice his usual sodas. How hard can it be? Andy–I mean,

Drew – is going to sell some of his photographs, Doug some of his drawings." When Joe didn't answer, she said, "Come on. It'll be fun."

Joe closed his eyes, pinched the bridge of his nose, and groaned, "I wish my life had background music so I could understand what the hell was going on."

When he opened his eyes again, he saw the others had quietly left the kitchen. It was only he and Darby, and judging by the set of her chin, he was going to lose. Silently, he watched her sweep up the hair clippings and tidy everything away. He didn't want to fight with her. He just didn't know what to do with her, was his problem. Darby Walker had him flummoxed. Watching her work around the kitchen quietly, time ticked by, and he softened.

He could make a few calls …

Finished tidying, she surprised him by coming to sit in his lap. She wrapped her arms around his neck and kissed him on the mouth.

He glanced at the door. "What are you doing?"

"I was informed in no uncertain terms today that if we think we're fooling anyone, we are sadly mistaken."

He rolled his eyes to the ceiling. "Shoot me now, Lord. Shoot me now."

"Want that sound track right about now?"

He laughed. "Yeah. How about Dazed and Confused?"

She kissed him again. "How was your day, Honey?"

"Not as exciting as yours, apparently," he growled, tightening his arms around her and nuzzling her neck. "So I hear you've got cookies in here somewhere … wanna share?"

TIDE POOL REFLECTIONS

"JUST A bit more," Drew instructed tersely, pulling away from her grip. "A l m o s t …."

"I can't hold on much longer," Darby panted, her fingers cramping even as the fabric of his sweatshirt began to slip from her grip. This was crazy dangerous. "Seriously! You're slipping!"

"Got it!" he shouted, jerking back and rolling onto his side across the uneven rock, then away from the jagged edge onto his back, her underwater camera safely gripped in his hands and his face split wide with a triumphant grin. "That's just gotta turn out good! The colors are incredible. Red. Yellow. Purple. Blue. I swear one was so white it was almost blue. And they were huge, the biggest I've ever seen, waving back and forth like they were listening to music. I can't wait to develop them."

Darby flexed her aching hands. "Me too. And just so you know, I won't be hanging onto you while you dangle over a cliff ever again. If your father saw what we just did to get those sea anemone, he would kill me."

"You know if I waded into the pools, they'd close up and there'd be no point."

"Still."

"And what's the worst that could happen? I get wet?"

"Or break your neck."

He grinned at her some more. "Or not."

She couldn't help smiling back. The boy had skills, just like his father.

He pulled at the hem of his T-shirt and dried off the camera, then glanced up at her shirt and frowned. "Hey, no statement on your T-shirt today. How come?"

"I'm trying to cut back."

"Seriously?"

"No." She grinned down at him. "Laundry day." She extended her hand. "Let's go." He took it, and she pulled him to his feet. Together they scrambled back up the rock face to the tree line. "We won't be telling your dad about how you got this particular shot."

"He's such a hard ass."

"He's the hard ass who loves you."

"Some days it feels like the opposite, like he hates me."

Darby stilled and turned to face him. "How can you even think that? Your father adores you."

"Yeah, he loves me so much he's hired nine different nannies to watch over me. Now that's love."

Turning to sit on the rocky curve of the cliff top, Darby took the opportunity to catch her breath. "Seems to me there's been some rewriting of history here."

Drew came to rest alongside her. "You weren't there; I was. It's been a revolving door, trust me."

"Have you ever talked about this with your dad?"

"You know how he is. Always so frigging serious."

"No, he's not. He has a great sense of humor. And watch your language."

Drew cocked his head to the side and shrugged. "Well, he has lightened up now that you're here." He smiled and nudged her with his shoulder. "Don't think you got me hooked, though. I'm still suspicious."

She nudged him back. "You're fourteen. It's your job to be suspicious."

They gazed from their perch on the rocky outcropping at the restless ocean, each thinking their own thoughts. Drew broke the silence, his voice soft. "I was headed into Vancouver the day I crashed my bike."

Darby turned to face him, alarmed. "Andy!"

"I could've made it," he defended.

"You mean you were running away to Vancouver?"

"Yeah. I had some money on me. I knew about a hostel I could stay at 'til I was on my feet."

Keeping fear from her voice, she asked, "What were you going to do when you got there?"

"Get a job in construction. I'm tall. People think I'm older than I look all the time. Plus, I'm strong."

She put her arm around his shoulders and squeezed him to her side. "Oh, Honey, if only that were enough."

He pulled away from her, propped his elbows onto his raised knees, and gripped his hands together, his expression scowled. "What? You think I don't have a clue? You made it, and I'm way tougher than you are."

She pressed her lips together, her mind frantic for where to start, how to tell him how dangerous his idea of Vancouver alone really was. A beautiful, blond boy like Drew would be swallowed whole in the sex trade within days, she knew. He'd never be the same again.

She gazed out at the water. "Okay. Did you remember your Social Insurance number?"

"My what?"

She looked over at him. "You know, the government ID number you need in order to be hired on a construction site?"

He didn't answer.

"And did you have enough money for a hard hat, steel-toed boots, work gloves, the basics? 'Cause they don't supply them. You have to have at least that much to start."

He dropped his head and stared down at the rocky ground.

"And an address and picture ID so you could open a bank account for your pay to go in, 'cause they all pay electronically these days."

He muttered, "They do?"

"Please hear me, Drew. This is so important. I've been there, I know what homelessness looks like. It's ugly and dangerous and ends lives early."

"You did it," he muttered again, only this time his tone was resentful.

"Because I would be dead if I didn't get out of my mother's house, Drew."

He brought his head up. "No shit?"

"No shit."

Another silence fell over them. Then Drew said, "I was pretty mad at my dad. He was coming down hard about summer school, and me hanging out with Doug, and then that jerk Mr. Pringle wrote this stupid letter I was supposed to bring to my dad …"

Darby sighed in sympathy. "Growing up is hard. Why make it harder by being on your own in a dangerous city?"

"You really don't think I'd have made it?"

"Nope."

"Why the hell not?"

Darby looked at his open and vulnerable young face and wanted to hug away his hurt confusion. "It's not about you, Honey. If you could make it on sheer determination alone, I have no doubt you could succeed at anything you choose. Except this."

"How did you do it?"

She dropped her eyes and stared sightlessly at the rock at their feet. "Sometimes, I don't know myself."

"It was scary?"

"It was terrifying."

"W-will you tell me about it?"

"Oh, Drew." Raking her fingers through her hair, she stared at him, assessing his eager expression of curiosity. Yeah, she'd made it. But she didn't want to romanticize her experience to an impressionable and competitive young boy. It might even be waving a red flag before a bull. But he'd opened up to her, told her a secret about himself she'd bet money no one else knew.

Life on the streets was not romantic in anyway, and if he harboured any lingering ideas of taking off to Vancouver when things got tough at home, which they would–every teen goes through tough times–she had to take this opportunity to convince him it would be a very bad move. Now was the time for honesty.

"All right, Drew, it's like this. When you live on the streets, you are one of many. But make no mistake, in spite of all the offers of friendship you will receive, there are no 'friends.' You really will be on your own.

"The people down there are most often drug addicts or lifetime drunks or are mentally ill and have no one stepping up to help or care for them and have run out of options, or they're underage kids escaping a home life that makes the streets look good in comparison, or maybe they got snagged by a pimp, or they're an illegal immigrant on the hook and it could mean their life if they tried to escape. Every story could break your heart.

"There is no loyalty. Everything is about the next fix, the next meal, the secret cardboard hidey hole, the buried change of clothes, the place in line for a bed at the shelter, the pecking order at the burn barrel, the treasure of a half-eaten Subway sandwich from a dumpster, a warm hat or jacket, a grocery cart that still has a quarter in it, a good corner to solicit your next John. All these things are valuable enough to knife someone in the side to get. It happens every day, all day; every night, all night.

"Nowhere is safe. It isn't safe to fall asleep. It isn't safe to trust a 'friend.' It isn't safe to tell a cop. It isn't safe to approach a stranger. It Isn't safe.

"You ask yourself: where can I sleep tonight, where can I pee, what will I eat, where can I get water that's safe to drink, where can I wash, where can I store my stuff, will it be here when I get back, how will I stay warm tonight?"

"In Vancouver?" he asked incredulously. "Why can't you talk to a cop?"

"They'll say, 'Move along now,' 'No, not here,' 'Keep on walking, buddy.' You'll be exhausted. You can't sleep at night, because that's when the crazies come out. So you stay awake, and keep moving, watching your back, protecting what's yours. Maybe a backpack with essentials, maybe a shopping cart—you've seen those, piled high with whatever can be scrounged that has trade value, or warmth, or maybe isn't too far gone and can still be eaten.

"During the day, if you can, you sleep out in the open, where other desperate homeless people wouldn't dare attack you or steal from you—too many witnesses. Of course, then the cops will roust you and again you have to move along. An hour's sleep here, half an hour there, and walking, always walking, searching for scraps, begging for change, sneaking into public washrooms where you can to drink, pee, wash.

"God, to have hot water, even for a moment. You'll still smell bad, since you have the same clothes on day after day, and people will cut a wide path around you with their faces screwed up in disgust or pity, but you get used to that. You comfort yourself because you know you washed a little at that gas station last Tuesday …

"Your hair gets grimy and greasy and begins to stiffen, then mat. It smells rancid, but that's not the bad part, the bad part is the bugs that live there and the sores they leave behind, sores that never heal. Your breath could stop a truck, you won't be able to tolerate the taste of your own mouth. Your teeth start to decay, and losing a tooth is always preferable to the pain of keeping it once it's rotten.

"God help you if you get sick." She paused before going on. "And God help you if you're pretty. It isn't only girls who are raped."

Drew's eyes were large in his head, his gaze riveted to her. "This all happened to you?"

"Some happened, for some I had a front row seat. I was lucky. I went to school during the day. I showered at school, shampooed my hair, brushed my teeth at school, though I was sleeping in the park, in bushes, or tied up in a tree so I wouldn't fall when I slept. Some nights I'd stay in the library if they didn't catch me hiding out in the stacks. I even spent two nights in a Walmart, just like that movie, if you can believe it. It was hard, though. They had a night crew unpacking stock, so it wasn't exactly like the movie.

"I was really lucky when I graduated from stealing part of a sandwich or maybe a half-eaten apple or leftover fries left on people's trays at the cafeteria at school—so humiliating to get caught—and dumpster diving in alleyways for food, to eating real food.

"Because I was clean, I got a job at the soup kitchen in exchange for meals, breakfast and suppers during the week, breakfast, lunch, and suppers on the weekends, except in the summer. I bought clothes at the Salvation Army, washed them at the coin Laundromat, and packed them with me everywhere I went. I had two backpacks. One for school, one for essentials.

"At first I stayed at one of three shelters at night—they don't let you stay too many nights—so I made the rounds, same as everyone. Because I didn't make trouble and helped out whenever I could, one of them broke the rules and made sure I had a bed every night, one near the lights, where others might think twice about trying to steal my stuff while I slept. Still, I learned how to sleep on my side, curled around my bags, which I'd tie to my body.

"Then came the lucky day I talked my way into teaching kids Art in the Park for the summer. That's when my life really turned around. I saved every penny I could manage. I found a dentist who'd work for cash, no questions. I cut my own hair and dyed it, used dramatic makeup that made me look older and screamed 'Don't piss me off.' I walked around looking as tough as I could, and always with someplace important to go. Using school and library computers, I applied for scholarships and grants. By then I had a post box—a real luxury—and that put me back in communication with the legitimate world. I bought a burner phone from a drug dealer I knew—."

"You knew a drug dealer?"

"I knew lots of drug dealers, Drew. Lots. There's two on every corner. Like I said, the reason half the people are down there is drugs. Or alcohol. Didn't touch the stuff myself, but I knew plenty who did. I knew pimps and prostitutes, runners, enforcers. I saw crack houses, cardboard cities, suicides, murder victims, rummies, knife fights, meth labs, grow ops. It's a whole other world, one that's hard to get clear of."

"Wow," Drew breathed, his face alive with wonder.

Afraid he was hearing this as an adventure, she added, "It's a place where people are killed for a sandwich or a fix or a warm hat. Life is cheap. They sweep the city, picking up 'stiffs' every morning—like road kill."

His expression changed to alarm.

She went on. "So then I had a phone number, somewhere a potential employer could contact me. That's when I started to get a shift here and there in the afternoons after school at a coffee shop near the shelter, then at a second-hand bookstore.

"Never in the evenings, though. I had rules about evenings."

"The crazies?"

She nodded. "Once I learned the ropes, I never stayed outside after dark. My number one rule: inside by dusk—every night, no exceptions, no matter what. Still, a rummy broke my right arm to get my winter jacket when I was seventeen. That was bad. I was worried I wouldn't be able to work at the soup kitchen anymore and would lose my source of clean, safe food. I was lucky, they were good to me. They worked around it, let me stay. That was the closest I came to falling all the way to the bottom, a place very few climb out from.

"Another time I lost my essentials backpack to a group of four girls who forced me into an alley and beat me up pretty severely for shits and giggles.

Someone called 911, and because I was dressed neatly and had a school bag, they thought I was a regular person caught on the wrong side of the tracks and actually helped me.

"It turned out to be another close call, though. They called social services and wanted to put me into the system. I knew that was the fastest road back to my mother's house, so while they were busy discussing me, I slipped away and hid behind a linens trolley until daylight and it was safe to hike back to my neighborhood. Of course that meant building up my essentials again, not easy when you're living inside an almost cashless society."

"How did you make money?" he asked, though his eyes were averted. She smiled at his tact.

"I had a camera by then. I sold pictures at Stanley Park, on weekends, when people came with their families. Sometimes I bought a huge bag of candies and mini chocolate bars, then parceled them out and sold them in little treat bags for a dollar. Sometimes I sold fruit: apples, cherries, Okanogan peaches. I got them off the fruit truck, cleaned and repacked them, of course. And flowers—same deal. If I found a large moon snail shell at low tide, I could always get good money for that too. The hard part was getting Sue down at the soup kitchen to let me boil it clean." She made a face. "What a stink!"

"How did you get out?"

"I worked. I kept my eye on the prize, which in my case was art school. If I could somehow win a scholarship or grant or bursary, anything that would further my education and give me a chance at a life, I was all over it. I stayed on at the soup kitchen, took any offered shift at the coffee shop and bookstore of course, still making sure I was safely inside before dark.

"The best things I got from the coffee shop and bookstore were their recommendations. The pay was nothing, but when applying for scholarships and grants, letters of recommendation are pure gold. The soup kitchen wrote up a good one for my 'volunteer' work there, omitting the important fact that I actually worked for food. The shelter did the same. Add in my summers spent teaching Art in the Park for the YWCA, and I had a half-decent résumé. It didn't tell the real story of course, but it looked good on paper, and that's what counted.

"Then, happy day, I won a full scholarship to art school. Oh, my God, such a happy day that was for me, you have no idea. No one does or probably ever will. And that's when I met Laura and Maggie and Hayley—at art school. A true blessing, my tribe—especially Laura.

"My scholarship didn't include living costs, so I was still hiking back and forth to the shelter, though what I was going to do when it started getting dark earlier, I hadn't figured out yet. When Laura got wind of that, she suddenly needed me to stay over in her dorm room. Too scared to be alone at night, she claimed. What a crock. I never went back to the shelter after that night. It seemed that Laura needed all kinds of support. She couldn't eat in the cafeteria alone, so could I help her out … ? Hated being alone in her condo in the summer, that sort of thing. She'll deny it to this day, but she saved my life."

Drew asked, "Is that why you're so scared of … ?" his voice trailed off, his eyebrows high on his forehead.

"No. That was from my time with my mother, and not something I want to talk about." She patted the ground between them. "I think we've had enough True Confessions for today. The bottom line is, I was damned lucky to get out in one piece. I honestly don't know anyone else who did. Pretty bad odds if you ask me."

"I-I didn't know."

"And I never want you to know. No kid should know. Now, let's get going back. Your dad's going to wonder what's happened to us. Plus, I have s'mores packs to make up for tomorrow's market. I think it's going to be fun, don't you?"

When she started to get up, Drew reached out and stopped her. "Darby?"

"What?"

"Thanks. For telling me about your life. The truth. And … and not treating me like a kid."

"You deserve the truth, Drew. Always."

TO MARKET, TO MARKET

PULLING UP to staff parking by the marina office, Darby couldn't believe her eyes. The grassy field was transformed, and in a very good way. Everything was alive with color and activity, with the borrowed church tables shaded under three rows of white canvas canopies. Every table also had chairs for the sellers and was piled high with wares and hand-lettered signs.

She hadn't even thought about being out in the sun all day, let alone standing in the sun. Of course the sellers needed shade—and a place to sit. There were blue and pink his and hers portable toilets stationed at each end of the park, and large plastic-lined garbage and recycling bins strategically placed among the tables as well. There was even a section of seats under a fourth canopy set up with tables and chairs that afforded market patrons a place to rest.

Again she hadn't thought of these things—not sexy, but absolutely necessary: sun protection, washrooms, garbage containers, rest areas. Joe had been right. It wasn't as simple as she'd claimed, and he'd come through, filling in where she'd failed to plan. A few calls, huh? Joe was a very practical man, and she was glad of it.

Already, a huge bunch of colorful balloons floated over one of the booths, and she could detect the scent of freshly mown lawn along with deep fried mini donuts wafting through her open car window. How could she be hungry when she'd just eaten breakfast? It was only 8:30 in the morning, a half hour before the market was set to open, and the winding highway was lined with parked cars on either side with people streaming in.

Shannon was bouncing in her seat with excitement and grappling with her door handle. "Let's go, let's go."

Darby shut off the car and released both of their seat belts. "This looks wonderful!"

Before she could even begin to unload her baskets of s'mores kits and Shannon's glued beach-stone figurines, Darby saw Joe approaching from across the grass, dodging distracted customers and running children, his stride easy, his tanned face relaxed and happy. Her heart skipped inside her chest at the sight. Joe MacKinnon affected her like no other man had ever done. Had she finally found and followed the right path and found her soul mate?

A troubling thought tumbled forward in her brain, something she'd been skirting around for weeks, she realized. She was living with her sister's family, sleeping with her sister's husband. Was this a followed path, or had she somehow stolen Nadine's rightful place?

Joe's expression clouded. Arriving at the car he took her box of s'mores kits and asked, "What's wrong?"

She shook her head. She didn't know how she was going to clear this last hurdle of insecurity, but today was not the day to hash it out. Today was a day for family fun. "Absolutely nothing. This is so much more than I imagined, and it's all because of you. I can't believe the turnout; I should have made twice as many s'mores kits."

Hugging her shoe box of stone Inuit sculptures to her chest, Shannon added, "And my Inuksuk."

"Especially your Inuksuk," Joe agreed, smiling down at her as they walked across the crisp, green grass.

Their table was prime, right next to the mini donut machine, which was enjoying a long line of patrons. Drew was already making sales from his display of photos at the MacKinnon table, using the matting Darby had given him to frame them up for the best presentation, each inside a plastic page protector from Staples. It was an inexpensive but attractive way to display his work, which was surprisingly good.

As agreed, Doug was off making a quick sketch of the market to copy on her printer and sell as limited editions. Darby quickly unloaded her s'mores kits, arranging them in an attractive display, each clear bag wrapped with curly, colored ribbon. Shannon busied herself setting her Inuksuk on the red linen cloth Mrs. Russell had given her, creating little vignettes that made sense to her.

"That looks good, Shannon," Darby complimented her. "Your Inuksuk look as good as the ones in the airport gift shops."

Shannon nodded as if this were a given. She'd been working hard on her Inuit place keepers and figurines for a solid week, scavenging beach stones and beach glass every morning, then gluing the prettiest ones into Inuksuit every afternoon.

Looking at Drew and Shannon standing proudly behind their creations, Darby murmured to Joe, "Look how proud they are of what they've done. This is so good for them."

Joe smiled and surveyed the whole market. "It's good for the whole town. I never thought people …" He stopped and looked back at her with affection. "But then I have you for that now, don't I?"

"You are no kind of saleswoman," Mrs. Russell announced, puffing up from behind Darby. "Don't you see paying customers right in front of you?"

Darby's eyes refocused from the park in general to her table. "Oh. I'm so sorry." Two women in wide-brimmed hats, their money in their hands, apparently forgotten, were staring at her T-shirt of the day that read, *Never trust an atom. They make up everything.*

One woman asked, "Who's Atom?"

Darby looked back at her blankly; Joe snickered behind his hand. Mrs. Russell reached past Darby, exchanging cash for two kits. "Here, let me. Harvey won't let me sell my own damned tomatoes over there. This I'm good at. You go bask in your success."

Darby looked down at Shannon, who was patiently explaining to another equally serious little girl that Inuksuit were traditional symbols of important places to the Inuit people. Darby was proud of her simple but clear explanation. Oh how she loved this little girl. She asked, "What about Shannon?"

"She'll be fine," Mrs. Russell replied. "Go on now. Be a tourist in your own town."

"How about we bring you back a pupcake?" Joe asked his daughter, his eyes crinkled with humor.

She raised her gaze to meet his, her expression long-suffering. "It's cupcake, daddy. Only babies call them pupcakes."

Joe's smile faltered. "Oh." After a moment of silence, he reached out his hand for Darby's. "Okay then. We'll–we'll be back in a bit."

When he was quiet as they walked along the line of tables, staring sightlessly at what was being offered for sale, Darby squeezed his hand.

He stopped, looked at her and said, "I missed it, didn't I?" She heard the devastation in his voice, could see he'd been cut to the quick by his exchange with Shannon.

"You're here now, Joe. That's what counts."

"I thought I still had time." His smile was bleak.

"All is not lost–you've still got 'taste bugs'."

He laughed then, and relaxed. Glancing at their clasped hands, he said, "You realize we're going public now and confirming all the rumors."

"PDA in action," she confirmed. "No going back now."

Hand in hand, they resumed strolling the aisle, this time taking an interest in what vendors were offering. Darby stopped before a table that featured stacks of colorful crocheted dish clothes and bought six. She'd never pull off that particular skill, no matter how much Mrs. Russell tried.

Doug planted himself in their path, his face flushed, a picture of frustration, his words coming in a whispered rush, "I can't get the mayor to leave me alone. Everywhere I look he's walking into my view. As soon as he heard I was drawing a limited edition garden market picture, he's been bird-doggin' me. I tried from the entrance; in he walks, all nonchalant, so I gave it up. I went over and tried from the pier, and sure enough, up pops the mayor. So this time, I sneak through the trees, and it's working, I'm almost done and in he strolls, 'Oh, are you sketching here?' he says, all innocent like."

"Make a quick drawing with him in it," Darby said, "Then finish the one you like best, minus the mayor. I'll handle the rest."

Doug's shoulders dropped in relief. "Thanks." His eyes shifted to behind her and Joe. He muttered, "Aaaand he's back …. It's like a stupid pop-up book."

Joe erupted in laughter. "Go, get outta here."

Doug beat a hasty retreat, and Joe handled the mayor, accepting his hand-delivered permit graciously and inviting him to walk along with them as they took in the market themselves for the first time. Mayor Mayer was only too pleased to give them a guided tour of the market, much to Darby's amusement. How did Bob Mayer find himself at the helm of so many civic events?

It was noon by the time they arrived back at the MacKinnon tables, carrying the dishcloths, a slab of homemade maple walnut fudge, a quart of garlic dill pickles, three bunches of sweet peas and one of Faye Crabtree's coveted apple pies. They found that Mrs. Russell had been successful in selling out the s'mores kits and had returned to the MacKinnon ranch with Drew to pick up more ink for Darby's printer. Doug's line drawings were a huge hit, and a secondary drawing of the marina, one he'd done for his own pleasure, had been requested by many in the form of a limited edition copy, the same as he'd done with the market drawing.

Shannon was grinning from ear to ear because her Inuksuk display was also empty, plus she had purchased a set of knitted finger puppets from a craft table next door with her very own money!

Mayor Mayer was visibly shaken when he learned that the fifty limited edition copies of Doug's garden market line drawing (Doug had cranked off copies in the marina office on Darby's trusty printer, signed them, and slapped matting over them) entitled First Annual Brennan's Point Garden Market had sold out at twenty-five dollars apiece, and had not included an image of Mayor Bob Mayer.

The injury in Bob's eyes was real, and surprisingly, Darby felt bad for the man. She reached out to Doug. "Got the special one ready?"

"Yes," he answered, sliding a single matted drawing out from under his sketch pad. This too was signed and inside a plastic page protector. He said, "This is my other drawing, the special illustration of the market featuring you, Mayor Mayer."

Bob Mayer's eyebrows furrowed. "There's a second market drawing?"

Darby smiled at him brightly. "There sure is. Doug wanted to do one just for you."

Bob still looked doubtful. "So why not make the one with …?" He flushed a little—Darby guessed that even he recognized his ego was out there for everyone to see—then plunged on. He was, after all, a politician. "The one with the town's mayor featured in it, the one you copy and sell?"

Darby handed him Doug's second drawing. He stared down at it wordlessly. She said, "Yes, those drawings were copies. You know, signed limited editions, but copies, nevertheless. Yours is a one-of-a-kind," she whispered conspiratorially. "You have in your hand the only original, signed by the artist."

Bob's eyes brightened and a smile bloomed across his face. "That's right, isn't it?"

Catching on, Doug added, "I might be famous one day. An early original is so much more valuable than a copy, every day of the week."

"Even more so after the artist's death," Mayor Mayer nodded thoughtfully. Their little group stared back at him, speechless. Seeing their expressions, he clasped the drawing to his chest as if afraid Doug would change his mind and demand it back. He quickly amended, "That's all supposition, of course. The main thing is, I have a nice little memento of today's market, right?"

A beat of silence remained. Darby filled it with a faint "Uh-huh," as the others found somewhere else to be. "Maybe you could show it around to a few of the Brennan's Point citizens while they're still here at the market," she suggested, eager to see the back end of the man. Bob thought hers was an excellent suggestion and hurried off, his mayoral paunch pointing the way.

The MacKinnon group drifted back together and exchanged mildly shocked expressions. Joe muttered, "Now there's our mayor at his finest."

Doug said, "You should run against him, Mr. M. You'd get in for sure."

"Nah. I'd tell people the truth, and then where would I be?" He put his arm around Doug's neck in a mock wresting hold. "So what's the tally? How much did you make for cancer research today?"

Darby watched Joe and Doug and marveled at the difference a summer had made in their relationship. She was so glad for Doug.

Relaxing back in the shade, she could see most of the tables were stripped of their produce or crafts or home baking, the sellers having moved their tables to form groups of two or three, where they could congregate under the shaded canopies and chat with neighbors and friends. The buying public had moved onto Carl's secret sauce burger or were lined up for the ice cream Kelly-Anne and her crew were still scooping from coolers. Some were picnicking on blankets beside the fiddlers whose cheery music had enlivened the entire morning. Dozens of colorful balloons bobbed along singly or in pairs, with the gently moving waves of attendees. A group of young people who'd set up a beach volleyball game garnered themselves quite the fan base from the market goers. A group of ladies under cover of the resting canopy had formed a knitting circle and were chatting animatedly to one another over their colorful projects.

It seemed that apart from food, the selling was over and the visiting just getting into full swing. What a great way to wind up the summer.

She glanced back at Shannon who was giggling in her father's lap now as they played with the finger puppets with no particular place to go. This result was so much more than she had ever envisioned, and it had all started with a deserted grassy park and Mrs. Russell's bumper crop of tomatoes.

No, that was wrong, it had started long before—it had really all started with a boy running away to Vancouver on a dirt bike and never making it out of town because fate had placed Darby in his way. She was so glad it had.

"Darby!"

Everyone turned at the urgency in Drew's voice. His face was dark with fury as he streaked across the grounds toward them, Mrs. Russell following close behind with a distressed expression.

He pulled up short in front of Darby. "Oh, you are good!" he said, throwing the ink cartridge at her feet and shaking his head in disbelief. "I'm just the dumb kid who believed everything you told me."

Joe jumped up, handing off Shannon to Mrs. Russell just as she arrived. He pulled his son away from Darby. "Whatever this is, we're taking it inside right now." His hand gripping Drew's arm, he marched his son across the grounds toward the marina office.

Darby was on her feet and running across the grass after the two MacKinnons, shocked at Drew's attack. "What's wrong?" she gasped. "What happened?"

"Inside first," Joe said tersely, "then we talk."

INSIDE DARBY'S TRUNK

JOE SHUT his office door behind them then turned to face his angry son. "Okay. Explain yourself."

Drew pointed to Darby. "She's full of shit."

"Andrew!"

"It's true. How do you even know she's Mom's sister? Did she tell you? Because if she's your source, it's bullsh–."

"Andrew!" Joe slammed his palm against his desk. "Watch your mouth!"

Darby stepped forward. "What happened?"

Drew rolled his eyes. "And here it comes, the injured act. The 'I don't understand' act, when she's had a plan all along, ever since she moved in."

"You're right, I don't understand. What are you talking about?"

"I'm talking about you moving in with our family, pretending you aren't looking for a cushy situation when all the time, you came complete with your own wedding dress!"

Fear slammed into her chest so hard she actually staggered back against one of Joe's old file cabinets. She started at Drew in horror. "God, Andrew. Tell me you didn't cut it up!"

"Cut it up?" Joe looked from Darby to Drew, then stopped and slowly looked back at Darby. "You own a wedding dress?" When she couldn't bring herself to answer him, his eyes snapped back to his son. "And why, first thing, does she think you'd cut it up?"

Drew's gaze never left Darby's face, his eyes bright with virtuous indignation. "Not only that, she got that government contract she was going after. She's been covering it up ever since you guys got back from Vancouver. I guess being Mrs. MacKinnon pays better than photography."

Joe's gaze jerked back to Darby. "Is this true?"

Darby ignored him. "Andrew. Did you cut up my dress?"

"You'll see what I did to it when you get back there. Have fun with that."

"Jesus! Andrew!" his father hissed. "What's going on with you?"

Darby whirled around and ran from the office, the building, her every breath a noisy struggle for oxygen. The dress. The dress. Everything was ruined. Her dreams of that one day ... God. The girls. The dress. She reached the car and fumbled to unlock it, barely aware of the sounds she was making. Finally, the lock gave way, and she pulled at the door. Joe's hand reached from behind her and held it closed. "You're in no shape to drive."

"Let me go!" she wailed, pulling frantically at the door.

"No. I'll take you. Slide over to the passenger's side."

"I don't need you. I don't need any of you!"

He pried the car keys from her hands and bundled her inside the car, taking over the driver's seat and starting it up. He reached across and fastened her seatbelt around her, then guided the car from the lot with maddeningly calm movements. Darby wrapped her arms around her torso and rocked in place with her eyes closed. "Drive fast," she instructed through clenched teeth. "Fast."

"We'll get there soon enough." He turned onto the highway. "Tell me about this dress."

"Just drive."

"Was it your mother's dress?"

She moaned, "God, do you know me at all?"

"I thought I did."

"Obviously, you don't." She turned her face to the window, her eyes still closed and concentrated on remaining calm. Get me out of here, far away from here. Take me anywhere. But first, let the dress be all right.

When the car slowed near the house, Darby's seatbelt was off, and she was out of the car before it stopped, running across the yard and up the steps and into the house. "Please, not cut up," she prayed.

Her bedroom door burst open at her shove, bounced back from the wall and slammed into her shin as she threw herself inside and onto the white gown spilling from the open trunk. She grabbed up the bodice, ran trembling fingers over the lace work and hand-beading, then lifted it up and examined the froth of skirt, her eyes searching for destruction … and found … none.

Clutching the dress to her chest, she sank to the bed and closed her eyes. "Thank you. Thank you," she whispered.

"The dress is all right?"

It was Joe asking. She opened her eyes and looked at him standing in the doorway, and was surprised to see Drew standing beside his father, his expression belligerent.

She had no words for them. None. Her relief was so great, she could not speak. She only shook her head and pressed her face into the dress, breathing in the scent of the sachet she and Laura and Maggie and Hayley had so carefully packed away with the dress. It was still perfect, still here, waiting for them to share, and wear, each in her turn, when the time was right.

"Why did Darby believe you'd slashed this dress?"

"Who cares? I didn't touch the stupid dress. I just wanted to scare her."

"Answer me, Andrew."

Darby looked up to see his gaze drop in shame. At least he understood what he'd done was wrong. "I kinda …. He looked back up at his father. "I cut up a bunch of her pictures, when she first got here."

"You what?" Joe's shock was plain, then he looked at Darby as if she'd betrayed him in some way. "And you didn't tell me?"

She let the dress drift into her lap. "I took care of it myself. I thought you had enough on your plate. So I made him clean up the mess and redevelop them, the old-fashioned way. They were the pictures I'd done for the proposal."

Joe's mouth tightened. "That's why you jumped to the conclusion Drew had cut the dress?"

She shifted her gaze to Drew. "The best indicator of future behavior is past behavior. And this dress means the world to me. The world."

Joe sat on the bed beside her. "Why is this dress important?"

If he'd been angry, she could have held out, but he was gentle, and it was that gentle tone that was her undoing. Tears sprang up into her eyes, making the room suddenly blurry.

She swallowed hard, forcing back a flood of emotion. It took several attempts before she could trust her voice. "Because," she said hoarsely, "it's the only promise of family I've ever had, my connection to my girls. Before them, I had nothing but what I carried on my back. I-I had no friends, no one I could trust, no safe place. Then I met Laura in art school, and through her I met Maggie, then Hayley, and they became my family. My only family. We were all orphans in some way, on our own and lonely. At school, we grew to trust each other. We had each other's backs, we filled in where life didn't. Those three girls were my salvation, my sanity, my connection to the real world. When it was coming close to school being over and time for us to strike back out on our own, alone, I panicked.

"I knew we each had our own path. Laura was drafted into her family's company. Maggie inherited a little cottage back on Vancouver Island and intended to start up her landscape business there. Hayley. Well, Hayley was the most vulnerable one of us all. She was … well, I can't say. It's too terrible to even tell you." She glanced over at Drew and away. "Then there was her dad … Let's just say he made her feel worthless, and that leaked into just about everything she did, including standing up for herself. She kind of followed us around until we took her in and loved her just as she was.

"Anyway, during that last year I was scared we'd lose touch and I'd lose them forever. Then I found this dress in a consignment shop. It was the most beautiful dress I'd ever seen, and it laced up in the back. I instantly knew all four of us could wear this dress when we married one day, so I put a deposit down on it without telling the girls. Then I brought them to the shop and let the dress do the talking for me. Or so I thought.

"They weren't convinced, at first. The last thing any of us was thinking about back then was marrying." She stroked the dress lovingly. "The thing was, they all had homes to go back to except me. I was actually going a little crazy. Seeing how much it meant to me, and … and other things …

"Anyway—Laura caved first and tried on the dress. It looked so perfect on her. Stunning, in fact. We could hardly speak she looked so beautiful. Then the other girls tried it on, well, except Hayley… and it felt as if this dress had been made especially for each of us and that I was meant to find it. We all fell in love with this dress. I knew it was a sign."

Joe smiled at this. Gratitude for his understanding flooded her.

She continued, her voice stronger. "We all promised that no matter where in the world we ended up in life, when it came time for us to marry and start a family of our own, we would each wear this dress, and we would all be there, no matter where we had to return from. It was a promise to stay a family, to have each other's backs. It was the only way I could let them go, you see? Laura put up the rest of the money on the spot. I agreed to keep it safe."

"You've been keeper of the flame ever since?"

She nodded. "Yes."

"And the contract? Why didn't you tell me about winning the contract?"

"Because when I got it, it wasn't important to me anymore. I'd ..." She bit her lip and dropped her chin to her chest, feeling suddenly shy. "I'd found something that meant more to me. Much more."

He murmured, "No longer undeclared?"

She looked back up at him, shook her head and whispered, "No."

He drew her into his arms—the dress forgotten between them—and kissed her lips so tenderly it was almost heartbreaking in its acceptance and understanding and love. "Will you wear this dress for me, Darby Walker?" he whispered.

A braying sound from the doorway broke the connection. Together they turned to see Andrew, his face red and twisted, tears streaming down his face. "So that's it? You get married, and I'm yesterday's news? You get a nice, brand-new family?"

Joe turned to more fully face his son. "What are you saying? You're part of this family, always will be. It's never been a question."

"So why haven't you ever wanted to adopt me? After Mom died, you just gave up."

Joe stared at him in disbelief. "How do you believe that? We've never been apart—not even for one day. I've made sure of it."

"Until something better comes along. I know you and Mom were splitting up before she got cancer."

Darby turned stunned eyes to Joe. He'd never breathed a negative word about Nadine. Joe opened then closed his mouth. Finally he said, "I didn't know you knew that."

"I'm not as stupid as everyone thinks I am."

"No one thinks you're stupid!"

"Tell that to Mr. Pringle."

Joe waved his hand dismissively. "Forget that idiot."

"So Mom gets cancer, you put the divorce on hold, you guys have Shannon, Mom dies, and you're stuck with me. I get it. Your bad luck."

"Andy! How can you say that? You and your sister are my number one priority."

"Shannon, yeah, she's your real daughter; me you got by default."

"Never by default!"

"You wouldn't adopt me, even when I kept asking you. You said you would– one day. You're always too busy. Now I know the real reason, don't I? The dumbest kid on the planet could get it. You don't want me around."

"I never did it because it didn't seem important–."

"To you, maybe!"

"You are my son!" Joe shouted. "It's never been a question."

Andrew's mouth opened, but no sound came out, only a silent howl of agony.

Joe jumped to his feet and closed the gap between them. Pulling his son into his arms, he soothed, "Andy. Andy."

His son flailed at him, punching ineffectually at his father's ribcage. Joe took the abuse, riding out his son's rage. "Son, I'm here."

Andy stopped punching and clutched at his father, sobbing out his hurt. Witnessing Joe's capacity to love this boy made Darby's heart swell with love for the man, and the boy, who had finally, at last, revealed his secret fear.

So this was why Andrew MacKinnon's mission in life was destroying what he saw as his father's chances to marry again, to start a family again. Andrew didn't fear his mother was being replaced in his father's heart, he feared that he would be replaced.

She tiptoed from the room, allowing father and son to come together in understanding and healing. This was a private matter, something that had been brewing inside Andy's heart for a very long time.

INTO THE ABYSS

"DARBY …," THE woman's voice pleaded in her ear, cool air brushing her skin and giving her goose bumps. "Find Shannon …"

Darby sat up with a start and glanced at the clock–6 a.m.–then out her window. The sky looked unnaturally dark and dangerous, but the window was closed–no cool breeze from there. She listened intently. The house was silent; not peacefully silent, it seemed to her, but tensely silent.

She could have sworn someone had been right here beside her.

Just a dream. She shivered and lay back down. Obviously, yesterday's emotional drama had taken its toll.

But it had been good, too. Joe had promised to begin adoption proceedings first thing Monday morning, and Drew now had no doubt about how much his father loved him. This had come as a result of hours of father and son pacing up and down the beach, talking together, working out what had come before, each explaining what events from their past had meant to them, learning about and understanding the other's point of view and motivation.

They had returned to the house long after Darby had served then cleared away dinner, preparing a plate for each and placing it into the fridge for when they were ready. By then, Shannon was already in bed for the night.

Darby had left them to their dinners, retiring to her room to allow for the healing between father and son to continue. As she'd dozed off for the night, she'd thought how very long ago it was that she'd smelled fresh hot mini donuts at Brennan's Point's First Annual Garden Market.

But this morning she didn't feel one bit rested. In fact, it seemed she was more tired now than before, as if she'd put in a long night of toiling over some unnameable task. She closed her eyes and nuzzled back into her pillow. Funny she should wake up from a dream of searching for Shannon, who was the very least of their worries. She was a steady little trooper, hard on the heels of her latest quest, her belief in herself unshakable.

"Wake up, Darby!" the voice insisted, more desperate this time. "Find Shannon, before it's too late!" Abruptly, Darby was awake again, fright coursing through her. Whoa. These dreams were getting too damned real. She pulled herself from the bed, convinced any chance of rest was over, in spite of the early hour. She'd get up and fix something nice for breakfast. Maybe some fruit-explosion muffins? Then she and Joe needed to talk.

She had a quick shower to get her bearings and dressed in clean jeans and a pink T-shirt announcing *I thought my Blood Type was A Positive, but it was a Typo.* Standing before the bathroom mirror she raised her black eyeliner pencil up, then paused and stared at her reflection. Did she really need a "Don't Piss Me Off" look anymore? Really? She let her hand drop, considering, then after a moment dropped the eyeliner back into her bag, unused, and zipped it closed. She left the bathroom and went to bake muffins.

The house was still strangely silent when she backed into Joe's room with a tray of juice, two coffees, butter, and warm muffins. He was still asleep. Little wonder after the emotional wringer he'd been through yesterday. Setting the tray beside the bed, she stroked his whiskery cheek with the back of her finger and whispered, "Joe."

His hand came up and brushed her hand away. "Nadine," he answered. His eyes opened. "Nadine?" he repeated, staring at her in puzzlement.

"Nadine?" she whispered.

His eyes focused. "Darby. I thought–."

"I know what you thought."

He frowned. "What?" He sat up, saw the tray and smiled. "Hey, this looks good." He hitched himself against the headboard, pulling the tray onto his lap.

Worry passed across his face. "There doesn't seem to be enough here for you, though." When she didn't laugh, he frowned. "What's wrong?"

"You just called me Nadine."

"No." His expression grew distracted for a moment, then cleared. "Yeah. Actually, I was dreaming of Nadine; some sort of message from beyond." He laughed. "Uh-oh, I'm starting to sound like you."

"You could do worse," she pouted, sinking onto the side of the bed. "I wanted to talk to you before the kids got up."

Joe split and buttered a muffin. "Okay. Shoot."

She was a little afraid to open the last can of worms in her insecurity arsenal. Was she being weak, or was she being brave? She stroked her lips with her fingertips, wondering exactly how to open up the subject.

"Okay, now you're making me nervous."

She snorted. He'd never looked less nervous, in fact he looked very sexy, propped up in bed, devouring muffins, his face unshaven, his hair loose around his thick, muscular shoulders, his tanned chest dusted with golden hair. It occurred to her he could be a model for the front cover of a bodice ripper romance. He would hate that.

She took the plunge. "I think I need to talk about Nadine."

He looked wary. "Okay. What about Nadine?"

"She's my sister, I don't know anything about her, and I'm about to marry her widower and help raise her children. It suddenly feels …" she dropped her gaze to her hands, "like a monstrous undertaking. I-I can't help wondering if maybe, on some level, just a little bit …" She looked up through her lashes to watch his reaction and paced the rest of her question. "You might be thinking of me as a substitute for the real thing?"

"The real thing being Nadine?" He gazed back at her, his eyes troubled, then set aside the tray. "Darby. I get it. You look like Nadine; I was married to Nadine. Please believe me when I tell you that what Nadine and I had was nowhere near perfect, but it was what it was and not what you and I have. You are so far from being a second Nadine; I can't even tell you how different you are.

"But if you need to hear a list of her faults and mistakes, you won't be hearing them from me. She died–heroically in my book. Of course, I speak well of her and will always speak well of her. She was the mother of my children. She gave her life to give Shannon life. I will be grateful for that for the rest of my life. All the rest–I leave behind."

Darby filled her cheeks with air and puffed it back out. "I know this is insecurity. I know what I'm asking for–."

He reached out and took her hands in his. "What are you asking for?"

"Some sort of proof, maybe, that it's me you love, not the ghost of Nadine." Seeing his expression, she added, "Am I being pathetic?"

"No. You're not pathetic. You're ... being a girl?"

"Stop. This is serious."

"Darby, how can I 'prove' something like that? It's impossible."

"I know. This is stupid. I woke up feeling so strange, on edge, like there's something I'm missing, something important. The truth is, I've always felt this way, ever since I moved in here, like I've just missed something, out of the corner of my eye.

"When I have these feelings, they usually turn out to be right. It worries me. I trust my gut, and my gut is telling me there's something going on here and I'm missing it." She recognized his confused expression and stopped. This was over the top, even for her. "Oh, forget it. I'm being stupid."

"Not stupid," he cautioned, obviously trying to understand, trying to find a way to help her. "Why don't we try another angle? What about your no-regrets philosophy? You told me once that it wasn't what people did that they regret, but what they didn't do."

"Yes, but this isn't just you and me experimenting, trying on a new life to see if it suits us. This involves Shannon and Drew."

"Don't forget Doug," he reminded her with a faint smile. "A late season draft pick of yours, I believe."

She didn't smile back. "What if you and I marrying turns out to be our biggest regret?"

He reached for her and drew her across the covers and into his arms. She snuggled against his shoulder and gnawed at the cuticle of her thumb. He stroked her hair and asked, "Do you believe that?"

"No. I'm no longer undeclared, remember?"

"Me either." He gave her a little shake that ended with a kiss on her temple. "You're the best thing to happen to this family. Just try getting away, Miss Walker."

He seemed so certain. And he was such a rock, someone to count on. She twisted her neck and looked into his clear-blues eyes and suddenly wondered–*what the hell am I doing? I love this man. This man loves me. This is crazy talk!*

She sat up and turned to face him. "So we're doing this thing?"

"We are absolutely doing this thing. And as long as we're clearing up loose ends, I have a bone to pick with you too."

"Oh?"

"That contract. I don't want you to give it up. It isn't a case of them or us. If we work together, it can be us, traveling, exposing the kids to places they'd never otherwise see, and you fulfill your contract. You've said you have three years of work in the can, right?"

Excitement spread from her center and raced through her body. "Yes."

"But not the coast?"

"Right."

He grinned. "Well. I just happen to know a fella who has a boat, and that fella can take you to places that have never seen a camera. How does that sound?"

"You'd seriously come with me?"

"Are you kidding? It would be a chance of a lifetime for the whole family. We'd have to schedule it, maybe do some homeschooling from time to time. I'd have to take time from the marina, maybe a couple of weeks, three or four times a year, but that could be arranged too. I'd be an idiot to make you walk away from this."

She threw herself into his lap, laughing. "Oh my God, Joe! I can't wait to start our life together. Get up, get up; let's go tell the kids, let's tell the world!"

Drew threw open the door, his eyes wild, a sheet of paper in his hand. "Shannon's gone up to the lime caves to find diamonds."

■ ■ ■

THE HORSES were skittish going up the trail toward the lime caves. Darby had a fight on her hands with her mount, Joe and Drew, being better horsemen, had it easier, though not by much. Overhead, the clouds crowded together, clashing and rumbling, lightning strikes coming more often and closer as precious minutes ticked by. If she'd been safely inside, Darby may even have enjoyed the show, but not today. All she could hear, over and over again in her head, was the woman's voice from her dreams pleading for her to find Shannon.

In her heart of hearts, she now believed that voice was Nadine's.

Joe shouted and swung off his horse, reached down by a sharp drop-off, and came up with Lily Kitty in his gloved hand. Terror spiked through Darby. It had to be a hundred-foot drop. God, please no. Let her be safe.

Joe fell onto his stomach, gripped the edge of the rock, and peered over, searching far below. After a lifetime of waiting, he glanced up and shook his head, sprang onto the balls of his feet and back up onto his horse. They moved onward, ever upward, only now they were forced to travel single file, Joe in the lead, Drew behind him, with Darby bringing up the rear.

Was that a barking dog? The sound came and went so quickly, she wasn't sure. It could be Buddy, and where Shannon went Buddy was usually close at hand. "Please be Buddy," she moaned.

A stinging drop of rain slapped against her face, like a flung pebble, then another, then more. She turned her face away as the sky opened up. She urged her mount forward, hunching her back against the assault as they inched their way along the narrow path until her horse refused to go any farther. The wind whipped more sounds past her. There it was again, the sound of a dog barking. Was it Buddy?

Joe and Drew were shouting. Had they found Shannon?

She grabbed her supply bag and slid off the horse, squeezing by the quivering animal. By running her hand along the rocky wall of the cliff, she traced her way toward the commotion. Joe and Drew were inside a cave, their flashlights bobbing up and down. Buddy was whining pitiably at them, leaping at them, running a few feet ahead, then returning to them. She pulled out her own flashlight, flicked it on, and followed them in, her heartbeat picking up at once.

Not far in she found both Joe and Drew flat on their bellies, peering down a fissure in the floor of the cave. Buddy was frantic in his whining now, moving rhythmically from foot to foot before the opening in the ground. Her heart sank at the sight of Shannon's pink backpack.

"Tell me she isn't down there." She dropped to her knees and trained her flashlight into the hole along with theirs. The hole was about two, two and a half feet wide at best and went on and on into the ground.

"Daddy," a thin voice cried from deep underground.

Oh, God. It was Shannon.

"Are you hurt, Sweetheart?" Joe asked, his voice cracking.

"I'm scared, Daddy," Shannon cried. "Come get me, Daddy."

Joe groaned in anguish, a series of options considered and discarded flashing across his face. He stared at Darby and Drew and called into the hole, "Daddy's going to get you out of there, I promise."

"How, Dad?" Drew demanded, his face stricken with fear. "How!"

"We'll drop a sling down to her, get her to tie it around herself, and we pull her up. Go get the ropes off the horses, Drew." The boy spun away and out from the cave into the downpour outside.

"What if she doesn't tie it right, and partway out she falls again?" Darby hated to say, but was compelled to point it out. "We're lucky she wasn't hurt this time. We may not be next time."

"Can you think of a better way?" he challenged, then said, "Sorry, I didn't mean that."

Shannon's voice drifted from below, panicked now. "Daddy, the water's getting in."

"Water?" Darby repeated. Drew was back with the ropes in time to hear his sister. Darby saw that the news of the water hit both he and Joe hard. "What does she mean? What water?"

On his feet with lightning speed, Joe seized one of the ropes, secured it to a second, then after securing it around his waist, tied off a sling at the other end to lower down to his daughter. His mouth formed a thin line, fear etched his face like a knife.

It was Drew who answered her. "Sea water. The tide's coming in. Once it reaches a tipping point, it can pour into these fissures like filling a bathtub."

It was as if a hand had reached into her chest, grabbed her heart, and made a fist. How long did they have left? Maybe an hour? Only minutes? She watched Joe lower the sling into the fissure, feeding it down as swiftly as it would go, precious seconds ticking by. When he tried to speak to Shannon, his voice caught. He swallowed and tried again. "Shannon, Honey. Can you see the rope Daddy's send down to you?"

"Nooooo," she wailed. "I can't see it, Daddy." Then a shrill scream echoed. Darby jumped in reaction, frantic to do something, anything to stop Shannon's terror.

"WHAT!" Drew yelled into the hole. "What happened?"

"Daddy! Something's down here with me! A monster is trying to get me! Daddyyyy!" Shannon's shrill scream raced up the fissure and up Darby's spine.

Darby sobbed and gripped the edge of the fissure hard to keep from screaming herself. "No!" she called down. "No, Shannon. Listen to me. It's okay. That's Daddy's rope, tickling you. There is no monster, I promise you."

Shannon stopped screaming, and began a hiccupping wail, "Daddy, come get me!"

Joe rocked his jaw and walked in a circle, his rage of helplessness overwhelming him, then he stopped over the hole. With a deceptively calm tone, he asked, "Can you feel the rope now, Honey?"

"Y-yes."

"How far down, Dad?" Drew asked.

"I'm thinking, twenty-five, thirty feet."

"We can do this," Drew said excitedly. "We can pull her up!"

His father nodded, his eyes burning with concentration. "Can you pull the rope around your tummy, Shannon, under your arms and around your tummy? We can pull you up if you can. Please, Honey, try."

A long silence, then Shannon started to cry again. "It's not working, Daddy."

Joe moaned deep in his throat and swung his arms out, clutching and unclutching his fists with barely restrained energy. Darby knew if he could claw his way to his daughter, he would be doing it now, at this very moment. Instead, he said, "Try again, Sweetheart. It'll work. Just pull the loop over your head, then under your arms to around your tummy. Please, Shannon. Please try."

"The water is so cold, daddy. It's up to my tummy." Her crying petered off to a relentless, droning wail of despair.

Through gritted teeth, Darby said, "Lower me down there. I'll tie her to me, and you and Drew can bring us back up."

"No!" Joe shot back. "Too dangerous."

"Then me," Drew burst out. "Let me. You know I can do it, Dad."

Darby jumped in, "You're too heavy. Your father and I could never get you back to the surface. It's got to be me."

"Shit!" Joe tugged his hair from his face and stared back at her, hope and fear warring in his eyes.

She began to shake, but plunged on, "I'm 105 pounds. Shannon's probably 40 to 45 pounds. That's 150. You can get us back out, right? You and Drew?"

"You can go down there and still function?" he demanded.

"Yes."

"Darby." He reached for her like a starving man and gripped her shoulders hard, looking at her with longing to believe her plan would work, but laced with fear she couldn't survive the ordeal.

She poured every ounce of determination she possessed into her voice. "I can do it if you can get us back out."

"Daddyyyyy," Shannon wailed. "Come get me, Daddy. The water's coming more and more."

"Yes, we can get you back out," Drew answered for his father, pulling the rope up, hand over hand until the empty loop was back at the surface, the sickeningly empty, sea water-soaked loop. Darby's heart flopped inside her chest. "Darby can do it, Dad. She has to, so she will. And me and you will get them back, no matter what."

Darby stared back at Joe, willing him to believe in her. She saw when he decided hers was the only way that would work. In a choked voice, he said, "I won't leave you down there in the dark, I swear to you."

"You won't," she answered, knowing it was true.

Joe grabbed the rope and reconfigured the end. This time he formed two loops, sliding one over Darby's head and around her body. She stared down into the hole, still trembling. "This way, we won't crush Shannon against you when we bring you back up," he said, his voice thick and gritty as he checked for fit around Darby's ribs. He stopped at finding her whole body quaking. "Darby ...?"

"Believe in me?" she begged, her teeth wanting to chatter as fear raged through her. Clenching them together she said, "I can do this." When Joe just stared back her, his expression agony, she whispered, "It's our only option, Joe."

With a jerk of his head, he returned to fitting the ropes securely around her body. Drew called down the dark hole to his sister. "Darby's coming to get you, Shannon. Hang on just a little longer, and she'll be right beside you."

Joe's eyes rose to Darby's. His voice breaking, he pleaded, "Go save my little girl."

Darby sat down at the edge of the hole abruptly—it felt more like a collapse—and let her feet dangle into space. Horror at the unknown below almost swamped her, her heart jackhammering inside her chest. Nausea swept through her, leaving her weak and dizzy with sweat.

"Here." Drew pressed her flashlight back into her hand. He murmured close to her ear, "This way it won't be so scary," and squeezed her arm. She gripped the flashlight with both hands as if praying, and nodded, then closed her eyes and kept them closed. "Okay," she moaned. "Lower me down."

She heard rather than saw Joe and Drew scramble, felt herself lifted into the air, swinging free, fright thundering through her so badly she almost cried out. She felt the cold sides of the shaft brush by her, and she opened her eyes and sobbed, the sound coming right back at her in such close quarters. Blackness rushed at her, broken by the shifting shaft of weak light from her flashlight. Still, the darkness was overwhelming in its ability to strip her of all personal power. The rope swung, smashing her face into the jagged rock. She yelped and dropped the flashlight. Horrified, she yelled, "Watch out, Shannon!"

"Darby!" Joe called from above.

"Wait!" she commanded, and made herself hold still. The flashlight clattered downward, then after a few seconds she heard the distant sound of it splashing safely into the water below. Shannon screeched in fright. Darby called out, "Shannon? You okay?"

"Darby," Shannon pleaded, "please hurry."

"Darby?" Joe called down again, the effort to remain calm very evident in his strained voice. This was killing him. "Talk to me, Darby," he pleaded. "Say something."

"I'm ..." She touched her face, found that her nose was bleeding profusely. And so what? It was a nose bleed; it was nothing, and it was strangely freeing.

Time to get herself together—she was no good to anyone freaking out. "I'm good. Keep lowering."

The shaft grew smaller and tighter the lower she went, and she had to push with all her strength against the fissure walls to work herself downward, scraping her arms and legs, skinning her knuckles, but she didn't stop. Once she was moving, helping reach Shannon, nothing had the power to make her stop, not the cuts and scrapes—she barely felt them—not the closeness, not the darkness, not the cold. "More rope," she called up to the receding circle of pale light above. "I need more rope. I'm stuck."

The rope slackened, and she twisted in the shaft, wiggling her hips past the obstruction. Suddenly, she was through and free falling before being brought up with a painful jerk, the sound of shouting and strain coming from above as Joe and Drew worked together to regain control. Dangling in space, she squeezed her eyes shut, wrapped her arms around her head, and moaned. Fright surrounded her, suffocated her, pressed her down so hard she barely knew where she was, where her huddled body ended and the sucking, gaping abyss took over.

It was the closet all over again. She swung in a slow circle. Frozen. Abandoned. Powerless.

Then she heard that voice—that whispery voice that had woken her this morning, this time warm against her ear. "It's all right, Darby," the woman's hushed voice breathed, bringing comfort and calm with it. "Find Shannon for me, Darby. Save Shannon."

Abruptly and acutely aware of her surroundings, Darby heard that Joe and Drew were calling down to her, heard Shannon calling up to her. She opened her eyes to blackness. She was back from her old nightmare and here in a new one, catapulted into giant soul-sucking black hole. She grasped the rope—her lifeline—pressing her cheek against it, breathing hard, fighting to regain some semblance of connection with reality. This was for Shannon. There was no hiding from fear here. She had to make this work.

"I-I'm okay," she croaked. "J-just give me a minute."

She made herself absorb her surroundings. There was more room here, but the space in which she dangled was now completely devoid of light. She'd have to rely on touch alone, but what horrors waited for her here in the darkness?

Let go of the rope, she told herself.

She clung to the rope and shivered even more.

Let go of the rope! You don't have time for this shit!

Crying now, she ripped her hands away from the rope and made herself reach out into the darkness, searching for clues, learning where she was and what she needed to deal with. The rock walls that surrounded her were farther away now and were uneven, cold, and unforgiving. She heard the sound of trickling water nearby and Shannon's soft, ragged sobs.

"Shannon?" she called out, her voice thin and unrecognizable to herself.

"Darby." Shannon's voice drifted up from below. She was maybe another ten feet away? She sounded strangely calm.

"I'm almost there, Sweetheart." Darby turned her face upward and shouted to Joe and Drew, stronger this time. "I'm going to need about ten more feet of rope. But slowly."

She felt herself descend in small, jerking measures, her hands outstretched and tracing the wall. Then her feet were in icy water and Shannon's little arms were around her legs like steel bands.

"Darby," she cried, "I knew you'd come."

"Let go of my legs, Hon." Darby tipped her head up and shouted. "Just a couple more feet, and we're good." It was disquieting how the sound of her voice, though shouted, seemed to be sucked into almost nothing in this closed space. Absorbed. Deleted.

Still, they'd heard her. She was lowered into the freezing water until her feet touched bottom, the water level reaching her waist. Pushing Shannon's icy-cold hair back, she kissed her wet face again and again, frantic with gratitude that Shannon was here, in her arms. "I'm here, Baby. I'm here." Shannon shook with the cold, her teeth chattering, the water level to her armpits now, the sound of the trickling water taking on a new and more dangerous meaning. While Darby had been dangling overhead, paralyzed on that rope, time and the ocean had raced ahead of her.

Stupid, stupid, stupid.

In darkness Darby ran her hands over Shannon's slight body, satisfying herself that she was okay, wet, cold and shivering, but miraculously okay. She almost laughed with relief—it was like finding herself. God, another human being, here in the darkness with her. She welcomed the renewed strength and determination Shannon's presence gave her.

"Hang on to me, Honey. You're daddy and big brother are going to bring us out of here together."

"I'm scared, Darby. Lift me up. I'm so cold."

"Oh, I will, Honey, as soon as I can."

Darby encircled Shannon with the second loop of rope, arranging it by touch alone as Joe had shown her, then hugged her tight, grateful for the solid feel of the child, certain Shannon's presence was as comforting to her as she was to Shannon. "You hang on to me, now. Don't let go, Okay?" Then she yelled up the shaft, "Okay. We're ready. Bring us up."

After a moment, they began to rise, inch by inch, with pauses, then jerks upward, with Darby holding Shannon to her with iron arms. They cleared the open area quickly. When they got to the narrow part, Darby shouted, "Stop. I have to figure this out. Give me a minute."

"What's wrong?" Joe yelled back.

"Just wait!" She held Shannon tight with her left arm and felt around with her right one, and after a moment, found a toe hold she could use. "Okay, Shannon. Here's the hardest part of our adventure. We have to get through this tiny hole, one at a time, but we're tied together. What would Dora the Exploder do?"

Shannon continued to shake inside her makeshift harness, but seemed to be considering the problem. "She'd go through the hole one at a time?" she said through chattering teeth.

"Right. That means that for this part, I'll need to untie you–."

"No!" Shannon wailed, pressing her face against Darby's chest, her skinny arms lashed around her waist like piano wires, her little body shuddering compulsively. "Don't leave me!"

Darby hugged her back, stroking her head roughly, feverishly. Oh, how she understood Shannon's terror at being left behind. "Know that I will NEVER leave you behind, Shannon, for as long as you need me. Never. Never."

Shannon continued to shake.

"What's happening down there?" Joe yelled down, worry edging his deliberately modulated tone.

"We're good. Just working things out," Darby yelled back. To Shannon she whispered. "Let's not make Daddy and Drew wait anymore, okay? Let's get out of here, together." She felt Shannon nod. "You have to take off your loop and let me push you through the hole. Once you get through, you hold on to something, anything you can find, until I get through and tie us together again, then we go home to Drew and Daddy, okay?"

"O-okay," Shannon stuttered against Darby's chest. The child's faith in her was humbling.

Darby yelled up at Joe and Drew. "We have to separate to get through an opening. I'm going to push Shannon through first. Just keep me steady here for a bit."

"You've got it," Drew yelled back.

Darby braced her back against one side of the shaft and dug her toe into the hold she'd found in the opposite side. Clutching Shannon to her, she shifted the rope over the child's head, sobbing as she did. This was the most dangerous part, this right here, with Shannon no longer tied to her. Please, God. Please, God. Please, God. Already, her outstretched, bracing leg was quaking with the strain. She had to do this, and do it fast, before her strength gave out.

"Okay, Shannon, reach your arms up into the hole and pull yourself through. I'm going to push you up from below."

Shannon did as she was told, slipping easily up into the opening and beyond Darby's reach. "You hanging onto something, Shannon?"

"Yes," was Shannon's trusting answer.

Darby shouted, "Pull up about a foot!"

The slack in the rope was taken up enough that she could abandon her toe hold and reach up into the opening. Gripping the inside edge of the rock, she pulled herself through until her hips jammed. Try as she might, she could not force her way out. Panic set in, and for one crazy moment, she believed she wouldn't be able to escape and thought—what if she couldn't get out? They had more rope, didn't they? She could tie Shannon with a new rope and they could still get her out, couldn't they?

Shannon cried, "Hurry, Darby. My arms are getting tired, I can't hold on anymore."

Darby dug her elbows into the sharp-edged opening, welcoming the pain, using it to center her focus. She rocked back and forth, squeezing through inch by inch, reliving the memory of squeezing through the wall beside the closet all those years ago, feeling first her clothing, then her skin tear as she wrenched her body through.

She was free! Bracing her body across the shaft, she pulled Shannon to her and looped her safely inside the rope once again, before sobbing with relief when the child was again anchored to her body. Okay. This was okay. She squeezed the tiny girl to her, beating back the image of Shannon falling from her arms. This was okay.

"I-I can't breathe," Shannon gasped against her chest.

Abruptly, Darby was laughing. Adrenaline dump. "Sorry! Sorry," she cried, "You are so brave, Shannon. Dora the Exploder absolutely could not have done what you just did." Then she tipped her head back, saw the beautiful circle of light above them and yelled out. "Okay. We're free. Pull us up."

The rope tightened around them, and then they were free floating once again, rising up again, only this time the space was so much smaller with the two of them. Darby pressed Shannon's face to her chest, protecting the child's head with her left hand which was smashed against the rocky shaft again and again—better her hand than Shannon's head—while clawing her way upward with her right hand, digging in and pushing with her toes, her knees, her elbows, any part of her that inched them ever upward and prevented them from slipping backward. She stared unwaveringly toward that circle of light above, a beacon of hope that grew bigger and brighter with each grunting pull from the two working above. She was still crying, barely aware of the hits she was absorbing on their bumpy ride to the surface, crying with relief and gratitude for Shannon, and for Joe and for Drew.

Seeing that precious light above them grow nearer and nearer, she felt something deep inside shift and she was fifteen-years-old again, being rescued from her own dark nightmare along with Shannon, surely and steadily, hand over hand, by people who loved her. A warm bloom of certainty enveloped her. This was her path, finally realized.

They broke the surface, the light blinding after the blackness of the fissure. Hands reached down and brought them out onto the cave floor, and everyone was hugging, arms and legs tangled, tears flowing. Where one body ended and another began could not be discerned, and did not matter. They were safe and together. Buddy leapt around them, barking and yipping with joy, licking anyone he could reach.

When they finally broke apart and Joe had satisfied himself over and over again that Shannon was unharmed, that Darby was all right, he went outside to get the leather bedrolls containing rough dry blankets to wrap them in. When he returned, Darby saw at once that he'd taken a moment while outside to let grateful tears fall, their traces tracking his grimy cheeks. Her heart swelled at his vulnerability as she watched him bundle Shannon securely into her blanket and bring her safely into his arms. Then she registered the state of his raw and bleeding hands. "Oh, Joe!" she exclaimed, reaching out to cradle one of them in her own, then looked at Drew's, whose hands were no better than raw meat inside. "Your poor hands!"

Drew looked her up and down, taking in her shredded clothes and bleeding cuts and scrapes. "And your poor … everything! You're kind of a mess, you know."

"Nothing a hot bath and a few dozen Band Aids won't cure," she replied, looking at Shannon held so securely in her father's arms, where every little girl in this world should be: safe in her father's arms. "I wouldn't trade a single scratch."

Joe had told her, "I won't leave you down there in the dark, I swear to you," and he'd kept his promise. She glanced out to the mouth of the cave and realized she wasn't anxious about being here inside at all. The sky was a beautiful clear blue. She murmured, "I see the storm's over."

Drew said, "I'll go get the horses turned around so we can head home."

"Thanks, Son." From the exchange between Joe and Drew, Darby wondered if Joe needed to formalize the adoption after all. But then, with Joe, a promise was a promise.

Shannon snuggled her face into Joe's neck. It looked like Joe wouldn't be letting go of his daughter anytime soon. Shannon said, "I knew you would come get me, you and Darby and Drew. The angel in the hole told me so."

Joe and Darby exchanged mystified looks.

"There was an angel in the hole with you?" Joe asked.

"She looked just like Darby, only different, all golden and angel-y. Then when Darby came down on the rope, she said goodbye and said I had a new mommy now."

Joe and Darby stared at one another in shock.

"Did you tell Shannon we're getting married?" Darby murmured.

"No ..." Then he made a face and shook his head. "Nah. She was scared out of her mind down there. Kids dream up all sorts of stuff when they're scared. It's a coping mechanism."

Darby looked at him doubtfully, remembering that voice in the darkness, urging her on. "You think?"

"Yeah."

He put his other arm around her and hugged her to him. It felt very, very good. "I love you, you crazy woman."

She looked up into his weary eyes and knew it was true. She said, "Let's go home."

Together they made their way out of the darkness and into the light, where Drew stood waiting with the horses.

The End

Read an excerpt from Book Two of the Wedding Dress Promise Series, a romantic suspense entitled 'After the Party.' You met Laura in No Regrets. Here is Laura's story.

AFTER THE PARTY EXCERPT

It looked as though the meeting was going to take place right here, dockside. Laura's jaw dropped as Dean quickly pulled off his sneakers and socks, stripped off his sweater and jeans.

"What are you doing? You can't go down there!

He placed his finger to his lips and shook his head once, then eased himself over the edge of the dock and slowly into the chilly water in order to not send the swaying motion back toward Richard and his companion. With practiced silent strokes and by staying in the shadows of the moored boats and the dock, he was able to make his way toward them and come within a few feet of where they stood. Laura could barely make him out. Then, he ducked his head close enough to the floating logs under the walkway that he disappeared completely into the shadows.

It took her all of thirty seconds to strip down to her bra and panties and slide into the cold water after him, shuddering with the chill. Like Dean, she stayed in the shadows and moved soundlessly between the boats and dock until she treaded water at his side. He was not happy to see her. With vigorous pantomime, he motioned for her to go back. She shook her head and pointed up at the two men towering over them.

The tugboat captain flicked his cigarette toward their hiding place. It hit the water and winked out so close to her she shocked he hadn't seen her face in the water. Holding her breath, she watched him pull a flask from the inside pocket of his worn vest, and saw that he also had a gun strapped to his side, hidden under the vest.

She hissed, "He's got a gun!" Dean just nodded, like this was an everyday thing to him, sneaking up on dangerous men carrying guns.

The tugboat captain twisted the cap off the flask and threw back a swallow. "I needed that," he told Richard, his gravelly voice a testament to years of smoking. "It's colder than a hooker's heart tonight."

She knew that voice! She tugged on Dean's arm and whispered close to his ear, "That's Rolly Taylor." Dean nodded, this time raising his finger to his lips.

"You'd know," Richard replied, with a shake of his head at the offered drink. It was clear he held the older man in disdain.

"Can't help being an asshole, can ya?'" Rolly shot back. These men did not like each other. The flask disappeared back into the folds of Rolly's grimy clothes. Laura half expected his hand to emerge holding his weapon. "So, why the second meeting? I thought we covered everything last night."

"Things have changed."

Rolly's expression became wary. "What things?"

"I've got a couple of snoops." A thrill of fear ran up Laura's spine. Richard knew they'd been searching Holly's office! Did he also know she'd been back and found the laptop? "I'm taking care of them, don't you concern yourself. You all set for the drop? There won't be much light."

"Don't bother me; in fact, it suits me to a T." Rolly pulled out a minuscule slip of paper, and carefully laid a trail of tobacco along it with stained fingers. "I know my way through the maze of docks at Brennan's Point and the tides that run through the islands like I know my own hand. Drunk or sober, I make the run and always come home."

"You damned well better be sober. You're no good to me drunk."

"Ah, quit your carpin'." Rolly licked the edge of the paper then rolled the homemade cigarette into a skinny tube. "You'd be nowhere without Rolly Taylor at the helm." He lit the cigarette and smiled grimly into the darkened harbor. "I seem to recall a time when you came to me, hat in hand, and pleaded for my expertise. Sure, you're a high roller. I get around; I know you hang with some of the big boys. But when the chips are down, it's ol' Rolly who's number one in your plans. Hell, without me, there is no plan."

"You've been well compensated for your troubles," Richard replied stiffly.

"You bet I have. It's the cash, plain and simple, that keeps me waitin' with my scow for the signal off Idle Island." Laura's grip on Dean's shoulders tightened at hearing her island was part of the scheme. Richard had been using the breakwater as a cover.

Rolly continued, "But, now I'm thinkin', maybe, with people snoopin' around, an' things changin' like you say, that it's time ol' Rolly got himself a raise."

"Brought you a little incentive." Richard reached into his breast pocket and extracting a thick envelope. He handed it to Rolly. "Come Friday midnight, you'll earn more in a few hours of orchestrated confusion than you'd make in three months of night shift at the plant."

Rolly opened the envelope and ran his thumb over the edges of the cash inside. He turned on Richard abruptly. "It's not enough, and we both know it. I'm makin' you a rich man. Three month's pay ain't going to cover it anymore. I know too much about this little operation for you not to cut me a bigger slice."

Richard eased away from him, his fear of the rough tugboat captain evident. Then, unexpectedly, he threw up his hands in a show of resignation. "You're right. It's not enough. Think of this as a down payment. In fact, the reason I wanted to meet with you tonight is to arrange for you to pick me up drop night. I want in on this one."

Rolly seemed stunned by Richard's request, as were Dean and Laura, shivering in the water a few feet away. What was going down this next drop? What was different?

"Hey," Rolly protested. "I work alone."

"Not this time. I need to be there this trip. I've got a connection I need to make, and riding along with you fits my plans perfectly. And," he forestalled Rolly's next objection, "I'm willing to pay. Big time."

"How big time?" Rolly growled. Laura could almost hear the numbers adding up in the greedy man's head.

"Fifty thou," Richard announced, with a show of confidence his offer would not be refused. Rolly whistled in appreciation.

"You got yourself a ride, Mister. Be on board by midnight. If you're not there, you miss the show."

"I'll be there," Richard said curtly. "You be ready to go."

Rolly tossed the butt of his cigarette into the water. Dean jerked away from the burning embers, slamming his head hard against a log. He groaned and made a splashing noise. Laura watched in horror as his eyes drifted closed and he sank under the surface.

Reflexively she grabbed him by his hair and brought him back out of the water. Blood streamed down the side of his face. Fighting panic, she glanced back at Richard and Rolly. They hadn't changed their demeanor. Clearly they hadn't heard Dean's moan. How long could she keep Dean afloat while he was unconscious; how serious was his head injury?

To keep his legs from floating out into the open, she wrapped hers around the trunk of his body, gripped the end of a cross timber and drew deeper into the shadows, bringing Dean with her. Something sharp jabbed into her back. She craned her neck and saw a huge rusty spike, the source of Dean's wound.

Abruptly Rolly stooped toward her—Laura's heart shot up into her throat, her brain screaming, "He knows, he knows!" Trapped holding Dean, she squeezed her eyes shut, waiting for rough hands to haul her from the water …

Nothing. No hands.

She opened her eyes and risked a peek. Rolly had untied his boat and was now back on board, disappearing into the cabin. Air whooshed from her lungs, leaving her weak with relief. Oh God. Oh God. Starting up the purring motor, Rolly maneuvered the scrubby tug away from the dock and guided her out to sea. Without a backward glance, Richard turned on his heel and stalked up the dock. The meeting was over.

Laura's teeth chattered with the cold and adrenaline dump. She wanted to weep with relief.

Dean's eyes were open. "What … happened?"

"They're gone. You hit your head and passed out." She waved her hand in front of his face. "You okay?" His eyes seemed slow in focusing. He ran his hand over his head, and she knew from his grimace when he located the wound. "Do you think you can swim on your own?"

His gaze changed from vague to lecherous. "Not with your legs wrapped around me like this I can't." Now here was the Dean she knew. Hastily, she unwrapped her legs from around his body and moved away, but came back the instant his eyes slide closed again.

"Dean! Stay awake, Dean." He opened his eyes wide, blinked and rolled them around in an obvious effort to remain alert. Fearing she'd never get him out of the water, Laura ran her hand along his cheek to keep his attention. "Stay with me. Concentrate on hanging on to me, and I promise I'll get you out of this." His eyes closed for a moment, and then he was looking back at her, more alert this time. He nodded, grimacing at the motion.

"Okay, here we go." She kicked with all her strength, drawing him along with her, moving mere inches at a time along the deserted dock, past dozens of moored boats toward the pylons where they had hidden their clothes. They'd come to the end of the docks so quickly; going back was a torturous path of stops and starts, of Dean fading in and out of consciousness.

"Concentrate on hearing my voice, Dean. Listen to my voice. Stay awake."

She kicked again and again, gripping the seaweed slick logs with one arm to pull them along while gripping Dean's slippery body with the other. She cut herself repeatedly on the sharp edged barnacles that clustered the underside of the dock, her limbs growing ever weaker as they made their way along each link. The muscles of her arms screamed for relief.

After what seemed an eternity, she located a rudimentary ladder, not far from where they had entered the water in the first place. "Thank you, God," she gasped, hooking her arm through one of the rungs and holding Dean's body close. Together, they bobbed in the water while she fought to catch her breath and gather strength to climb out. "Okay, Dean, you're going to have to get up here on your own. It's only three rungs, and you're home free. I can't lift you. It's either this, or we try to go all the way back to shore. It's a long way. It's your call."

"Yup, yup," he muttered. "I'll get up."

She guided his hands to the ladder, watching him ready himself to make the attempt.

"Okay." He gripped the rungs of the ladder and lurched out of the water. Pitching onto the dock with a groan, he slumped motionless where he landed. She scrambled out after him, knelt beside him, her every muscle quivering ….

The 4 Book Wedding Dress Series, No Regrets, After the Party, The Wish List and The Contract are available at www.Amazon.com and at www.Amazon.ca

ABOUT RONNIE ROBERTS

I live in northern Canada where I live half the year at our family cabin on 100 acres along the Peace River, where my family practices living mostly off the grid. Not quite preppers, we do love being self-sufficient. I had an embarrassment of zucchini from the garden this year which has resulted in a relish so good I want to dive into a tub of it and rub it all over my body! (Must put that recipe onto my website ….) The rest of the year we live in town in the house my husband and I designed and built together.

Since we've been on the Peace River acreage, and don't allow hunting, the wildlife is gradually making a comeback, which we cherish. We love the black bears lumbering by the garden,, the moose looking up from eating reeds in the back channel, the whitetails trotting down the path ahead of our side-by-side, the frogs hoping along the riverbank, the eagle teaching it's eaglet to fly, the partridge hiding in plain sight,(aren't they just the silliest birds ever?) the rabbits dashing through the brush, the beaver 's beautifully built oasis, the coyotes' howling at twilight.

This is a place of great peace and beauty and where I love to write. I hope my stories bring you happiness in the form of romance, mixed with some gentle humour, with a side of suspense and adventure. These stories are meant to provide an enjoyable escape and fun, with uplifting happy endings for the busy women out there keeping this world going round. Writing woman's fiction with strong, flawed but empowered woman is my passion. Being female is awesome, something to celebrate!

I do love writing about relationships, which, lucky for me, come in all sizes and varieties—endless writing material for the romantic that lives within us all! I hope you enjoyed reading the book you have in your hand as much as I enjoyed writing it.

One Last Thing:

If you enjoyed this story, would you be so kind to leave a review on Amazon? Reviews are the lifeblood of writers, the word of mouth we depend upon to keep doing what we love to do, which is write more books! Thank you in advance for your support. You make writing a pleasure!

If you'd like to receive the inspiring short story for The Wedding Dress Promise Series for free, please go to my website at www.RonnieRobertsBooks.com and sign up and look around. Love to see you there!

Made in the USA
Lexington, KY
12 February 2015